Alyson Richman is the daughter of a painter and an engineer, and her novels have been published in more than ten languages. She lives in Long Island, New York with her husband and two children.

Hertfordshire Libraries

Kings Langley Library
Kiosk 1

Customer ID: *****7636

Items that you have borrowed

Title: The Gypsy bride [text(large print)]
Due: 02 December 2021

Title: The lost wife [text(large print)]
Due: 02 December 2021

Total items: 2
Account balance: £0.00
11/11/2021 14:06
Checked out: 2
Overdue: 0
Reservations: 0
Ready for collection: 0

Thank you for using Hertfordshire
Libraries
Enquiries / Renewals go to:
www.hertfordshire.gov.uk/libraries
or call: 0300 123 4049

03 AUG 2013

BUN

Please renew or return items by the date
shown on your receipt

www.hertsdirect.org/libraries

Renewals and enquiries: 0300 123 4049

Textphone for hearing or 0300 123 4041
speech impaired users:

L32

Hertfordshire

THE LOST WIFE

During the last moments of calm in pre-war Prague, Lenka, a young art student, falls in love with Josef. They marry — but soon, like so many others, they are torn apart by the currents of war. In America Josef becomes a successful obstetrician and raises a family, though he never forgets the wife he thinks died in the camps. But in the Nazi ghetto of Terezín — and later in Auschwitz — Lenka has survived, relying on her skills as an artist and the memories of a husband she believes she will never see again. But, decades later, an unexpected encounter in New York brings Lenka and Josef back together . . .

ALYSON RICHMAN

THE LOST WIFE

Complete and Unabridged

CHARNWOOD
Leicester

First published in Great Britain in 2011 by
Hodder & Stoughton
London

First Charnwood Edition
published 2013
by arrangement with
Hodder & Stoughton
An Hachette UK Company
London

A catalogue record for this book is available
from the British Library.

ISBN 978–1–4448–1556–6

Published by
F. A. Thorpe (Publishing)
Anstey, Leicestershire

Set by Words & Graphics Ltd.
Anstey, Leicestershire
Printed and bound in Great Britain by
T. J. International Ltd., Padstow, Cornwall

This book is printed on acid-free paper

To Charlotte, Zachary, Stephen,
and my parents with love.

With special thanks to the Book Revue.

I am my beloved and my beloved is mine
SONG OF SOLOMON 6:3

1

New York City
2000

He dressed deliberately for the occasion, his suit pressed and his shoes shined. While shaving, he turned each cheek carefully to the mirror to ensure he hadn't missed a single whisker. Earlier that afternoon, he had even bought a lemon-scented pomade to smooth his few remaining curls.

He had only one grandson, one grandchild for that matter, and had been looking forward to this wedding for months now. And although he had met the bride only a few times, he liked her from the first. She was bright and charming, quick to laugh, and possessed a certain old-world elegance. He hadn't realized what a rare quality that was until he sat there now staring at her, his grandson clasping her hand.

Even now, as he walked into the restaurant for the rehearsal dinner, he felt as though, seeing the young girl, he had been swept back into another time. He watched as some of the other guests unconsciously touched their throats because the girl's neck, stretching out from her velvet dress, was so beautiful and long that she looked like she had been cut out from a Klimt painting. Her hair was swept up into a loose chignon, and two little jeweled butterflies with sparkling antennae

1

rested right above her left ear, giving the appearance that these winged creatures had just landed on her red hair.

His grandson had inherited his dark, unruly curls. A study in contrast to his bride-to-be, he fidgeted nervously, while she seemed to glide into the room. He looked like he would be more comfortable with a book between his hands than holding a flute of champagne. But there was an ease that flowed between them, a balance that made them appear perfectly suited for each other. Both of them were smart, highly educated second-generation Americans. Their voices lacked even the faintest traces of the accents that had laced their grandparents' English. The *New York Times* wedding announcement that Sunday morning would read:

Eleanor Tanz married Jason Baum last night at the Rainbow Room in Manhattan. The rabbi Stephen Schwartz officiated. The bride, 26, graduated from Amherst College and is currently employed in the decorative arts department of Christie's, the auction house. The bride's father, Dr. Jeremy Tanz, is an oncologist at Memorial Sloan-Kettering hospital in Manhattan. Her mother, Elisa Tanz, works as an occupational therapist with the New York City public schools. The groom, 28, a graduate of Brown University and Yale Law School, is currently an associate at Cahill Gordon & Reindel LLP. His father, Benjamin Baum, was until recently an attorney at Cravath, Swaine & Moore LLP in New

York City. The groom's mother, Rebekkah Baum, is a retired schoolteacher. The couple was introduced by mutual friends.

At the head table, the lone living grandparent from each side was introduced to each other for the first time. Again, the groom's grandfather felt himself being swept away by the image of the woman before him. She was decades older than her granddaughter, but there was something familiar about her. He felt it immediately, from the moment he first saw her eyes.

'I know you from somewhere,' he finally managed to say, although he felt as though he were now speaking to a ghost, not a woman he had just met. His body was responding in some visceral manner that he didn't quite understand. He regretted drinking that second glass of wine. His stomach was turning over on itself. He could hardly breathe.

'You must be mistaken,' she said politely. She did not want to appear rude, but she, too, had been looking forward to her granddaughter's wedding for months and didn't want to be distracted from the evening's festivities. As she saw the girl navigating the crowd, the many cheeks turning to her to be kissed and the envelopes being pressed into her and Jason's hands, she had to pinch herself to make sure that she really was still alive to witness it all.

But this old man next to her would not give up.

'I definitely think I know you from somewhere,' he repeated.

3

She turned and now showed her face even more clearly to him. The feathered skin. Her silver hair. Her ice-blue eyes.

But it was the shadow of something dark blue beneath the transparent material of her sleeve that caused shivers to run through his old veins.

'Your sleeve . . . ' His finger was shaking as it reached to touch the silk.

Her face twitched as he touched her wrist, her discomfort registering over her face.

'Your sleeve, may I?' He knew he was being rude.

She looked straight at him.

'May I see your arm?' he said again. 'Please.' This time his voice sounded almost desperate.

She was now staring at him, her eyes now locked to his. As if in a trance, she pushed up her sleeve. There on her forearm, next to a small brown birthmark, were six tattooed numbers.

'Do you remember me now?' he asked, trembling.

She looked at him again, as if giving weight and bone to a ghost.

'Lenka, it's me,' he said. 'Josef. Your husband.'

2

New York City
2000

She had slid the painting out of its cardboard tube the night before, flattening it like an old map. For over sixty years she had taken it with her wherever she went. First hidden in an old suitcase, then rolled into a metal cylinder and buried under floorboards, eventually pushed behind several boxes in a crowded closet.

The painting was created with thin black and red strokes. A kinetic energy shone through each line, the artist working to capture the scene as quickly as possible.

She had always felt it too sacred to be displayed, as if the mere exposure to light and air or, perhaps worse, the stares of visitors would be too much for its delicate skin. So it remained in an airtight box, locked away like Lenka's thoughts. Weeks before, while lying in bed, she decided that the painting would be her wedding gift to her granddaughter and her groom.

LENKA

When the Vltava freezes, it turns the color of an oyster shell. As a child, I watched men rescue swans trapped within its frozen current, cutting them out with ice picks to free their webbed feet.

I was born Lenka Josefina Maizel, the eldest daughter of a glass dealer in Prague. We lived on the Smetanovo nábřcežci embankment, in a rambling apartment with a wall of windows overlooking the river and bridge. There were red velvet walls and gilded mirrors, a parlor with carved furniture, and a beautiful mother who smelled like lily of the valley all year long. I still return to my childhood like it was a dream. Palačinka served with apricot jam, cups of hot cocoa, and ice skating on the Vltava. My hair piled underneath a fox hat when it snowed.

We saw our reflections everywhere: in the mirrors, the windows, the river down below, and in the transparent curve of Father's glasswares. Mother had a special closet lined with glasses for every occasion. There were champagne flutes that had been etched with delicate flowers, special wine goblets with gilded rims and frosted stems, even ruby-colored water glasses that reflected pink light when held up to the sun.

My father was a man who loved beauty and beautiful things, and believed his profession created both using a chemistry of perfect proportions. One needed more than sand and quartz to create glass. One needed fire and breath as well. 'A glassblower is both a lover and a life giver,' he once told a room filled with dinner guests. He lifted one of the water glasses from our dinner table. 'Next time you drink from one of your goblets, think of the lips that created the subtle, elegant shape which you now sip from, and how many mistakes were shattered and recycled to make a perfect set of twelve.'

He would have every guest enraptured as he twisted the goblet to the light. But he had not meant to be a salesman or a spectacle that evening. He truly loved how an artisan could create an object that was simultaneously strong and fragile, transparent, yet capable of reflecting color. He believed there was beauty in both the flattest surface of glass and those rippled with soft waves.

His business took him all over Europe, but he always walked through our front door the same way he left. His shirt white and crisp, his neck smelling of cedar and clove.

'*Milačku*,' he would say in Czech as he grasped Mother's waist between two thick hands. 'Love.'

'*Lasko Moje*' she would answer as their lips touched. 'My love.'

Even after a decade of marriage, Father remained beguiled by her. Many times, he returned home with presents bought solely because they reminded him of her. A miniature cloisonné bird with intricately enameled feathers might appear by her wineglass, or a small locket with seed pearls in a velvet box might be placed on her pillow. My favorite was a wooden radio with a brilliant sunburst design radiating from its center that he surprised Mother with after a trip to Vienna.

If I were to close my eyes during the first five years of my life, I could see Father's hand on that radio dial. The wisps of black hair on his fingers as they adjusted the tuner to find one of

7

the few stations that featured jazz, an exotic and invigorating sound that was just beginning to be broadcast over our airwaves in 1924.

I can see his head turning to smile at us, his arm extending to my mother and me. I can feel the warmth of his cheek as he lifts me and brings my legs around his waist, his other free hand turning mother into a spin.

I can smell the scent of spiced wine wafting from delicate cups on a cold January night. Outside, the tall windows of our apartment are covered in frost, but inside it is warm as toast. Long fingers of orange candlelight flicker across the faces of men and women who have crowded into the parlor to hear a string quartet Father has invited to play for the evening. There is the sight of mother in the center, her long white arms reaching for a small canapé. A new bracelet at her wrist. A kiss from Father. And me peering from my bedroom, a voyeur to their glamour and ease.

There are quiet nights, too. The three of us nestled around a small card table. Chopin on the record player. Mother fanning her cards so only I can see. A smile curled at her lips. Father feigning a frown as he allows my mother to win.

At night, I am tucked in by a mother who tells me to close my eyes. 'Imagine the color of water,' she whispers into my ear. Other nights, she suggests the color of ice. On another, the color of snow. I fall asleep to the thoughts of those shades shifting and turning in the light. I teach myself to imagine the varying degrees of blue, the delicate threads of lavender, or the palest dust of white.

And in doing so, my dreams are seeded in the mystery of change.

LENKA

Lucie arrived one morning holding a letter. She held the envelope out to Father, and he read it aloud to my mother. *The girl has no previous experience as a nanny*, his colleague had written. *But she has natural talent with children and she is beyond trustworthy.*

My first memory of Lucie is that she looked far younger than her eighteen years. Almost childlike, her body seemed lost in her long coat and dress. But when she first knelt down to greet me, I was immediately struck by the warmth flowing through her outstretched hand. Every morning when she arrived at our door, she brought with her the faint scent of cinnamon and nutmeg, as if she had been baked freshly that morning and delivered warm and fragrant — a delectable package that was impossible to turn away.

Lucie was no great beauty. She was like an architect's straight edge, all lines and angles. Her hard cheekbones looked as though they had been hammered with a chisel; her eyes were large and black, her lips tiny and thin. But like a dark forest nymph stolen from the pages of an old-fashioned fairy tale, Lucie possessed her own unique magic. After only a few days of working for my family, we all became enchanted by her. When she told a story, her fingers worked the air, like a harpist plucking imaginary strings. When there were chores to be done, she hummed songs that she had heard her own mother sing.

Lucie was treated not as a servant by my parents, but as a member of our extended family. She took all her meals with us, sitting around the large dining room table that always had too much food. And although we did not keep kosher, we still never drank milk when we ate a dish that had meat. Lucie made the mistake her first week of work of pouring me a glass of milk with my beef goulash, and Mother must have told her afterward that we didn't mix the two, for I never remember her making the mistake again.

My world became less sheltered and certainly more fun after Lucie's arrival. She taught me things like how to trap a tree frog or how to fish from one of the bridges off the Vltava. She was a master storyteller, creating a cast of characters from the various people we'd meet during our day. The man who sold us ice cream by the clock in Old Town Square might appear that night at bedtime as a wizard. A woman, from whom we bought apples at the market, might later emerge as an aging princess who had never recovered from a broken heart.

I have often wondered if it was Lucie or my mother who first discovered that I had a talent for drawing. In my memory, it is Mother handing me my first set of colored pencils and it is Lucie, later on, who buys me my first set of paints.

I know it was Lucie who first began taking me

to the park with my sketchpad and tin of pencils. She would stretch out a blanket near the little pond where boys sailed their paper boats, and lie on her back and watch the clouds as I drew page after page.

In the beginning, I drew little animals. Rabbits. Squirrels. A red-breasted bird. But soon I was attempting to draw Lucie, then a man reading a newspaper. Later on I began more ambitious subjects, like a mother pushing a pram. None of these first sketches were any good. But just like any young child who is first learning to draw, I taught myself by doing it over and over again. My observations eventually began to connect with my hand.

After hours outside of drawing, Lucie would roll up my sketches and bring them home to our apartment. Mother would ask how we had spent our day and Lucie would take the sketches she loved best and tack them up on the kitchen wall. My mother would carefully look at my work and then wrap me in her arms. I must have been close to six the first time I heard her say: 'Lenka, you know I was the same way at your age — I always had a pencil and piece of paper in my hands.' That was the first time I ever heard my mother draw a comparison between us, and I can tell you, as a child, whose dark hair and pale eyes resembled more her father than her elegant mother, the thrill of the two of us sharing something struck me straight to my heart.

That first winter Lucie was with us, Mother wanted to come up with a gift that showed her gratitude. I remember her discussing it with Father. 'Do what you think is best, *Milačku*,' he had said absent-mindedly while reading the newspaper. He always gave her free rein when giving gifts, but she always felt she needed to ask permission before she did anything. In the end, she had a beautiful capelet made for Lucie in blue wool with velvet trim. I can still see Lucie's face when she first opened the package — she was hesitant to accept it at first — almost embarrassed by the extravagance.

'Lenka has one coming, too,' Mother said gently. 'What a handsome pair you'll make skating on the Vltava.'

That evening, Mother caught me watching Lucie from my window as she walked off in the direction of the tram.

'I suppose I will have to order a cape for you tomorrow,' she said, touching my shoulder.

We both smiled, watching Lucie, her body seeming inches taller, as she stepped elegantly into the night.

Although our home was always filled with the melody of clinking glasses and the colors of my drawings, there was also a quiet but palpable sadness within our walls. When Lucie left each evening, and the cook packed up her bag, our spacious apartment seemed too large for our little threesome. The extra room next to mine became filled with packages, baskets, and stacks of old books. Even my old crib and pram were silently pushed into a corner, draped with a long white sheet, like two old ghosts, forgotten and misplaced.

There were stretches of days, whole patches of time, when I remember seeing only Lucie. My mother would take almost all of her meals in her bedroom and, when she did appear, she would look bloated and puffy. Her face showed clear signs that she'd been crying. My father would come home and quietly ask the maid about her. He would glance at the tray outside of her room with the plate of untouched food — the cup and saucer with the tea that had grown cold — and look desperate to bring the light back into his darkened house.

I remember Lucie instructing me not to question these episodes. She'd arrive earlier than usual in the morning and would try to distract me with a few things she had brought from home. Some days she'd pull from her basket a photograph of herself when she was six years old, beside a pony. Other times she'd bring a string of glass beads and braid it into my hair like a garland of twisted ivy. She'd tie a sash of blue silk around my dress and we'd imagine I was a princess who ruled over a kingdom where everyone had to whisper. The only sound we allowed ourselves was the rustle of our skirts as we twirled around the room.

At night, there would be visits from the family doctor, who'd gently close the door of Mother's room and rest his hand on Father's shoulder, talking to him in hushed tones. I would watch them, failing to discern what ailment my mother could possibly have that would prevent her from appearing during the day.

As I grew older, it became clearer that these shadows in my childhood were my parents' difficulties in conceiving another child. We tiptoed around conversations of families where there were many children and I learned not to ask for a brother or sister, for on those few times I did, it had only brought my mother to tears.

Something in our household changed after my seventh birthday. Mother spent weeks with what seemed like a touch of a stomach ailment and then, suddenly, the color in her cheeks returned. In the weeks that followed, she stopped wearing the slim-fitting skirts and jackets that were in vogue, opting for ones that were more loose and flowing. She grew peaceful and her movements became slower and more cautious. But it wasn't until her belly became gently rounder that she and Papa announced they were to have another baby.

One would have thought that Mother and Father would, after all these years, have celebrated at the announcement that I was to have a baby brother or sister. But they treaded upon the subject with great caution, fearing that any display of excitement or joy could undermine the health of the pregnancy.

This, of course, was a Jewish custom, the fear of bringing a curse on one's good fortune. Lucie was confused by this at first. Every time she tried to bring up the subject of the pregnancy, my

14

mother would not answer her directly.

'How beautiful and healthy you look,' she'd say to Mother.

To which Mother would just smile and nod her head.

'They say if you crave cheese, you're having a girl,' said Lucie. 'And if you crave meat, it will be a boy.'

Again, only a smile and a nod from Mother.

Lucie even offered to help prepare the nursery in advance, to which my mother finally had to explain her hesitation to do anything until the baby actually arrived.

'We appreciate all your good wishes and offers to help,' Mother explained, gently. 'But we don't want to bring any attention to the baby's birth, just yet.'

Lucie's face seemed to immediately register what Mother was saying.

'There are people who believe the same thing in the countryside,' she said, as if suddenly Mother's behavior finally made sense.

Still, Lucie tried ways to express her joy at my parents' good news without directly mentioning it. When the lilacs were in bloom that spring, she'd arrive with fistfuls of the fragrant branches, the stems carefully wrapped in strips of wet muslin, and arrange them in vases around the apartment. I remember watching Mother, with her increasingly rounded stomach, walking between each room smiling, as if their perfume had put her into a trance.

Sometimes Lucie would come with a basketful of dark bread that her mother had baked and leave it on the kitchen counter with a jar of homemade honey.

But it wasn't until the baby was born that her most beautiful gift appeared.

My sister Marta was born at sundown. The doctor came into the living room where Father and I sat on the sofa, and Lucie on one of the red velvet tufted chairs.

'You have another beautiful daughter,' he said to my father.

Father clasped his hands and rushed toward the bedroom. Lucie took his place on the sofa and took my hand.

'So you have a sister now,' she said quietly. 'What a gift.'

We waited until Papa said I could come in and see them.

He came back a few minutes later and told us we could both come and see the two of them.

'Lenka, come meet your baby sister.'

Lucie gave me a little push, an unnecessary gesture, as I could have leaped from my chair. All I wanted to do was run into my mother's room and kiss both her and the new baby.

'Lenka' — my mother looked up from the bundle in her arms and smiled at me in the doorway — 'come.' She patted her hand on the bed with one free hand while holding the tightly swaddled baby in her other arm.

I was in awe of the sight of them, but I remember a little pang of jealousy striking my heart when I leaned in and saw the tufts of red hair on my sister's infant head.

'Congratulations!' Lucie said as she came in

16

and kissed Mother on both her cheeks.

A few minutes later she returned, carrying a stack of embroidered linens. The edges were trimmed in a scallop of looping pink thread.

'I had hidden them in the closet,' Lucie said. 'I embroidered one set in pink, and one in blue, just in case.'

My mother laughed. 'You think of everything, Lucie,' she said as Lucie set the linens on the night table.

'I'll let you and Lenka have a few moments with the baby.' She smiled and gave me a pat on my head.

I gazed at my new sister. She was Mother in miniature form. The small rounded chin, the milky green eyes, and the same hair.

My reaction, however, was not what I had anticipated. Tears filled my eyes. I felt a tightening in my throat. Even my heart felt as though someone had thrust their hand inside my chest and was gripping it with all their strength. All I could think of was that I was to be replaced — forgotten — and that all of my parents' attention would now be directed at this little creature with its angelic face and tiny, reaching hands.

Of course this was not the reality, but the fear still gripped me. And I suppose that is why in the first few months of Marta's life, I clung so closely to Lucie.

Slowly, I grew to see that Marta's arrival did not mean I would be replaced. I was soon holding her in my arms. I read her my favorite books and sang her the same songs that had lulled me to sleep.

I also discovered my new sister was the perfect model for my ambitious attempts at portraiture. I used Marta's first milestones as my inspiration. I started with her sleeping in her pram, and then moved on to her crawling at the beach during summertime. I loved to draw her in pastel. The soft blending of the pigments made it easy to create the roundness of her cheeks, and the length of her growing limbs.

I loved to paint her as well. Marta's skin was the opaque white of heavy cream, and her hair the deep red of paprika. Those features, which had presented themselves at birth, grew even more pronounced as her baby fat melted away. Marta had the same high forehead as Mother — along with her small straight nose and upturned mouth. As I watched Marta grow before me, it was almost as if I was able to witness my mother's own transformation from infancy into girlhood.

Marta became more independent with each passing day. Lucie no longer had to get on bended knee to help her with her shoes or constantly change her because she had stained her dress. Her once-chubby body grew long, and her desire to express her own opinion grew as well.

But as Marta grew older, our relationship began to change. She was no longer a little doll that I could dress and pretend to be in charge of. We were rivals not just for my parents' attention, but also for Lucie's. And even though there were more than seven years between us, we still would bicker and Marta would often throw tantrums

18

when she did not get her own way.

Still, once Marta turned eight, there was one thing that we had in common that we both loved to discuss more than anything else: Lucie's love life. After we returned from school, we could spend hours trying to find out if she had a boyfriend. I would pry into who had given her the small gold necklace that suddenly appeared around her neck, or the new silk scarf she tucked underneath the collar of her capelet. And Marta would ask if he was handsome and rich, before bursting into tears and begging Lucie to promise that no matter what — she'd never leave us.

3

LENKA

In the autumn of 1934, Lucie announced that she was getting married to a young man by the name of Petr whom she had known since childhood and who now had a job as a clerk at a pharmacy near her parents' house in Kalin. Mother took the news as if it was her own daughter announcing her engagement.

When Lucie arrived for work the next day, Mother and the seamstress, Gizela, were already waiting for her with a dozen bolts of white silk propped against the walls.

'We're making you a wedding dress,' Mother announced. 'I will hear no words of refusal.'

'Get undressed, down to your slip and corset,' Gizela ordered.

She withdrew three pins from her pincushion and began wrapping the measuring tape, first around Lucie's bustline, then her waist, and finally her hips.

Lucie trembled as she stood silently in her underclothes.

'Really, this isn't necessary at all. I'll wear the dress my sisters wore. Petr doesn't care if it's worn or stained!'

20

'We will not hear of such a thing!' my mother said, shaking her head. She walked over to Lucie, who was quickly getting dressed. Her kiss reminded me of the way she kissed Marta and me.

Lucie wore her family's lace veil, a simple covering that fell just to her collarbone. Her garland was made from daisies and wild roses. Her bouquet was a mixture of asters and yellow leaves. She walked down the aisle on her father's arm, the black ringlets of her hair artfully arranged beneath her headpiece, her gaze looking firmly ahead.

We all wept when they exchanged their vows. Petr was as young as Lucie, no more than twenty-five, and I felt giddy for both of them. There was a beauty in how physically opposite they were. He was so much taller than she, with broad, flat features and a head full of blond hair. I noticed how large his hands were when they reached out to lift Lucie's veil, and how tiny her face was when he lifted her chin. His kiss was light and thoughtful, so quiet and gentle. I saw Mother take Papa's hand in hers and smile at him as if remembering their wedding day.

They left the church for the reception at her parents' home. It was a rustic farmhouse with exposed beams and a red tile roof. There were crooked apple trees and fragrant pear trees already in bloom in the garden. A white tent had been erected, the poles wrapped with thick yellow ribbon. On a small, makeshift stand, four men sat playing the polka.

It was the first time I had been to Lucie's childhood home. She had been with my family for years, yet I knew little of her life outside of the one she shared with us. We were united as tightly as a family, but it was always within our apartment or the city of Prague as the backdrop. Now, for the first time, we were seeing Lucie in her surroundings, with her family and her friends. From the corner of the garden, I gazed at the faces of her sisters and saw how they resembled each other. The small features, the narrow chin, and the high, straight bones in their cheeks and jaw. Lucie and her father were the only ones with black hair, as the rest of the family was fair and blond. They were a loud, noisy bunch compared to us. There were large pitchers of Moravian beer and *slivovice* — a homemade plum spirit. There were platters of rustic farm food like sauerkraut and sausages, and the traditional dumpling stew.

Marta and I were clapping and laughing with everyone as a circle formed around Lucie and Petr. We could hear the cheers for the ceremonial plate to be smashed. It was a Czech tradition, not so different from the Jewish one of the groom's breaking a glass. Unlike the Jewish ritual, though, which symbolized our people's years of sadness, the Czech one was meant to show the unity of the newly wedded couple. After the plate was broken, Petr was given a broom and Lucie a dustpan, and together they cleaned it up to show their future together.

Lucie only stayed with us a year after she got married. She became pregnant in March, and the daily trip to Prague became too exhausting for her. By this time, Marta was nine years old and I was sending out applications to art school. But we missed her greatly. She would still come to visit at least once a month, her belly popping through the blue velvet cape from Mother that she still dutifully wore. She was round like a little dumpling, her cheeks rosy and her hair glossier than ever.

'If I have a girl, I will call her Eliška, after you,' she told my mother. The two of them were now united in that secret sisterhood of mothers, with Marta and me looking on from the outside.

As Lucie's body changed from her pregnancy, mine finally began changing as well. I had been holding my breath for some time waiting for my body to catch up with the other girls in school — all who seemed to develop before me. That autumn I spent increasingly more time in front of the mirror. I stared at my reflection; the image of the little girl was receding, while a woman's face and body were coming to the surface. My face, once cushioned with baby fat, was now thinner and more angular, while my body was softer and more curvaceous. In what seemed like a final coup d'état over my body, my breasts seemed to grow several inches overnight and I soon discovered I could no longer close the buttons on some of my blouses.

Part of me wanted to give in to all these

changes, overhauling my appearance completely. I came home one day with a fashion magazine and pointed to a photograph of Greta Garbo. 'Please, Mama,' I begged. 'Let me bob my hair!' I was rushing to be grown up, my head filled with the idea that I could transform into an American movie star overnight. Mother placed down her teacup and took the magazine from me. She smiled. 'Keep your braids a little longer, Lenka,' she said, her voice tinged with wistfulness. 'It's taken you years to get your hair this long.'

And so my braids stayed. My mother, however, came to welcome some of the modern trends coming into Prague. She loved the new style of wide-legged trousers, a full blouse peeking out from a high, nipped waist. She bought these fashions for both herself and me, and even had Gizela, her seamstress, make several pairs of pants for us from a pattern book she ordered from Paris.

Unfortunately, my closetful of new, modern clothes failed to alter my perception of myself. I still felt as though I was trapped in a state of awkwardness. I wanted to be more confident and more feminine, but instead I only felt unattractive and insecure. My body seemed completely foreign to me now. For years, I had stared at a girl with braids and a body that seemed like it was cut from a paper-doll book. Now, with the changes of adolescence, I was more self-conscious about how I moved — even how I used my hands to express myself. An arm might now graze my breast when it earlier could move freely in front of me. Even my hips seemed to get in the way when I thought I could squeeze between two chairs.

I tried to focus my attention on my portfolio for art school. This was something that was tangible and something in which I had confidence. In my last year at high school, I had progressed from simple watercolors and pastels to a love of oil paint. When I was not doing homework, I spent my time painting or drawing. Our living room was full of the framed portraits I had done over the years. The small sketches I had done of an infant Marta were now replaced with a large portrait I painted of her in the white dress and pale blue sash she had worn to Lucie's wedding.

I hoped my portraits could express more than just the appearance of my subject, but their thoughts as well. The hands, the eyes, and the position of the body were like the instruments of a clock, and I only needed to orchestrate them in such a way so as to portray my subject's inner life. I imagined myself as El Greco, arranging my father in the large recess of his intricately carved chair, the red velvet seat a striking contrast to his black suit. I painted his hands, with the blue ribbons of his veins, the carefully manicured nails, and his laced fingers gently resting on his lap. I painted the blue green of his eyes, reflecting the light. The blackness of his mustache, resting above two closed, pensive lips. My mother, too, offered to sit for me.

Mother's name, Eliška, when abbreviated to Liška, meant 'fox,' and was a nickname my father called her lovingly. I thought of that as I painted her. I asked her to pose in a simple housedress, made of white starched cotton with an eyelet neck and trim on the sleeves. It was the way I loved her most, without her typically powdered face or her elegant wardrobe. My mother, simple and natural. Her pale skin, once revealed, was slightly freckled, like speckles of oatmeal floating in a bowl of milk.

She was always quiet after she studied one of my completed paintings. As if she wanted to say something, but instead held back.

She never spoke of her own time in art school, and certainly there was an air of mystery surrounding her former life as a student. She never displayed the paintings she had done before her marriage. I knew where they were because I had stumbled upon them around the time that Mother first announced she was pregnant with Marta. Lucie and I had gone to the storage cage in the bottom of our apartment building to look for a pump for my bicycle. Each apartment had a small locker, and Mother had given us the key for ours. I had never been down to the basement, and it was like a dark cave filled with everyone's misbegotten things. We passed old furniture draped in heavy white cloth, leather trunks, and boxes stacked to the ceiling.

Lucie took the key and opened our locker. Papa's bike was there, along with labeled boxes of china and even more boxes of glasses. We found the pump. It sat next to at least a dozen canvases that rested against the wall, covered by a white sheet.

26

I remember Lucie moving them cautiously. 'I think these are your mother's,' she said, whispering even though we were the only ones in the basement. Her fingers worked gently to separate each painting so we could both see the images.

Mother's paintings shocked me. They were not elegant, meticulous reproductions of great masters, or sweet, bucolic landscapes of the Czech countryside. They were sensual and dark, with palettes of plum and deep amber. There was one of a woman reclining on a divan, her pale arm resting behind her head and a naked torso with two rosy nipples and a blanket draped carefully across two crossed legs.

I later wondered about these paintings. The bohemian woman who painted them before she became a wife and mother was not my mother who was running her household upstairs. I tried to revise my image of her, imagining her as a young art student and in the arms of Father when they first met, and wondered if that part of her had disappeared completely, or whether it occasionally resurfaced when Marta and I were fast asleep.

Lucie never mentioned these paintings again. But years later — when I desperately tried to create a full and accurate picture of my mother — I would return to them. For the contrast of the woman and her paintings was impossible to erase from my mind.

I was accepted to Prague's Academy of Art in 1936, when I was seventeen years old. I walked to school every morning with my sketch-pad underneath my arm and a wooden box filled with oil paints and sable-haired brushes. There were fifteen students in my class, and although there were five girls in total, I quickly became friends with two girls, Vêruška and Elsa. Both girls were Jewish and we shared many of the same friends from our grade school years. A few weeks into our first semester, Vêruška invited me to her house for Shabbat. I knew little about her family except that her father and grandfather were both doctors, and her older brother Josef was now at university.

Josef. I still can see him so clearly. He arrived home that night wet, his curly black hair slick from the rain, and his large green eyes the color of weathered copper. I was standing in the hallway when he first arrived, the maid just slipping my coat from my shoulders. He had come through the front door just as I was heading toward the living room.

'Josef,' he said, smiling, as he put down his book bag and handed his coat to the maid. He then extended his hand to me and I took it, his broad fingers wrapping around mine.

I managed to utter my name and smile at him. But I was battling my constant shyness, and his confidence and good looks had rendered me mute.

'Lenka, there you are!' Vêruška chimed as she bolted into the hallway. She had changed from the clothes I had seen her wearing in class that afternoon into a beautiful burgundy dress. She threw her arms over me and kissed me.

'I see you've met my brother.' She went over and pinched Josef's cheek.

I was blushing.

'Vêruška.' He laughed and swatted her away. 'Go tell Mother and Father I'll be there in a moment.'

Vêruška nodded, and I followed her down the hallway to a large living room where her parents were deep in discussion.

The Kohns' apartment was not unlike ours, with its antique red velvet walls, the dark brown wooden rafters, and large glass French doors. But there was a somber quality to the household that unsettled me.

My eyes scanned the parlor. Around the perimeter of the room there was evidence of the family's scholarly life. Large medical journals in heavy bindings were stocked on the shelves along with other collections of leather-bound books. Framed diplomas from Charles University and a certificate of commendation from the Czech Medical Association hung on the walls. An imposing, large grandfather clock chimed to sound the hour, and a baby grand piano sat in the corner of the room. On the sofa, Vêruška's mother sat with a piece of needlepoint on her lap. Short and round, Mrs. Kohn wore simple dresses that hid her soft, plump physique. A small pair of reading glasses dangled over her large breasts, and her hair was wrapped plainly and practically in a bun at the nape of her neck.

Vêruška's father also seemed to wholly

29

contrast with mine. Whereas my father's eyes emanated warmth, Dr. Jacob Kohn's were clinical. When he first looked up from his book, it was clear he was surveying whoever stood before him.

'Lenka Maizel,' I introduced myself. My eyes fell to Dr. Kohn's two perfectly white hands, the nails meticulously filed and clean, as they unclasped and he stood up to greet me.

'Thank you for joining us this evening,' he said, his voice tight with restraint. I knew from my mother that Dr. Kohn was a distinguished obstetrician in the community. 'My wife, Anna . . . ' He touched her shoulder gently with his hand.

Věruška's mother smiled and extended her hand to me. 'We're happy to share Shabbat with you, Lenka.' Her voice was formal and exact.

'Thank you. Thank you for inviting me.'

Dr. Kohn nodded and gestured for me to sit down.

Věruška was her bubbly self and plopped down on one of the deep, red sofas. Quietly smoothing my dress over my legs, I sat down beside her.

'So you are studying art with our Ruška,' her mother said.

'I am. And I am in good company. Your Věruška is the great talent of our class.'

Both Dr. and Mrs. Kohn smiled.

'I'm sure you're being too modest, Lenka,' I heard a soft, low voice say from behind me. It was Josef, who had walked in and was now standing behind his sister and me.

'It is a noble trait, modesty,' Dr. Kohn added. He folded his hands.

'No, it's true. Vêruška has the best eye in our class.' I patted her on her leg. 'We're all jealous of her.'

'How can that be?' Josef asked bemused.

'Oh, make him stop, Mama,' Vêruška protested. 'He's twenty years old and still taunting me!'

Josef and I locked eyes. He smiled. My face reddened. And suddenly for the first time in my life, I felt I could barely breathe.

That night over dinner, I could hardly eat a morsel. My appetite had completely vanished and I felt terribly self-conscious with every movement I made at the table. Josef sat to the left of his father, his large shoulders extending past the back of his chair. I am too shy to meet his gaze. My eyes focus on his hands. My own mother's hands were smooth but strong. Father's were large and covered in a thin veil of hair. Josef's hands were unlike the small white hands of Dr. Kohn. They had the musculature one sees in a statue — the wide dorsal, the ribbon of pronounced veins, and the thick strong fingers.

I watched the hands of the Kohn family closely, as if each pair reflected the emotions running through the room. There was a tension during the dinner that was unmistakable. When Dr. Kohn asked his son about his classes, Josef gripped his knife and fork even tighter. His knuckles stiffened, the veins grew even more pronounced. He answered his father succinctly, without any detail, never once taking his gaze off his plate.

Vêruška was the only animated one at the table. She threw her hands about like a lithe dancer. She peppered the conversation with little bits of gossip: the neighbor's daughter who had grown so fat she looked like a cream puff; the postman who was caught having an affair with the maid. Unlike her more reserved parents, she took great relish in her every detail. There were great swirls and flourishes in her descriptions. When Vêruška spoke, you couldn't help but think of a rococo painting — all her subjects engaging in clandestine acts of love, their affairs painted in large voluminous brushstrokes of vibrant color.

I sat there, an observer of their household, all the contrasts in high relief to me. The elegant white cloth set with the Sabbath candles, the platters filled with meat and potatoes, the asparagus arranged like piano keys on a long, porcelain tray. Dr. Kohn, serious with his spectacles; his carefully, measured voice. His hands that never gestured, but remained at the edge of the table. Josef, the quietly bemused giant whose eyes looked alight with fire and mischief whenever he looked my way; his sister bubbly and effervescent as a tall flute of champagne. And Mrs. Kohn, who sat silently at the opposite end of the table with her hands folded, round and plump like a stuffed capon.

Eventually, dessert was served. Dry apple cake

with a faint taste of honey. I thought of Mother and Father at home, how they loved their whipped cream. Chocolate cake, raspberry torte, palačinka. Anything was an excuse to have an extra spoonful.

'You don't have much of an appetite, Lenka,' Dr. Kohn commented as he looked at my barely touched plate.

I took my fork and tried to force down another bite.

'I think I had too much lunch,' I said with a nervous laugh.

'And are you enjoying the Academy as much as my daughter?' He looked at Vêruška and smiled. It was the first time I saw him smile all evening.

'Yes. It is challenging. I don't have Vêruška's talent, so I must work harder to keep up.'

'I hope Vêruška isn't too much of a distraction in class. As you can see, it's hard for my daughter to keep still — '

'Papa!' Vêruška interrupted.

He smiled again. 'She's full of life, my daughter. I don't know what our household would be like without her and her stories . . . '

'It certainly would be much quieter . . . ' Josef murmured, smiling.

I smiled, too.

Josef saw this and seemed to be amused by my affection for his sister. 'We should have a drink to Vêruška!' He looked over at me then lifted his glass. 'And to her friend, who is clearly too modest.'

Everyone lifted their glasses and looked in my

direction. I felt my face redden with embarrass-ment.

And of course, it was Vêruška who took great pleasure in pointing it out.

❦

The dessert plates were cleared. Behind the kitchen door, there was the sound of porcelain and cutlery being rinsed and stacked away.

Dr. Kohn stood up. We all followed. He walked over to a pedestal with a gramophone. 'Mozart?' he asked with a raised eyebrow. He was holding a record in one perfectly white hand. 'Yes. A little Mozart, I think.'

He took the record from its sheath and placed the needle down. And the room was filled with a rain of notes.

❦

I drank one small glass of sherry. Vêruška had two.

Afterward, when the music faded and the decanter was taken away by the maid, Josef excused himself from our company. Moments later he was standing in the hallway like a summoned guardian. It was clear he would be the one to escort me home.

I insisted that I would be fine. But neither Josef nor his parents would hear otherwise. My coat was slipped over my shoulders, Vêruška kissed my two cheeks. I closed my eyes, momentarily distracted by the smell of sherry mixing with her perfume. 'I'll see you Monday in class,' she said, before squeezing my hand.

I turned to leave and walked into the iron-caged elevator with Josef. He was wearing a dark green coat, his mouth and nose covered by a thick wool muffler. His eyes, the same color as his coat, peered at me like a curious child.

We walked for a few minutes without speaking. The night was black. The sky like velvet, studded with only a few bright stars.

We felt the cold. It was the cold one feels just before a snow. A dampness that slices through cloth, skin, and bone.

On Prokopská Street, he finally breaks the silence. He asks me about my studies. What subjects do I like? Have I always loved to draw?

I tell him I struggle in anatomy class, and at this he laughs. I tell him I love to paint most of all.

He tells me he is in his first year in medical school. That he has been told he will be a doctor since the day he was born.

'Do you have an interest in something else?' I ask him. The question is bold, but the wine and sherry have made me more confident.

He ponders the question briefly, before stopping to think about it further. We are steps away from Charles Bridge now. Long branches of light come from the gas lanterns. Our faces are half gold, half shadow.

'I love medicine,' he says. 'The human body is part science, part art.'

I nod. I tell him I agree.

'But part of it can't be learned in books, and

that's the part that's the most daunting to me.'

'It's the same way with painting,' I tell him. 'I often wonder how I can be so insecure at times with something I love so much.'

Josef smiles. He turns away for a moment before returning his gaze to me.

'I have this memory from my childhood. My sister and I found a wounded bird. We placed it carefully in a handkerchief and brought it to our father.

' 'What's this?' he asked us, when we placed it down on his desk.

' 'He's sick, Papa,' I remember Vêruška saying. Her voice was so small and pleading. We had brought our father something we were so confident he could fix.'

I was looking at Josef now. His eyes were full of memory.

'My father took the kerchief with the trembling bird and cupped it in his hands. I could see the small creature's body soften from the warmth of my father's palms. He held it for what seemed like several minutes before the bird's movements stopped.'

Josef took a breath.

'The bird had died in his hands.'

'Oh, how terrible,' I said, bringing my hand to my mouth. 'You and Vêruška must have been devastated.'

'You probably thought I was going to tell you I wanted to be a doctor because I saw my father resurrect something so frail and wounded, didn't you?' He was shaking his head.

'But you see, Lenka, I return to that incident

over and over again. My father must have realized he couldn't have saved the bird. So he gently held it in his hands until its life flowed out from it.'

'But how painful for you and Věruška to see . . .'

'It was,' he said. 'It was the first time I realized that my father couldn't heal every broken thing. That, sometimes, even he could fail.'

He looked at me again. 'I try to remember that when I feel I disappoint him.'

I wanted to reach out to him as he said this, but my hands remained at my side.

'What is it about you, Lenka, that I want to tell you every story from my childhood?' He turned to me, and his face transformed into a grin. He gave a little laugh and I could tell he was trying to lighten the mood.

'Your eyes are wide open. I feel as though I could step inside them and make myself at home.'

I was now the one laughing. 'You're welcome to come in. I'll even make you a cup of coffee.'

'And will you put the gramophone on? Put on a little Duke Ellington on for me.'

'If you like,' I teased.

'And will you offer me your hand to dance, Lenka?' His voice was now full of light and playfulness.

'Yes!' I tell him. I cannot suppress my urge to giggle.

He laughs. And in his laugh I hear bliss. I hear feet dancing, the rush of skirts twirling. The sound of children.

Is that the first sign of love?
You hear in the person you're destined to love the sound of those yet to be born.

We walk farther, across the bridge, down the Smetanovo embankment until we are in front of the large wooden doors of my apartment building.

'I hope I will see you again,' he says.

We smile at each other, as if we both know something that neither of us is brave enough to say.

Instead we simply say good-bye.

There is no kiss between us, just the slightest graze of hands.

Věruška, Elsa, and I continued to be a threesome at school that winter of 1937. Dressed in our heavy cloth coats and fur hats, we would climb up the lengthy stairs of the Academy, peel off our layers, and find our seats at our easels. The classrooms were hot, and condensation fogged the windows as our live model stood naked against a draped chair.

Sometimes, I would lie in my bed and try to imagine Josef. I would try to conjure up what his shoulders might look like or the cleaving of muscles in the center of his chest. But my imagination could never convince my hand. My drawings were awkward and almost all of them ended up as crumpled pieces of paper in the waste bin.

I discovered that I did have one talent, which was when I concentrated on drawing my subject's face. Perhaps it was those years of shyness, my natural tendency to observe, but I found that I was able to see things that my other classmates had often overlooked. When drawing an old woman, I would find myself gazing at her pale, watery eyes.

While others concentrated to get the drape of skin just so, the weight of the flesh falling from a once-robust frame, I focused on the fallen skin of her eyelids. I thought of how I might draw their delicate flesh, like two paper-thin curtains, a veil over her already shaky eyesight.

I smoothed the contours of her face by smudging the charcoal with my thumb. I gave her softness, when the skin on her face was more like parchment than satin. But by doing this, her features — so carefully drawn — were like a frieze telling a story against a stretch of white marble. They seemed as if they were cut from stone.

Another skill I tried to develop in painting class was to bring a certain psychology to my canvases. I used colors that were not typical, sometimes blending pigments of blue and green to my skin tones to convey sadness. Or I might place dots of lavender inside the irises of the eyes for melancholy, or scarlet for passion.

I was intrigued by the paintings of the Secessionists, Schiele and Kokoschka, with their kinetic line and emotional message. Our teacher, Joša Prokop, was hard on me and did not praise me as readily as he did some of my classmates. But near the end of the semester he began to praise my efforts to take risks with my drawings, and I felt myself growing more confident each day. Still, I continued to work late at night on improving upon my weaknesses. Marta would sometimes indulge me and let me draw her. She would unbutton her cotton gown and let me sketch her collarbone or her neck. Sometimes she would even let me draw her back so I could concentrate on drawing the delicate wings of her shoulder blades.

The more I worked, the more I was able to see the human body as connected pieces of a puzzle. With time, I taught myself how each vertebra linked to another to create a stance of posture. I studied anatomy books to learn how each bone conjoined with another, and I came to see that our skin was nothing more than a tarpaulin that stretched over an extremely efficient machine.

When I was not at home or at school, I was at Vêruška's. Every invitation I received to go there, I accepted just so I could hope to steal a glimpse of Josef. At night, I dreamed of being able to paint his dark, pensive face, the thick black of his curls, the green of his eyes.

No longer did I dress without a thought as to how I looked. While in class, I dressed conservatively and in dark colors, often in trousers and a sweater. When I went to Vêruška's, however, I picked out outfits I thought accentuated my figure. I was now approaching my eighteenth year and feeling all the pull of my desire. I wanted to draw attention to myself, something I had never done in the past.

I began rummaging through my mother's vanity when she was out of the house, and started applying powder to my face and applying a faint trace of lipstick and rouge. I was more careful with my hair, no longer braiding it like a schoolgirl in two ropes near my ears, but putting it up and twisting it above my neck.

I've often wondered if it is impossible to dress purely for your own indulgence and not in the hope of catching a man's eye. Some women love the feel of silk in their own hand, the weight of velvet on their skin. I think my mother was like that. She always told us there were two types of women. Those who are lit from the outside and those who are lit from within. The first needs the shimmer of a diamond to make her sparkle, but for the other, her beauty is illuminated through the sheer light of her soul.

My mother had a fire that burned in her eyes. Her skin flushed not from the color of rouge but from the rush of her blood. When she was deep in thought, her complexion changed from milk to rose. When she was angry, she streaked crimson. And when she was sad, she became a shadowy blue. My mother was elegant, but she dressed not for the approving eyes of her husband or any crowd, but for her own secret ideal. A fantasy cut from a nineteenth-century novel, an image that was both timeless and eternal. A romantic heroine clearly her own.

4

JOSEF

My grandson tells me that I'm not a romantic. I don't disagree with him. For his impression is shaped by what he has observed over the years. He doesn't know me the way I was before the war, when my heart soared for a woman whose name he wouldn't recognize, whose photograph he has never seen.

I married his grandmother in 1947, in a dimly lit apartment within walking distance of the East River. There were snowdrifts piled high outside the fire escapes, and the windows were so foggy they resembled frosted glass.

I don't think I had known Amalia more than three months when I proposed to her. She was from Vienna, another transplant from the war. I met her in the public library. She was hunched over a stack of books, and I don't know if it was the way she wore her hair or the cotton wrap dress that was inappropriate for the climate, but somehow I knew she was European.

She told me she was a war orphan, having left Austria just before the war. She had not heard from her parents or sister in months.

'I know they're dead,' she told me flatly. I

42

immediately recognized that tone of voice: dead to emotions, a mechanical reflex that functioned solely to communicate. She ticked off only the necessary points of conversation like a finger to an abacus, with nothing more.

She was wan, with pale skin, honey-colored hair, and wide brown eyes. I could see her clavicle rising like an archer's bow from beneath her skin, and a tiny, circular locket resting between her small breasts.

I imagined that within that gold locket there was a photo of a lost love. Another tall, dark boy lost to the war.

But later, after several weeks of meeting at a small café near my classes, I learned there had been no boyfriend left to die in Austria.

Although she was forced to wear the yellow star in the weeks following the *Anschluss*, her family was initially able to keep their apartment on Uchatius Strasse. One afternoon, as she walked home from school along the Ringstrasse, her eyes lingered on the cobblestones. She said she had gotten used to walking with her head down, because she wanted to avoid eye contact with anyone. She no longer knew whom she could trust, who was a friend, or who might report her if she looked at them the wrong way. She had heard too many stories of a neighbor who was falsely accused of stealing, or one who was arrested for breaking a newly issued law affecting the Jews. On this particular day, her eyes caught sight of an envelope fluttering from underneath a bicycle tire. She claimed she didn't know what made her reach out to grab it, but when she took hold of the envelope she saw the return address was from America: Mr. J. Abrams on East Sixty-fifth Street in New York City.

She immediately recognized that it was a Jewish name. She told me that knowing there was a Jew somewhere across the ocean, in the safety of America, gave her a strange sense of comfort. That evening, she wrote to him in German, not even telling her parents or her sister. She told him how she found his name, that she needed to take a chance, to tell someone — anyone — outside of Europe what was happening in Austria. She told him of the yellow stars that her mother had been forced to sew on their coats. She told him of the curfew, and the loss of her father's business. She told him how the streets were now lined with signs that said JEWS FORBIDDEN, how windows were smashed with hate, and how the beards of those who maintained the Talmudic code were shorn by young Nazis searching for fun. Lastly, for no other apparent reason other than that the day was approaching, she told him her birthday was May 20.

She had not really expected Mr. Abrams to write back. But then, weeks later, she did receive a reply. He wrote that he would sponsor her and her sister to come to New York. He gave her directions on whom she should speak to in Vienna, who would give her money, and who would secure their visas and transportation out of this wretched country that had forsaken them. He told her she was a lucky girl: they shared the same birthday and he would help her.

He told her there wasn't enough time for a lengthy correspondence. She should do what he instructed her immediately, and not diverge from the plan. There could be no discussion, he could not arrange for her parents' transport.

When she told her parents of the letter she had written and Mr. Abrams's reply, they were not angry as she had feared, but proud that she had shown such initiative and foresight.

'What could two old people do in a new country anyway,' her father said to his daughters as the three of them sipped their favorite drink — hot chocolate. It was his nature always to make light of things when the family was pressed into a difficult situation. 'When this Nazi horror is all over, you will call for us, and your mother and I will come.'

She and her sister then traveled by train to Danzig, where the steamer was to depart from. But when they boarded the ship an SS officer looked at their passports with the word *Jude* stamped on it and blocked their path.

'You can get on.' He pointed to Amalia. He then pointed to her younger sister, Zora. 'You will stay.'

Amalia cried to the soldier that she would not leave her sister. It was not fair; they both had their papers, their tickets, and passports all in order.

'I decide who boards this ship. Now you can get on alone, or you can both get off together.'

Amalia turned to disembark with her sister. She would never leave her. To abandon your own sibling simply to save yourself was an act of treason she was not willing to commit.

'Go . . . Go . . . ' her sister insisted, but she refused. And then her sister did the unthinkable . . . she ran off alone. She ran down the plank and into the crowd. Her black coat and hat blended in with what seemed like a thousand others. It was like finding a single raindrop in a downpour. Amalia stood there screaming her sister's name, searching for her frantically. But it was of no use. Her sister had vanished.

The steamship's horn had signaled its impending departure, and Amalia found herself on the gangplank alone. She didn't look at the officer as he examined her papers for the second time. She was sure by his lack of interest in her that he didn't even remember that she had been the victim of his willful and incomprehensible cruelty less than an hour before. She walked into the belly of the ship, carrying her battered black suitcase. She looked back one more time — hoping against hope that Zora had somehow sneaked on board — and then stood by the railing as the anchor was lifted and the boat pulled away. Zora was nowhere to be seen in the faces waving at the dock. She had vanished into the fog.

I tell you Amalia's story because she is now dead. Dead fifteen years next October. Mr. Abrams gave her money when she arrived in New York. She met him in his office on Fifth Avenue, an office paneled with dark red wood and with a swivel chair that he turned to face the park.

She told me that when he turned to her, Mr.

Abrams asked her where her sister was. He shook his head when she told him how Zora had not been allowed to board.

'You were very brave to come alone,' he commended her. But she had not felt brave. She instead felt the weight of her betrayal, as if she had left her only sister for dead. He took some money from a drawer and handed it to her along with a piece of paper with the name of a Rabbi Stephen Wise. He promised he would help get her a job and a place to stay.

The rabbi got her on her feet, setting her up with a seamstress on the Lower East Side, where she worked for twenty-five cents an hour sewing flowers to the brims of black felt hats. She saved what little money she could after paying her landlady for the room she shared with two other girls from Austria, in a vain hope of bringing her parents and sisters over one day. In the beginning, there were letters from them, ones that arrived with thick black lines applied by a censor. But eventually, after the war had begun in Europe; her letters began to be returned to her unopened. She heard her roommates repeat vague rumors of concentration camps and transports, hideous things she couldn't possibly believe to be true. Gas and ovens, one girl even told her. But that girl, a Pole, was prone to drama. There could be little truth in her stories. Amalia told herself that girl was mad.

She grew even thinner than she was before. So thin you could see right through her skin. Her hands began to bleed from working with a needle and thread so many hours, and her eyesight grew poor. She almost never went out, except to the library, where she practiced reading English, still saving every penny she made to fund her family's future passage. That first day I met her there, I asked if I could take her to Café Vienna, a hole in the wall on the corner of West Seventy-sixth and Columbus Avenue. Every night it was filled with a hundred fragmented Jews; each of us had someone we were searching for. People showed photos and wrote names of the missing on matchbook covers. We were all adrift, the living lost, trying to make connections in case someone had heard of someone else who had arrived — who had survived — or who knew something. And when we weren't shaking a hand of someone who knew a friend of a friend of a friend, we drank whiskey or scotch. Except my Amalia. She only ordered hot chocolate.

So I eventually learned whose faces were in the locket, you see. Even though I never saw them until our wedding night, when she took off the necklace and laid it on our nightstand. I came back from the bathroom while my new wife lay sleeping, opened up the tiny gold circle, and silently peered inside.

What do you do with black-and-white faces that do not speak but continue to haunt you? What do you do with letters that are returned to you from across the ocean? The dead do not answer their mail, but your wife still sends them letters all the same.

So I think of what my grandson says about me, that I have no sense of romance.

Did Amalia and I ever really speak of those we left behind? No. Because if we did, our voices would crack and the walls would crush us with the memory of our grief. We wore that grief like one wears one's underclothes. An invisible skin, unseen to prying eyes, but knitted to us all the same. We wore it every day. We wore it when we kissed, when our bodies locked, and our limbs entwined.

Did we ever make love with a sense of vitality, or unbridled passion and lust? It seemed to me that we were both two lost souls holding on to each other, fumbling for some sense of weight and flesh in our hands — reassuring ourselves that we were not simply two ghosts evaporating into the cool blankness of our sheets. We each could barely stand to think of our lives and families before the war, because it hurt like a wound that would never heal. It stank with rot and clung to you like soaking-wet wool.

Amalia and I were at battle with our memories. That is what I remember mostly of our marriage. We feared we might drown in all those lost voices and other lost treasures from our homelands. I became a doctor, and she the mother of our two children. But every night in the thirty-eight years that I held her, it was as if she wasn't really there.

5

LENKA

Josef became my secret. I carried his image with me every morning as I walked the steps into the Academy. When Vêruška would mention her brother in passing, I was helpless to stop my cheeks from turning red.

At night, I would imagine his voice, try to conjure up the exact inflection of his speech when he had asked me if I liked to dance. And then I would imagine us dancing. Each of our bodies softening into the other like warm clay.

When Vêruška and Elsa spoke of their crushes, I listened intently. I watched as their faces came alive at the prospect of a secret tryst and how their eyes widened when they described the heat of a stare or the graze of a certain hand. I asked them questions, and made a concentrated effort to show enthusiasm regarding the boys whose affections they courted. All the while I was keeping a secret that I sometimes felt would choke me.

I struggled with whether I should tell my friends how I felt about Josef. There were several opportunities to confess my feelings. But every time I got close to opening up, I feared Vêruška's disapproval. How many times had I heard her complain about Josef being the focus of her parents' attention, or the afternoons she loathed to return home because her father insisted on complete quiet in the house so Josef could study.

'Let's go to Obcencí dům for cake,' she said, trying to rouse us all one afternoon after class. 'It's final-exam time for Josef, and I'll have to walk on tiptoe if I go home now.'

'Why doesn't he study at the medical library?' Elsa shook her head.

'I think he'd prefer that,' Věruška said as she placed her sketch-pad in her satchel. 'But my father wants to make sure he's really studying.'

'Your poor — '

'Don't say it!' Věruška lifted her hand up to Elsa. 'Poor nothing. He's their diamond. Their treasure. Their only *son*.' She let out a mocking sigh.

My eyes flickered with the thought of him hunched over the dining room table, his fingers running through his hair as he struggled to concentrate.

So for now, I kept him a secret. Every word he had said to me on our walk home was committed to memory. Every one of his gestures now moved across my mind like a carefully choreographed dance. I could see his eyes turning to me, envision his hands on my cheeks, feel his cloud of breath in the winter air.

First love: there is nothing like it. All these years later, I can remember the first time I looked up and saw Josef's face, the flash of recognition that defied words.

51

It was in those first glances, those first exchanges, that I sensed not the uncertainty of love between us, but rather the sheer inevitability of it.

And so at night, I allowed those feelings to swim through my body. I closed my eyes and colored my mental canvas with strokes of red and orange. I imagined myself traveling to him, my skin against his, like a warm blanket, wrapping him in sleep.

Vêruška, Elsa, and I spent much of the autumn of our second year struggling with our classes. We were being pushed harder than in our first year. Life-drawing class, which had once been off-limits to female students, was now part of our curriculum. We had not yet seen a male model, as only women had appeared on the small draped bed in our classroom, but we all still struggled to get the accuracy of every limb, curve, and angle.

At lunchtime, we sat in the school's courtyard and ate our packed sandwiches while enjoying the sun and fresh air. Elsa would sometimes bring little samples of cream and perfume from her father's apothecary. Everything was packaged in little glass vials that were elegantly labeled.

'Try this,' Elsa said to me. 'It's rose oil.

'It's my favorite,' she said as she moved my hair behind my ear and dabbed a little of it on my neck.

'Oh, that's such a nice smell,' Vêruška agreed.

'How come you never tell us about your crushes, Lenka?' She poked me. 'Elsa and I blabber on and you never mention a single boy!'

'What if I'm afraid you'll disapprove?'

'Never!' She let out a little squeal. 'Tell us!'

I laughed. 'I'm not sure you'd be able to keep a secret, Vêruška,' I teased.

She giggled and reached for the little vial of rose oil from Elsa's hand.

'I don't need for you to tell me,' she said as she applied some oil behind her own ears. 'I already know.'

'Who?' Elsa was now in on the excitement. 'Who is it?'

'It's Freddy Kline, of course!' Vêruška said between giggles.

Freddy Kline was a very short classmate of ours. He was sweet and kind, but I suspected he didn't have any interest in girls whatsoever.

I laughed.

'Vêruška, you've found me out.'

Those afternoons of laughter would soon fade. My own father's business began suffering as I entered that second year at the Academy. By the winter of 1938, his clients stopped placing new orders. Only one was honest enough to tell him it was because he was nervous to be associated with a Jew. Lucie was the only Gentile we knew who remained loyal to us. She continued to visit with the baby, a round cherub who now walked and made little noises,

53

and brought a much-needed vitality to our otherwise concerned household.

The contrast of Lucie's baby on my mother's lap revealed how she had begun to age. The strain of Father's failing business and the unspoken fear of rising anti-Semitism had begun to wear on her face. As if visited by an etcher's point, her face was now feathered with thin lines that made her appear sadder, and perhaps more fragile, than before.

I hold the image of my mother with Lucie's baby, Eliška, on her lap, like a postcard from a long-ago holiday. I have the sensation that I was once in the parlor in our apartment on Smetanovo nábřeži, a tuft of red upholstery beneath me and a cup of tea resting between cupped hands. Here I am, a daughter looking at her mother aging before her eyes. I see my nanny's child with her life stretched before her, in dark contrast to my mother's. I have never actually painted this image, even though I think of it often. Like poetry that is recited but never written down, more powerful because it is held solely in the mind.

I continued to throw myself into my studies during that second year at the Academy. While Věruška toted her sketchpad to the Café Artistes every afternoon, and sat seductively among the brooding intelligentsia, I walked back to our family's apartment to work on my homework assignments and keep an eye on my parents.

I knew that Marta's presence would have been enough, but I was increasingly worried about them. My own life had not changed yet. I was still attending school, and socializing occasionally when I felt like it. But the financial burden of supporting his family under deteriorating conditions was weighing on Papa. Like rain running down a gutter, his concern trickled down on all of us.

They had already let the maid go, and Mother's visits to the seamstress, Gizela, had ceased. Mother had taken to doing her own cooking, too. Papa was trying to sell off most of his inventory in an effort to downsize and raise money. There were whispers about perhaps trying to emigrate to Palestine, but how could they start anew in a country where they had no family, and no knowledge of the language or culture?

I lay in bed every night with my eyes shut and my ears hearing bits and pieces of their heated discussions. I loathe to admit it now, but I was still a self-absorbed young woman at the time. I did not want to believe that my family was suffering and that our life was beginning to unravel. I only wanted to distract myself. And so I would go to my room and try to think of something that made me happy. I thought of Josef.

Tensions began to escalate throughout Europe that June and my parents welcomed the news

55

when I told them that Vêruška's family had
invited me to spend two weeks at their summer
home in Karlovy Vary. I was overjoyed to learn
that Josef would be escorting us on the train.

Although my parents were happy that I'd have
a distraction, Marta was not so pleased.

'Do you really have to go?' Marta was twelve
now and had become particularly sullen when
not included in what she perceived as my
entertainment. I was folding my dresses as neatly
as I could because I didn't want them to be
creased.

'Marta.' I sighed. 'You would be bored silly.
We're probably just going to take our sketchpads
and draw by the river all afternoon.'

'Josef will be there.' She stuck out her tongue.
'That's why you want to go, I know it.'

I snapped my leather valise shut and walked
past Marta, tugging playfully on one of her
braids.

'It's only for two weeks,' I reassured her. 'Take
good care of Mama and Papa, and don't eat too
much chocolate.' I blew up my cheeks like a fat
toddler and winked at her. I remember how her
pale skin reddened with fury in response.

At the station, Vêruška and her brother stood
together. Josef was in a pale yellow suit; Vêruška's
sundress was poppy red. When she saw me she
leaped to greet me and thrust her arm through
mine.

Josef stood there watching us. His eyes were

firmly on me. When I met his gaze, he turned his eyes in the direction of my suitcase. Without asking, he took it and carried it in the direction of the porter, who had a trolley filled with his and Věruška's things.

The ride to Karlovy Vary would take three hours by train. Věruška's parents had a house in the country, only a short ride from the famed spa where one drank the curative waters.

It was my first trip there. 'Take a cure for us,' Papa had said sweetly. 'You'll come back even more beautiful.' My mother looked up at me from her needlepoint when Papa said this, and I had the distinct feeling that she was trying to memorize the way I looked, as though her young daughter was becoming a young woman before her very eyes.

I had packed a small sketchpad, a tin of vine charcoal, and some pastels so I could sketch the countryside during my two weeks at their house.

After nibbling on smoked fish sandwiches and some tea at the station's café, the three of us headed back to the first-class compartment where the porter was already waiting with our things.

Josef unbuttoned his jacket and folded it on top of our suitcases on the upper rack.

It was unseasonably warm, even for the month of June, and I envied the casual way Josef had taken off his coat. There was little I could do about the heat, and I was jealous that I could not also lose a layer. Certainly my dress was not too heavy, but with my slip and stockings, and the closeness in the compartment, I worried I might start to perspire. The thought of stains spreading underneath my arms was horrifying. I wanted to sit there in my dress like a medieval Madonna, not a tattered street urchin with moisture under my arms. My plan to attract Josef was coming undone.

We still had another twenty minutes to wait before the train departed for our long trip, and I hoped that Josef would open the window. Instead, he just sat across from Vêruška and me, his legs crossed and his fingers absentmindedly running through his hair.

'Josef!' Vêruška complained shortly to her brother. 'Why don't you please pull the window down?' He stood up and forced it open. The noises of the station rushed into our compartment. Families juggling their luggage, hasty farewells, and porters crying out that the train would be leaving in fifteen minutes. I closed my eyes and wished we were already there. But the breeze coming in from the train window cooled me, and I sensed that Josef had not actually forgotten about his overheated train companion. For he continued to look up from his book and sneak glances in my direction.

We pulled out of the station on time, and Vêruška chatted for nearly the entire trip. Josef had taken a book out of his suitcase and I envied his ability to tune out his sister. If the trip had been less bumpy, I might have pulled out my sketchbook and asked to draw sister and brother, but I knew my hands would not be steady enough with the sensation of the wheels underneath me.

We took a horse-drawn carriage when we arrived in Karlovy Vary, passing the town with its multicolored façades and peaked rooflines. Josef spoke to the driver, giving him directions, and when he caught me staring at him, he returned my gaze with a slight smile. We had not really talked during the train ride. I had returned Vêruška's chattiness with a diligent and attentive ear and Josef had managed to read his book in its entirety.

When we arrived at the Kohns' home, deep within the mountains, I knew almost immediately that I'd have ample opportunity to sketch. The scenery was lush and majestic, with stretches of verdant green that reminded me of illustrations of fairies and wooden kingdoms from my childhood books. The smells of wildflowers, tails of lupine, and star asters dotted the landscape. The house itself was beautiful and old, with a broad porch and a Bohemian turret that looked as though it could pierce the sky.

We were greeted warmly by an old woman named Pavla, who I later learned had been Josef and Vêruška's nanny when they were little. Josef bent down to kiss Pavla on both cheeks, his large hands nearly enveloping the entirety of her tiny round head.

'Your parents arrived last night and decided to stay at the spa until this evening,' Pavla told them. 'I've made your favorite cookies with the jam in the center. Would you like them now with some tea?' I had to suppress the urge to laugh, for she spoke to them as if they were still three years old.

Josef shook his head no, but Vêruška, who was always hungry, eagerly jumped at the invitation. 'Oh yes, Pavla! That would be wonderful!' She turned to me. 'You will need to take a cure at the spa after two weeks of Pavla's cooking. We will be as big as stuffed geese when we return to Prague.'

'I just need to wash up and then I'll join you,' I promised. I was eager to unpack and change my clothes.

'Let me take your suitcase, Lenka,' Josef offered. His hand was already wrapped around its handle.

I went to stop him, but he was already walking in the direction of the stairs. 'It's this way,' he said.

I walked behind him, winding my way up the steps, his shadow and mine two moving cutouts against the white walls. When we arrived at the guest room, he placed my suitcase on the floor and walked over to the window that faced the mountains. There below was a garden filled with roses and a large outdoor seating area with an old wooden table and some white-painted iron chairs.

'Here,' he said, opening up the two glass doors. 'Now you can breathe in all the fresh air you need.'

'And hopefully there won't be any dying birds in the garden. It would embarrass me greatly if I couldn't resurrect one for you.'

I laughed. 'Hopefully your medical powers won't be needed for birds or for Věruška's or my sake!'

'Well, I'll let you rest before dinner, then. You must be tired from the journey.'

I looked at him and nodded. 'A little rest would do me good.'

As I walked with him toward the door, I could feel the heat spreading across my face. It wasn't until he had left the room, and closed the door completely behind him, that I was actually able to settle in. Only then, as the redness of my skin began to dissipate, did I take off my sandals, stretch my legs across the bed, and close my eyes. My head filled with thoughts of Josef as the breeze brushed against my skin.

That afternoon I was breathless as I walked through the house. The crystal chandeliers sparkled in the sunlight. There were large pieces of carved Bohemian furniture, and beautiful china already in place on the dining table next to tall, handblown cobalt wineglasses. In the middle, Pavla had arranged a handkerchief vase full of daisies.

By evening, the same handkerchief vase was rearranged with roses. The dining room, which hours before was filled with sunlight, was now dark except for the low flickers of candles. Tall, etched goblets were filled with red wine. Rounds of white porcelain lined the table and a tall silver pitcher cast a warped reflection.

I had forgotten how different Vêruška and Josef's parents were from mine. After engaging in a few obligatory pleasantries with me, Dr. Kohn questioned Josef about his studies for the rest of the meal.

'What reading have you brought with you, Josef?'

Josef paused for a second over the cutting of his meat. '*Lady Chatterley's Lover*, Father.'

'Really now, Josef.'

'Really, Father. The anatomy descriptions are proving quite helpful to my studies, among other things.'

Josef looked over his wineglass in my direction. He was smiling and the top of his lip was stained darker from the wine. He looked like a little imp — a mischievous boy hoping to make me smile.

Vêruška and I nearly choked on our wine laughing, but Dr. Kohn did not seem to find any humor in his son's antics. Whereas Vêruška's little anecdotes were smiled upon, the elder Kohn tolerated far less levity from his son.

'*Your* studies are important, Josef.'

Josef's face reddened. 'Of course they are.'

'Being a doctor is not just a profession; it is an honor.'

'I realize that.'

'Do you?' Dr. Kohn brought a napkin up to his lips. 'I often wonder if you do.

'I have lost count of the exact amount of

children I have brought into this world,' Dr. Kohn proffered. 'But nothing was more important to their parents, and I am blessed to have helped them.'

'Yes, Father.'

'The practice of medicine is not something to be taken lightly.'

As Dr. Kohn spoke sternly to Josef, I tried to picture the wounded bird in his palms. I wished that he could be as soft with Josef, allow himself to smile in his company, and not question him so relentlessly. This man, who had known exactly what to do with a fragile, injured bird, lacked those instincts with his own son.

I could see Josef struggling under his father's glare; his jaw was stiff and his face was now serious.

When I looked over at Věruška, it was the first time I saw her resembling her mother. They were like two china dolls, their heads tucked downward, their eyes staring motionless at their plates.

In the reflection of the silver pitcher, I saw my own face. A forced smile that belied a frown.

6

JOSEF

It used to bother Amalia that every evening after I returned home from the hospital, I would lock myself in my study for half an hour. She always had dinner on the table for me. The usual fare: a pot roast, a basket of rye bread, and an overboiled green vegetable. The only time I ate my dinner while it was still warm were nights when there were no deliveries, which was rare.

There was no lock on the door to my study, but Amalia and the children knew not to disturb me there. My days at the hospital were long and hectic and I needed a few minutes of privacy in order to clear my head.

I had become an obstetrician because I was tired of being haunted by death. There was something reassuring about my hands being the first ones to touch a new human being as it was born into this world. To usher life into this world is a gift, let me tell you, it's a miracle every time it happens.

I kept a list of each child I delivered, from the first one in 1946, to the last one I did before I retired. In a ledger bound in red leather, I had columns for the infant's name, sex, and birth weight, and whether it was a vaginal or, less common, cesarean delivery.

I wonder if after I die my children will find my ledger. I hope they will understand that it was not an act of vanity on my part. I had delivered 2,838 children by the time I retired. Every name I recorded was as meaningful to me as the first. Every time I placed the tip of my pen on the space in the lined paper, I paused to think of the million and a half children who perished in the Holocaust. I imagined that after so many years in the profession, my feelings of honoring the dead would lessen, but they never did. If anything, as I grew older, as I became a father and grandfather myself, those feelings only intensified. When I looked at my children, I now understood how my own father must have felt at the threat of extinction for his family. How many times did I cradle them when they were babies in my arms and wonder what evil could have wanted to extinguish this joy, this singularly most perfect creation?

My love for my children was so intense that it occasionally triggered something approaching panic. I found myself obsessed with every aspect of their well-being. I rode Amalia's waves of concern during their painful teething episodes and their first fever or flu. I looked at our children's pediatrician with distrust. He had grown up in the comfort of Forest Hills, and had no experience with the threat of typhoid or diphtheria. Part of me realized I was behaving irrationally and another part of me thought such vigilance was something that just came with being a parent.

There was a pain, a bittersweetness in my heart that my father had not lived to see me embrace my role as both a parent and a physician. Why was it now, years after my father's death, that I could finally understand all those lines on his face? Had it taken me this long to recognize that I now looked just like him? Now, when I imagined his eyes, I could see the look he carried for a patient who might be in distress, or that quiet devastation — so personal that it defied words — that overcame him when he lost a child in delivery.

I could finally peel away the layers of his formality, his rigidity, and see the human part hidden beneath. I could see how I wrestled with my own expectations that I held for my son — ones that probably would never be achieved — and understood how frustrated my father must have been with me.

There were some nights I wished I could bring him back and have him sit across from me. I would tell him how I now understood what he was always trying to convey to me, that a sanctity existed within our profession. That I finally understood that my hands were blessed to hold something as sacred as a squirming, hollering newborn experiencing its first moments of life.

But these are only a few of my many regrets. These thoughts, I tuck away among so many other things. Just as Amalia's locket remained shut, my returned letters to Lenka were hidden among old shoe boxes from Alexander's and Orbach's. I find myself alone in my office with the door closed, seeing solace in a ledger of 2,838 names.

7

LENKA

Those two weeks in Karlovy Vary were magical. I awakened every morning to the scents of Pavla's freshly baked bread and wet grass on the breeze. We took our breakfast outside to the sounds of birds and the sight of an occasional scampering rabbit. Pavla brought wild strawberries to the table, a bowl full of homemade preserves, baskets of warm rolls, and a pot of freshly brewed coffee on a silver tray. Vêruška had no desire to sketch or paint while we were there, and made it clear to all who asked that she intended only to indulge herself in plenty of rest and good food.

During breakfast, I usually tried to watch Josef out of the corner of my eye. He would typically arrive after me, his black hair tousled from sleep. He was quiet in the morning, concentrating on his food rather than on conversation. When Vêruška arrived, her nightgown peeking from underneath her linen robe, I always felt somewhat relieved to hear her chatter.

After breakfast, I'd pack a small knapsack with my sketchpad and a tin of oil pastels and venture outside to draw. I didn't know when I'd have a chance to get to the countryside again, and wanted to draw from nature as much as I could.

By the time I'd leave the villa each morning, Josef was usually reclining on one of the Kohns' iron chaise chairs with a book on his lap. His feet would be stretched out and his ankles crossed. Sometimes he would look up from one of his books, but other times his gaze never ventured from the page.

'You're off to go sketching?' he asked that first afternoon. The second and third time I left he nodded to me without remark. After four days of this, he looked up from his medical book and asked if he could come along.

I had imagined him asking me this question nearly every night. In my mind, I had always been bold and told him, 'Certainly.' But now, with his question hanging in midair, I stood silently like an awkward child, my head racing.

I looked down at my sundress as if it would answer for me. The cotton of my skirt was creased, my shoes scuffed from days of walking the terrain outside the garden.

'If you prefer to be alone, I understand,' he said softly. 'I wonder where you go every afternoon.'

I finally managed to turn to him and smiled. 'Every day it's a little different. I'd be happy to have you come along.'

We walked the first half of the way in silence, our footsteps on soft, quiet earth. Without a cleared path, I had learned not to be bothered by jutting branches or the thorns from the wild bushes. I could hear Josef's breathing from behind, which grew more rapid as we walked uphill. I began to worry that I couldn't find the place I had come to only the day before. But just as I began to lose hope, the small valley opened up before me and I turned to face Josef.

'This is it,' I told him, and pointed down below. He walked closer, nearly grazing my shoulder as he came to take a better look. He was so close to me at this point, I could smell the faint scent of his soap coming off his skin.

'I used to walk these woods with Vêruška,' he said, turning to me. 'We looked for strawberries in the summer and mushrooms in the fall.'

'We would carry baskets and bring home everything we found to Pavla. She'd show us how to wash everything. With delicate things you have to be careful.'

He smiled and looked at me. 'I have never seen the valley from this angle, though. It's amazing, but you're showing me something new. I thought I knew every corner of this forest.'

I laughed nervously. 'I found it almost by accident . . . I was walking and I saw that fallen tree over there.' I pointed to an old hollow log. The brittle bark had intrigued me, and its dark center made an interesting composition with its bright green moss. 'But after I finished my sketch of it, I walked further on and discovered this.'

Josef pointed to the left of the valley, where the cupola of the town's church seemed to pierce through the low-hanging clouds. 'You have a bird's-eye view here, don't you?'

'I wish I had the talent to do it justice.' I sighed as I dropped my satchel from my shoulders.

He shook his head. 'I'm sure your talent is as deep as your modesty.'

He was staring at me and not moving. We were alone for the first time and I felt fear flooding through my body.

My fingers gripped the handles of my satchel and I stiffened as we stood there awkwardly in the silence of the forest.

His arm extended for a second, and I felt faint as it reached closer to me.

'Can I see what you've done so far?' Josef reached not for me but for my satchel.

I saw his hands gesturing at the sketchbook.

I knelt down and pulled out my book. The heavy white parchment was full of sketches from the past week. Some were better than others, and my favorite was the one of the fallen tree.

I turned to the page and showed it to him. I could feel his breath against my neck. I felt cold and my body shuddered as he moved closer. Still we were not touching.

I whispered quietly, 'It's still not finished.'

Josef took his finger to the smudges of green and brown on the base of the page and touched it lightly.

'It's beautiful. So delicate . . . It's as though it's almost moving.'

'It's flawed,' I said, pointing to the image of the tree. 'The perspective is off.'

'I think it's perfect,' he said.

I folded the sketchpad and put it on the

ground. He reached for it again and I went to stop him.

'Lenka,' he uttered as our hands grazed for the first time.

That first touch. A feather against my skin.

He finds the small birthmark on the inner part of my forearm and glides his finger over it. There is the slightest pull coming from him as if he were guiding me to turn to him.

'Lenka.' He said my name again.

Hearing it said, I lifted my face to him.

We hesitated before I felt his hands travel from my arms to my shoulders. He took a deep breath, as if he were taking the air from my own lungs and swallowing it for himself.

His palms brushing along my neck, before resting on my cheeks.

His lips on mine.

His kiss is like lightning in my chest. Firefly wings beating against a glass jar.

I close my eyes. Josef Kohn touching me, his hands gently mapping those hidden surfaces of my body, his mouth traveling over my naked skin.

❧

That night we gaze at each other over candlelight, the serenade of his parents' and Věruška's voices are a muddled melody in our ears. Neither of us has much of an appetite for our food or our wine.

The dining room is white. White walls. White curtains. A crystal chandelier hangs in the center of the round table, its light perfect and soft.

But inside I am burning. Crimson. Scarlet. Ruby red. The heat of my body searing against my cotton dress.

'Are you all right, Lenka?' Věruška whispers to me over dinner. 'Your cheeks are flushed.'

I tapped my finger to my glass and tried to smile. 'It must be the wine . . . '

'But you haven't had a sip. I've been watching you.'

I shook my head. 'I'm fine.'

She raises one of her eyebrows and casts me a puzzled look.

I try not to lift my head. I know if I lock eyes with Josef, I will reveal myself to the others.

So I keep my head bowed like a nun deep in prayer.

But my thoughts are the furthest thing from pure.

He comes to me in the middle of the night. He opens the door with a slow, careful movement of his hand.

His black hair is unruly, his features full and ripe. He holds a candlestick and places it down.

'Lenka,' he whispers, 'are you asleep?'

I raise myself to one elbow. Darkness envelops the room. A flicker of candlelight. A sheaf of moonlight. He pulls back my bed-sheet and I curl forward, raising myself to my knees.

I wrap my arms around his neck. He touches my nightdress, the pad of his finger like a match.

Is this what a kiss from the man you love feels like? All fire and heat. The color of purple. Indigo. The blue red in our veins before it meets the air.

I want to kiss him forever. My body, like sand beneath him, shifting to his shape, the pressure of his weight against mine.

'Give me your hands,' he whispers.

I raise my palms in front of me. He takes hold of them. His fingers interlace with mine.

And then he falls against me. Kissing my neck, moving his hand up and down the length of my body, over my nightdress, then under it.

He is both tender and curious at the same time, like a little boy who is finally given the chance to explore what has been forbidden. But there is also the strength of someone more grown. More attuned. Someone who knows exactly what he hungers for.

The hunger. That desire to eat both the flesh and the core of the fruit. To want to lick every ounce of the juice from my fingers. To swallow every seed. To know a taste in its entirety.

How have I grown this hungry?

Josef moans softly, kissing me again. I feel his breath and heart racing against my chest.

'I could kiss you forever, Lenka,' he says.

I wrap my arms around him tighter.

He pulls one of my hands against his chest.

'I think I have to leave or I'm going to do something I'll regret.'

He kisses the pads of my fingers and then presses them to his heart.

He rolls over and pulls his nightshirt on. I

watch his legs walk across the floorboards, his reflection caught in the standing mirror. He reaches the door, touches the handle, and turns to look at me one more time.

'Josef,' I whisper. 'I miss you already.'

How could it be that those two weeks slipped away so quickly? I awoke that next morning as if in a trance. I had slept maybe an hour at the most. The mirror in my room is no longer full of Josef's reflection, but mine. My braids are half undone, my nightdress unbuttoned at the top. But my face is saturated with color and my eyes are bright even without sleep.

I smelled Josef on me. I imagined that he had left a trail of fingerprints on my body, imprinted the path of his tongue as it had traveled along my neck, my cheeks, my collarbone, and my belly. I did not want to ponder the dreaded reality that the next day would be our last in Karlovy Vary. We would soon be in the compartment of the train. Our eyes averted, Věruška chattering on, and each of us bobbing our head to pretend that we were listening, when our thoughts were only of each other.

The night before, we had agreed to leave separately early after breakfast and meet at the valley where we shared our first kiss. From there, he would take me to his favorite spot.

I arrived before him and was wearing a sundress the color of the sky. I carried a basket full of strawberries I had gathered on the way.

75

The strawberries seemed to be ripening with each minute that passed. I could smell their perfume and yet the smell made me hungry for something altogether different from the fruit. All I could think about was Josef in my arms. The weight of him pressing into me. The salt of his skin. The taste of peaches on his tongue.

I glanced at my watch. He was late and my heart beat nervously. What if he didn't come? My head was racing with thoughts that were unbearable to me.

'Lenka!' I finally heard his voice and the sound of it made my entire skin come alive.

'I was beginning to worry,' I said, rushing to him.

'It took me a while to get away from Pavla,' he said. 'She kept trying to feed me more sausages!'

I laughed and I must have sounded mad because my laughter was more of a release of all that I was keeping inside than a reflection of my amusement at Pavla's doting.

'Mother and Father decided at the last minute not to take a cure today but to rest at the house instead, and that delayed me as well.'

'You are here now,' I said softly. His hands were now reaching for mine and I let him take the basket from me. 'That is what matters.'

He kissed me and this time there was no hint of hesitation.

We walked until we were at a clearing with a beautiful natural lake. Secluded by rocks and large trees, it was an oasis in the middle of the forest.

'I used to swim here as a child with Ruška. I taught her how one summer.'

'You didn't tell me that we were going to go swimming!' I said with concern. 'I didn't bring a bathing suit.'

'That was my plan . . . It's such a warm day, Lenka, it would be cruel not to suggest a dip!'

I watched him as his fingers moved deftly to unbutton his shirt.

'There is nothing indecent about swimming in our underclothes.' He grinned.

I watched him strip down to his undershirt and underpants. The night before, I was like a blind person feeling the planes of his body, only able to see glimmers of it in the flashes of candlelight. But now I could see all the contours and details of his body.

He was dark from having taken in the sun over the past few days. The musculature of his shoulders and back made them look as though they had been built up in clay.

'Come on!' he said playfully with a gesture for me to join him. He ran over the thatched earth and jumped from one of the tall rocks.

Suddenly a huge splash of water leaped out at me, causing me to squeal.

'You've soaked me!' I laughed as he came up for air.

'You sure you don't want to join me? You're already wet.'

There was part of me that did, but the daylight made me feel more modest and less daring than

I had felt the night before.

'When I have my suit, silly!' I answered.

'We'll be leaving tomorrow . . . ' he hollered back. 'When will you ever have another chance?'

I thought about it and decided to go against my nature.

'Turn your head, Josef Kohn,' I said as I took off nearly all my clothes.

He turned his head, though I'll never know if he cheated and looked. I leaped from the nearest boulder and dove headfirst into the water. The sensation of the cold water on my skin, wrapped as I was in nothing more than my drenched underpants and camisole, was thrilling.

As I swam close to him, he reached for my slippery arms and pulled me close, applauding my bravery with another perfect kiss.

8

JOSEF

Amalia painted the walls of our apartment the color of chicken fat. She bought carpet the color of earth, and heavy brown furniture with thick upholstery from two Jewish brothers on the Lower East Side. She dressed in simple cotton prints, a ribbon tied around her tiny waist, her hair pulled back, and her face with no adornment except for a few drops of beet juice rubbed onto her lips.

She always drank her coffee without milk, her tea without sugar. The radio in our living room played Benny Goodman or Artie Shaw, but she never danced. Instead, she would tap her foot against the chair leg when she thought I wasn't looking. Her face always changed when I placed the needle down on our record player and played the music of Billie Holiday. Those dirges, doleful and blue, pulled Amalia someplace far away. Someplace inside her head, where I was not invited to follow.

Black bodies swinging in the southern breeze,
Strange fruit hanging from the poplar trees.

Sometimes I would see her bite the edge of her

lip, as if she were stifling an urge to cry. Other times I would watch her nod, as if in a silent dialogue with the singer. Although I never saw Amalia mouth a single word from any of the songs, when the record came to an end, she would rise and walk to the record player and reposition the needle, Holiday's voice, once again, filling the room.

Our son's toys and teddy bears filled the playpen, dolls and pots and pans would fill the same space when our daughter arrived three years later. Our neighbors on East Sixty-seventh Street remained strangers. Every day, Amalia pushed her vinyl grocery cart, filled with fruit, bread from the German baker, and the meat from the kosher butcher, with a well-practiced nod to our doorman, Tom. She forced herself to smile to others on the elevator. If our children were with her, her arms reached for them like a sinking sailor's to a life ring. Maybe it was the close quarters in the elevator, all those tight bodies packed into a small space, that unnerved her. Or maybe it was just that Amalia didn't really like to make small talk.

'Hungry?' she would ask our daughter.

'Here, toast and butter.'

At night: 'You upset? Hospital problems?' she'd ask me. I'd nod, slipping into faded pajamas.

In our bedroom there were no photographs, no paintings, no mirror. The only familiar sound was the clink of her old locket falling into the drawer.

She unbuttoned her housedress without ever

speaking. Her naked body ever childlike, even though she had birthed two of her own. Slender, pale limbs, two tiny nipples on a chest that always beat quietly.

I held her and dreamed of others.

She let go of me and did the same.

9

LENKA

In Karlovy Vary we packed our bags like mourners dressing for a funeral. None of us wanted to return to the city. Pavla packed us a basket full of sandwiches and small tea cakes along with a thermos of tea.

The night before, I could not eat a single morsel of dinner. I felt changed by that first swim, the sensation of Josef's kiss. The memory of his skin, wet and slippery next to mine. How would I ever bear the train ride home with him, with Vêruška in the same compartment? I worried as I descended the stairs to find them waiting for me in the hallway and nearly tripped over my feet.

Vêruška giggled. 'You can be so clumsy, Lenka, but somehow you always manage to look beautiful.'

I considered it a strange comment because Vêruška was the one who always looked beautiful. Her cheeks were always flushed from some sort of mischief and she was never plagued by shyness. No one could light up a room like Vêruška, especially when she was wearing one of her favorite red dresses.

When I looked at Josef, I could feel the weight of his concern. It would be difficult not to look at each other. Not to touch.

Once in the car, he pulled out his book, though I never saw him turning more then a few pages. Every few moments I felt his eyes sneaking a glance at me. I attempted weakly to draw, though I failed. I tried to steady my hand as my pencil wobbled from the wheels of the train.

Both of us welcomed Věruška's chatter. We listened to her rattle on about the various boys in our class. Tomáš, who was loud and boorish but had a face that could melt stone, or Karl, the quietest boy, who still seemed intelligent and sincere. I had no such archives in my head. There was Josef and no one else.

I had only been gone for two weeks, but when I returned home, everything seemed changed. I walked into a silent apartment. My mother sat on one of the red velvet chairs, her powdered face streaked with tears. My father, hands to his forehead, pressed his elbows against the mantel.

My sister whispered to me that there had been an incident at Father's warehouse. A bottle of alcohol with a wick soaked in petrol had been thrown through the glass window, setting the place ablaze. Everything was destroyed. Papa, she whispered, had found everything in ashes. Only one wall remained, and on it, someone had scrawled ŽID. Jew.

I ran to my mother and embraced her. She held on to me so tightly I thought her nails might tear the cloth from my back.

'I am so frightened, Lenka,' she cried. I had never heard her voice so full of fear before. That terrified me.

My father's hands were now thrust into his hair. His knuckles white as marble, the striations in his neck pulsing blue.

'We are Czech.' He cried out with anger. 'Whoever calls me Žid and not Czech is a liar.'

'What did the police say?' I asked them. My suitcase was still at the front door and my head was a blaze of images and thoughts I couldn't sort out.

'Police?' My father turned, his face turning in a blind rage. 'The police, Lenka?'

And then, just as my mother had surprised me, my father did the same. But this time it was by the insanity of his laugh.

10

JOSEF

I bought a television for Amalia in January of 1956 as a gift for our tenth anniversary. The man at the appliance store had tied it with a large red ribbon and I was so pleased to have found the perfect gift. When I walked through the door that evening, Rebekkah burst out, 'Oh, Daddy!' and rushed toward me with such emotion that I was afraid I might drop the darn thing before I even had a chance to plug it in.

The box that talked. The box that broadcast a hundred happy faces beaming back at us each night. Amalia did smile. I caught the flicker across her face, like a line drawn in the sand before the water washes it away.

We ate on trays in front of the television that night. Plates of breaded chicken cutlets, wilted asparagus with a moat of melted butter, and baked potato without any sour cream.

I loved our new television not because I particularly enjoyed the broadcasts (I couldn't believe Milton Berle was the best the Americans could come up with), but because it provided a welcome distraction to our household.

With my children on the sofa, their little chins

held up by their hands and their heads tilted toward the screen, I could watch them without interruption. I have never been a great one for small talk. My books have been my primary companions.

Even my patients, whom I care for dearly and whose pregnancies I monitor as diligently and as compassionately as I can, I do not pepper with personal questions.

I watch my daughter in front of the television and notice that her profile is identical to my wife's. She has the same thin face, skin the color of navy beans, and hair the color of sun-bleached wheat. Her mother has made two tight braids for her that she plays with when she watches. On her elbows, with her legs stretched behind her like two straight sticks, I see her body is all sharp angles like her mother's. The circle of her collarbone pronounced like its own necklace, and the razor edge of her jaw. I see the flash of her grin, those broad white teeth that are mine.

My son is soft and round. His chubby limbs remind me of myself at his age. His skin is deeper, browner than my wife's and daughter's. His eyes look sad even when he's happy. His kindergarten teacher told us he appeared to have no interest in playing with the other children, that he could spend hours on a puzzle yet have no patience to learn to tie his shoes. I can hear no criticism of him. I love my children like a tiger. I love my wife like a lamb.

Amalia. Sitting there with your knees pinned together, your fingers gingerly in your lap. The black-and-white image from the screen paints you blue. I look at you and wonder how you were as a child. Were you feisty like our daughter, all words and fire? Or quiet and thoughtful like our son?

I imagine you running home before the war, with the fateful letter from America in your hands, your face bright like a full moon. Those large brown eyes and cheekbones that could slice bread. When your parents packed you off to safety, did something else get packed away as well?

Under the forgiving buzz of the television, I unpack my own memories.

My own mental suitcases unlock. My father's spectacles — a silver and round pince-nez — no longer on his narrow face, but floating in a bottle-green ocean. I see my sister's childhood bear with its brown, matted fur. Its torn velvet paw, its glass eyes and ribbon mouth. I see my mother rushing to pack what is dear to her: her wedding handkerchief, the portraits of us as children, all her jewels that she hides in the silk seams of her coat, which she opens and recloses like a surgeon. And books that I left behind. Those that littered the shelves of my room, piled at my nightstand, toted on my back. My favorite novel about the Golem. What I would do to have that book now and read it to my son.

11

LENKA

In Mala Strana, in a café with ice-colored walls, I order a hot chocolate for Marta.

'Tell me the story about the Golem,' she says again.

I tell her the legend that was first told to me when I was a little girl. How under Czech lore, Rabbi Loew ben Bezalel, the chief rabbi of Prague, created a protective spirit by mixing the clay and water from the Vltava River with his own hands.

My own hands, white like powder, tremble as I try to remember the details of the myth. 'The rabbi, he created this Golem to protect the Jews,' I tell her. 'Rudolf the Second — the Holy Roman emperor of the time — had declared that all the Jews either be killed or expelled, but the Golem rose up from the earth and dust and became a living warrior. He killed anyone who hurt the Jews.'

There is steam rising from Marta's untouched cup of cocoa. Her eyes are filled with tears. Her red hair limp behind her ears. I drink my coffee black without sugar.

The emperor, seeing the destruction cast upon

his city and its people, begged the rabbi to stop the Golem. In exchange, he promised to stop the persecution of the Jews. 'To stop the Golem's deadly and vengeful path,' I explained, 'the rabbi only needed to erase the first letter of the Hebrew word *emet* or 'truth' from the creature's forehead. The new remaining word would thus read *met*, which translated as 'death.''

This act of ending the Golem's life was done with the understanding that should the Jewish people ever be threatened within the walls of Prague, the Golem would rise again.

I took a deep breath and looked at my sister. Her crying had stopped and her color was less pale. Still, she was clearly shaken from the fire at Papa's warehouse and by the motive of the attack.

To reassure her, I added what was always my favorite part of the story. Legend has it that the Golem's body is stored in the attic of the Old New Synagogue. There he waits to have the missing letter on his forehead replaced so he may avenge any who seek to harm the Jews.

I can see the eyes of my twelve-year-old sister at the end of this story, like a child who still wants to believe that magic could exist.

'Will the Golem wake up and protect us now?' she says, staring down at her cold cocoa.

I tell her he will. I tell her if not Rabbi Loew's Golem, I will take the clay from my modeling class and make one of my own.

12

JOSEF

I have always believed in the mystical. One cannot study the science of conception and the practice of obstetrics without being in awe of how the human body can create new life. In medical school, we learn that everything that is essential to life exists in the midline of the body. The same can be said about love.

The mind, the heart, the womb. Those three are all threaded in a sacred dance.

A woman's pelvis is like an hourglass with the capacity to tell time. It both creates and shelters life. When the mother's diet is insufficient, nutrients are pulled from her own teeth and bone. Women are built to be selfless.

As a young man, I fell in love with a girl who loved me. Her smile was a golden rope around my heart. Wherever she pulled me, I followed.

But sometimes even the thickest rope frays and one gets lost.

I still dream of her. The first girl whose hand ever laced through mine. Even when there was another woman in my bed, I'd dream only of her. I'd try and conjure her face at twenty, then thirty or forty years of age. But as the years passed and I grew older, I stopped imagining her with a face that was lined or with hair tarnished like silver.

Every person has an image or a memory that they hold secret. One that they unwrap, like a piece of hidden candy, at night. Pass through there and you will fall into the valley of dreams.

In my dreams, I imagine her naked. Long white limbs, reaching to thread through mine. Hands reaching to undo damp, fragrant braids. Chocolate-brown hair falling over a collarbone as sharp as an archer's bow.

She crosses her arms over her breasts.

I kiss her hands, the pale of her fingertips. I turn up her palms and lift them from her breasts to my cheeks. She finds my temples, then my hair, pulls me toward her lips, and kisses me.

The kiss. The kiss. I am haunted by that kiss.

Sleep.

If only I didn't have to wake so soon. The beeper sounding that I am needed. The number at the hospital telling me I must go.

To sleep, where I am young again. To wake, where I am old, with weary limbs. The sound of that beeper that tells me where I need to go.

13

JOSEF

I no longer could stomach the taste of strawberries after I arrived in America. It wasn't that their sweetness could not compare to those we had every summer, but because they reminded me of Lenka.

Lenka, sitting under the shade of our garden in Karlovy Vary, her white shoulders bare in her cotton sundress. Her blue eyes. Her clavicle, the shape of a heart I long to kiss.

I sit across from her. Watch her as she scans the long wooden table that Pavla has crowded with plates of smoked meats, jars of homemade jam, and a basket of warm rolls. But it is the bowl of handpicked strawberries that delights her. She reaches for the bowl and brings one berry to her perfect mouth.

Her mouth. Her mouth. Am I such a beast because I cannot suppress the urge to bite it? Nibble at its tender flesh. Feel the softness of its inside. Run my tongue over her teeth. Feel the velvet of her tongue.

Sitting there, I watch her. All I can do to stifle my urges is to stare at her. How stupid I must look in this memory. Awkward and hunting her all the same.

When I walk next to her, I can barely breathe. I cannot speak. Four years older than she and I feel like I am without experience. There have been other girls, but their faces and their touch have all vanished from my memory.

I walk behind her. The taut muscle of her calves, the gentle slope of her backside, the glimpse of her neck, are a seduction all their own.

When she places her sketchbook down, I can feel the heat of her body next to mine. I can smell her. I want to breathe her into me like a child's first breath. I want to wrap my arms around her and melt her heart against mine.

I want to taste her. I want the sweet syrup of her mouth. I want the flesh of her tongue. I want to kiss her more than anything in the whole world.

The kiss. Am I too forceful? Am I too eager? That mouth sealed to mine . . . the taste of freshly picked strawberries.

I am gasping. My mouth open. My heart cracked like a smashed pomegranate. Ruby seeds heaping in my hands.

But then I awake.

I open my eyes and Amalia is reaching to turn the radio alarm off.

She kisses me.

Dryly. Absently. The taste of water.

My Amalia kissing me.

There isn't the faintest taste of strawberries in her kiss.

It is the taste of a snow cone without the juice.

Ice, without the color blue.

14

LENKA

Like a line drawn in the sand, I can mark the unraveling of my life, from the moment I returned to Prague. Those two weeks in Karlovy Vary were the last moments of calm. I had left Prague without the shadow of Hitler and returned with his threat heavy upon the city.

Suddenly it seemed I could not escape hearing his name everywhere. Would he invade Czechoslovakia or not?

We began to see parades outside our apartment window — men in lederhosen and women in traditional skirts, marching and chanting German national songs. Swastikas appeared on storefronts. Ugly, angry slashes. Glaring like a scar.

I returned to the Academy, but my heart was not in it. Vêruška also seemed somewhat changed. The liveliness of her eyes and the fullness of figure — all of the things that had made her appear buoyant in the past — had diminished.

We did not speak of the growing fear within our families. There were more pauses in our conversations. Instead, there was a silent exchange in our eyes when we looked at each other. We giggled far less often.

Now, over the radios at home, we heard of the German presence encroaching on the Sudetenland, the area on the Czech-German border. Our minister of foreign affairs, Dr. Basel, had ordered Czech troops to patrol the division line, but everyone doubted they could keep the Germans out for long.

I had not heard of any specific hardship falling upon the Kohns like we had suffered. I didn't see how Dr. Kohn's practice could be affected. His patients were almost exclusively Jewish. Jews would still remain loyal to Jews. Babies were not like crates of crystal that people did not really need. Still, who really knew the worries of others?

Elsa's beautiful lips now twitched when she talked. I noticed it almost immediately when our classes resumed.

I didn't ask her about her father's business at the apothecary. She still smelled of gardenia and tuberose. But I suspected that, like my father's, the growing anti-Semitism was affecting his livelihood as well.

Roth's Apotek, with its florid Art Nouveau sign, was almost a banner for Jewish mercantilism. It was in a prime location, on one of the side streets just off the center of Prague's Old Town Square. In the past, every time I passed it, there were people coming and going, their packages wrapped in Roth's brown paper and recognizable purple ribbon. The sign outside said EST. 1860; the family had owned it for decades.

I had not heard of any windows being

smashed there, or any Nazi slogans being written on its walls. But who knew? In such a short time it seemed like everything had changed.

At the break, my two girlfriends and I ate our packed lunches outside. The warm sun hit our bare legs and struck our faces with rays of honey-colored light.

This was our third year at the Academy, and we had always imagined when we were first-years that by this time we would feel like we owned the halls. Instead, we now were all preoccupied with concern for our parents and our life as we knew it in Prague.

'I wonder if we'll be able to finish our studies,' Elsa said. Her words sliced through the air like a rapier. 'Papa says he's not so sure.'

Vêruška scowled. 'Of course we will! The Czech troops won't let the Germans cross over our borders.'

I said nothing because I didn't know what to believe. Everything I knew about the political situation was gleaned from what I overheard during my parents' discussions at night. And one thing was certain: they were becoming less confident with each passing day. A different Lenka was emerging, one that existed as two halves — one half wanted to feel alive, to feel happy, to saturate myself in the feelings of first love — but the other half was full of dread. All I needed to do was to look at my father's face when he returned home from work in order to see the writing on the wall. I hate to admit it now, but there were several nights when he walked through the door when I didn't want to lift my eyes.

Things happened so quickly that autumn of 1938. On October 5, our president, Edvard Benes, resigned, realizing that the Nazi occupation was imminent. We had been defeated, without lifting a single weapon. There would be no resistance from our government and no protection for the tidal wave of anti-Semitism that the Nazis would soon unleash.

We began to hear slurs on the street: 'Jewish shit, you'll be dead by Christmas.' Elsa reported that her brother went into a café after school with friends and was told, 'Jews out!' Suddenly the fear that we saw on our parents' faces was now also on our own.

We began to hear of neighbors who were trying to secure visas, though neither Elsa nor Vêruška mentioned that their families were trying to do so. People we had known for years suddenly left without saying good-bye. We became watchful and guarded.

That year, I started learning a new art.

The art of being invisible.

Mama, too, no longer dressed to be noticed. She dressed to disappear.

Black coat. Charcoal-gray scarves over a dress the deep shade of graphite.

We no longer drank from colored crystal. Instead, the ruby-red wine goblets and the cobalt water glasses were all sold for far less than they were worth.

When I opened my tin of oil pastels in drawing class, I held the sticks of orange and leaf green

97

and felt an acute pain typically associated with hunger.

One professor began picking on the Jewish boys in our class. He criticized their drawings more than was deserved. He tore Arohn Gottlieb's sketch of a still life right down the middle and told him to leave his class at once.

We began to hear stories of schoolgirls who were attacked in Poland. Girls who were attacked by their own classmates after class, their faces scarred by boys who held them down and clawed at their faces.

Věruška, Elsa, and I now kept our heads down when we were in class. Though it appeared a posture of shame, for us, it was born from fear.

One afternoon over lunch outside, Elsa collapsed in tears. 'I can't take this anymore,' she said. She had grown thinner over the past two weeks. Her white skin was translucent and as thin as tulip petals, her blond hair wispy as straw. 'I can't draw. I can't even see what I'm supposed to be studying.'

Her hands were shaking as I took them in my own. 'Elsa, everything is going to be fine.'

'No, it's not,' she said. As she turned to look at me, there was a wild look in her eyes. And her lips were bright red, but not from lipstick. They were raw and chewed.

I now saw Josef whenever I could. We met in a small, secluded café on Klimentska Street nearly every other day. We had yet to tell our parents. I wish I could tell you that we kept our romance a secret because we didn't want them to have yet another burden, the pressure of making something too soon out of our courtship, but that would be untrue. We kept it to ourselves because we were young, in love, and selfish. It was our own perfect little secret and we wanted to keep it all to ourselves.

I felt as though I were existing on air. I barely ate and I was incapable of resting at night, my head was so filled with thoughts of Josef and our next plans to meet. And although I had no appetite and could not sleep, I felt more energized than ever before. Even my paintings changed. My brushstrokes were freer. I was more generous with my use of color and texture. Even my sense of line changed in my drawings. My hand loosened, as if it had finally gained a sense of confidence, and my subjects became more alive than ever.

That November, as we both tried to navigate between our studies and our courtship, the threat of war rattled like a storm outside our window. We heard it, but we tried to keep the window shut a bit longer. Each moment was more intense than the one before it. In between learning that his favorite color was green, his favorite author was Dostoevsky, and his favorite composer was Dvořák, we learned how to stretch out our kisses or how the other liked to be touched. There was heat even when there were pauses of silence between us. As I look back on it now, it was during those periods of calm, when we walked down the street and there were no eyes upon us, that I felt the happiest. We didn't need to talk, so synchronized were our thoughts. He would slip his hand in mine and nothing else seemed to matter. For a few moments I allowed myself to feel secure.

This was a fantasy I wanted to suspend for however long I could. But it was far from realistic. As tensions increased in Prague, we soon found ourselves behaving like every other Jew around us. We kept our heads down now when we walked home, and we avoided all eye contact with others. It was as if all the Jews in Prague wished they could vanish. We heard of Jews in Germany near the Sudetenland being forced from their homes and made to crawl to the Czech border and kiss the ground. The Czech guards forced them back, so they were pushed into a no-man's-land between two countries, neither of which wanted to accept them. Every time it rained and the temperature dropped near freezing, I thought of these men, women, and children. To live like hunted animals with wolves at your heels.

At the start of 1939, we felt all was lost. Our government, now headed by Hácha, ordered the police to coordinate with the Germans in suppressing the supposed threat of communism within Czechoslovakia. It was difficult for me to fully comprehend what this meant for us, but my father's reaction to the news made it all too clear. That night, he raised his hands to the ceiling and said this was a death sentence to all Czech Jews.

My mother said to be quiet, not to speak like that in front of Marta and me.

I smiled at Marta, who was holding back tears. 'We need to get visas,' Mama told him.

'Who in America will sign an affidavit for us?'

'We can buy false papers!' she cried.

'With what? With what, Eliška?' And his high-pitched cry reminded me of shattered glass. 'It's too late now. We should have left when the Gottliebs and the Rosenthals did. There is no money left to buy the papers and passage,' he said helplessly, his palms turned up toward the sky.

One day, Elsa did not come to class. Věruška and I exchanged a worried glance. 'Maybe they've been able to get out, somehow,' Věruška said flatly. I immediately wondered if the apothecary now stood empty, its shelves bare, and the smell of gardenia and rose replaced by stale air. Perhaps Elsa and her family had gotten on a boat with no time to say good-bye.

But what if it had been something terrible. I was worried.

I decided to pass Elsa's father's apothecary on the way to meeting Josef. Through the broken glass, I could see her sitting by the counter, her face in shadow.

I stood there staring at her. If I were to go in, I'd be late for Josef and cause him to worry. If I didn't, I would be distracted when I saw him by this haunting image of my friend, her face as shattered as the store's glass.

I walked in; my footsteps on the tile were the only sound. Elsa looked up at me, her blue eyes lifting like a porcelain doll. Her mouth trying to twitch into a smile.

'We missed you in class today,' I said softly as I approached her.

'I'm not coming back,' she said. 'I can't concentrate there anymore, and anyway, Papa needs me here to run the sales counter. He had to let Fredrich go, so Papa's now working the pharmacy in the back.'

'I thought perhaps your family had left,' I said.

She looked at me as though she were trying to read my face. 'We're trying to, Lenka. But everything requires money now, and we hardly have any left.'

I nodded. I knew this feeling all too well.

'Is there anything I can do?'

She shook her head. Elsa did not look helpless; she looked resigned.

'I'll bring Věruška the next time I visit,' I said, trying to sound upbeat.

We parted with a kiss, and I hurried off to meet Josef, my heart far heavier than it had been that morning.

He was waiting for me, his throat wrapped in a thick black scarf, his hands wrapped around a cup of steaming tea.

'I was worried about you,' he said, standing up to greet me with a kiss. His lips were still warm from the tea.

'I'm sorry,' I told him. 'I went to check on Elsa. She wasn't in class today.'

He raised his eyebrow and shook his head.

'I don't think any of us are going to be in class much longer.'

'Don't say that,' I said, reaching over the table to kiss him one more time.

He placed his hands on my cheeks and held them there. His fingers were so long they nearly touched my ears.

'Kiss me again,' I told him.

His mouth on mine was like new air being pumped into my lungs.

'We should get married, Lenka,' he said as he slowly pulled away from me.

I laughed. 'Get married? Neither of our parents even know that we are courting.'

'Exactly.' He smirked. 'Exactly.'

At night, I dream of myself in a white veil. My family's black coats and scarves are replaced by ripe colors of red and gold. Their faces are no longer frightened and worried, but radiant and full of joy. I see Papa being lifted on a chair, and Mama and Marta clapping as he bounces about on sturdy shoulders.

We drink wine in tall rosy goblets, and eat dumplings with the tenderest meat. The chuppah is threaded with flowers. Daisies, asters, and irises the color of jam.

On my honeymoon night, I lie beside him. He lays his hands above my head on the pillow. He kisses my temples, my heart, my belly, and then below.

I close my eyes and pass through a world where there is only love.

15

LENKA

By the end of January, it seemed as though it would only be a matter of time before the Germans finally invaded Czech soil.

'We must get married,' Josef implored me. 'I've told my parents that I'm in love with you.'

I blew puffs of steam in his face as I stood next to him in the cold. 'How can we get married now? The whole world's turned upside down.'

He pulled me closer. 'If we don't get married, there will be nothing good left in this life for me.'

He kissed me again, his arms enveloping me in their warm woolen sleeves. I felt like my heart was flooding with emotion whenever I was near him. But our situation was becoming more and more desperate.

'How can I tell my parents for the first time I am dating you, and in the next sentence, tell them I am to be wed?'

'These are strange days . . . things are not as they once were. Listen,' he said, shaking me a little by the arms. 'My parents are in the middle of negotiating exit visas for us. I need to marry you so they can secure one for you, too.'

'What?' I asked incredulously.

'Father is buying them on the black market. We have a cousin in New York who is sponsoring us.' He was now looking at me with such a ferocious intensity, I was frightened. 'Lenka, you need to understand . . . we need to get out of here. The Czechs will sell every Jew out if it means maintaining their sovereignty.'

I shook my head. 'I can't marry you unless you also secure visas for my parents . . . and for Marta.'

'That's impossible, Lenka, you know that.' His voice was now full of force and it surprised me. 'You will go first with my family, and then when we are settled you can send for them.'

'No,' I said. 'Promise me you will also get my whole family passports, or otherwise, the answer is no.'

16

LENKA

We told my parents the next evening. I brought Josef home and my parents, though shocked by the sudden announcement, did not protest. Perhaps delirious and worn down from their own desperation, they would have married me off to even a lesser man if he had promised us safety outside of Czechoslovakia.

Josef appeared remarkably calm as he told Papa of his plans to take care of me, and to take us all out of Prague.

'And your parents? They support this decision?' Papa asked.

'They love Lenka, as do I. My sister adores her. We will all take care of her.'

'But you will come with us. You, Mama, and Marta,' I interjected. 'Dr. Kohn is arranging papers for all of us.'

Josef looked at my father and nodded.

'We've either sent away or sold off her dowry,' Papa told him sadly.

'I am marrying her for love not for money. Not for crystal.'

Papa smiled and let out a deep sigh.

'This is not how I imagined your betrothal,

Lenka,' he said, turning to me. His eyes lifted toward my mother, who was standing at the threshold of the parlor, Marta's thin arms around her. My sister was thirteen now, but still seemed childlike to me.

'Eliška, do you think you can make a wedding in three days?'

She nodded.

'So be it,' Papa said as he stood up to embrace Josef. 'Mazel tov.'

My father's arms lifted to wrap around Josef. I saw Papa's head rest on Josef's shoulder, his eyes squinting shut, and the faint trickle of a father's tears.

We registered in the city hall and arranged with the rabbi to be wed in the Old Town Synagogue.

For the three days leading up to the ceremony, my mother was a woman possessed. She first unwrapped her own wedding dress, an elaborate white silk gown with long lace sleeves and a high-collared bodice.

I was at least three inches shorter than Mama, but for the alterations, she did not call the seamstress Gizela. Instead, she took out a large wooden box and did the job herself.

The silver shears sounded like blades over ice as Mother cut through the skirt. I was standing on a small stool, the same one that Lucie had stood on the weeks before her marriage. The irony of it had not escaped me as I looked into the gilded mirror in our living room. I looked at my reflection, with my mother now on her knees, the pins in her mouth, her scissors slicing through her own dress. I wanted to cry.

'Mama,' I told her. 'I love you.'

She looked up, but she didn't answer. Still, I saw the strain in her throat, her watering eyes telling me she loved me, too.

I was married at sundown in an ancient brick synagogue with four stained-glass windows, fingers of moonlight illuminating the old stone floor. My chuppah was snow-white silk wrapped around four wooden poles. Candles flickered in iron-roped chandeliers; the rabbi was pale and wizened beneath a tall black hat.

We had only invited our families to the ceremony, along with Lucie and her daughter and husband, Petr. I had not thought she could come, but she arrived with baby Eliška, now old enough to walk beside her and hold her hand. She wore the blue capelet Mother had given her years before, and her hair was braided behind her head. I smiled at her when I walked down the aisle with my parents on either side of me.

At the steps to the bimah Josef stood alone waiting for me. We touched fingers. My parents kissed my cheeks and walked up the steps to the chuppah. At the rabbi's instructions, Josef lifted my veil in accordance with tradition, confirming that I was indeed his bride.

Then my veil was again placed over my face.

We stood before the rabbi and heard the seven marital blessings. I walked around Josef, promising he would be the center of my life. We wrapped our fingers around the wedding chalice and drank the ceremonial wine as the rabbi asked us to repeat: '*I am my beloved's and my beloved is mine.*' We slipped bands over our fingers — a sign of unbroken, seamless love — and Josef broke a single glass underneath his foot.

We kissed as the rabbi pronounced us man and wife, the taste of salty tears as my lips parted over his.

That evening, Josef takes me to an apartment on Sokolská Street. He says he needs to tell me something, but I silence him with one finger over his soft, ripe mouth.

He tells me again that we need to speak. 'Urgent matters,' he says. And I tell him, what could be more urgent than this?

He leans into me and I can taste the powdered sugar on his lips from Mother's palačinka.

'Lenka,' he whispers, and I kiss him again. His hands touch my throat, his fingers reaching to the nape of my neck. 'Lenka.' My name said again, but this time like a psalm, a prayer, a wish.

I can feel his heart beating through his shirtwaist, the white cotton dampening from our heat. I pull his hands from my face and turn my back to him so that he will undress me.

His fingers are nimble over the scale of

buttons. He pulls back the cloth, places a single kiss between my shoulder blades, and presses his cheek to my back. I hear him inhale the scent of my skin; I feel him drop lower, offer another kiss to the small of my back, as he kneels even lower to the ground, his hands gliding over my thighs as the material falls to the ground.

I step out of a puddle of white silk, naked except for a corset of lace and whalebone. Josef's vest is unbuttoned, his dark throat exposed from his open collar. His hair a black lion's mane.

I am no longer a shy student but a wife. I unbutton him as he has done to me. I wrap my hands over the curve of his shoulders, and trace my finger down the line of his chest.

I feel the weight of his belt buckle in my hands and unlatch it. My hands now feel the back of his thighs, his sex swelling between us.

Does he whisper my name one more time before he lifts me and brings me to the bed? I can't remember. I only recall the sensation of my body inching under him, my legs wrapping tightly around his waist, my thighs sealing around his ribs. There is the sensation of him threading through me. Like a needle inching through the cloth. 'Josef,' I whisper into his ear. 'Josef.' I say his name again.

His name is an anchor in that bed of naked limbs and twisted sheets. I say it and he, too, whispers mine. And I bite his shoulder as we both climb to a peak and fall.

If the sound of clinking glass reminds me of my parents, then it is the sound of rattling porcelain that will forever remind me of my marriage to Josef. Over breakfast the next morning, white coffee cups and saucers, jiggling in his nervous hands, he tells me there will be no passage for my parents.

The table is set like a scene from the theater. The basket of warm rolls, the pots of jam. A china coffeepot. Two folded napkins. A vase with one, tired rose.

I tell him I don't understand what he is saying to me. I tell him I thought he promised me their safe passage.

'There are laws . . . restrictions, Lenka. Our cousin writes he can sponsor only my family and no one else's.'

'I am not your family,' I whisper. My voice trembles.

'You are my wife.'

And I think, though I don't have the strength to say: *And my mother is my mother. My father my father and my sister, my sister.*

'I have already told your father and he wants you to come with me.'

As he speaks, I can feel the blood running through my veins and my heart stopping as if it were tied off by a tourniquet. I know my eyes are too much for him and that he feels my anger, my disappointment, cauterizing his skin and slicing him to the bone. For months now, I know I have been selfish. I have heard my parents' desperation at night, and have seen it on their faces. I have felt it as I saw the riches

112

of our once-lavish lifestyle vanish. But only now, with the threat of being separated from my family, do I feel myself forced into a reality I'm ill-prepared to accept.

'Josef,' I say. 'How can I accept this?'

'We don't have a choice, Lenka. This is the only way.'

'I can't. I can't.' I say it over and over again. Because I know it's the truth. I know that if I go with him and something happens to my parents, to Marta, I will never recover from the guilt.

'You can't be telling me that you refuse to come?' He buries his forehead in his palms.

'Yes, I am, Josef.' I am crying now. 'That is what I'm telling you.'

'What can I do, Lenka?'

'You need to get us all visas. That's what you promised . . . ' I am shaking so much that I can't even stand up. I reach for a chair and collapse.

'Your father wants us to go . . . ' Josef's arms are now wrapped around my shoulders.

'I cannot do that. Don't you understand me?' Suddenly I wonder if our whole courtship has been a fantasy. That he doesn't realize that I can be stubborn and willful. That as much as I love him, I could never abandon my family.

I feel sick. I feel the heat of his body flowing through mine. The warmth of his breath, the wetness of his tears on my neck. But for the first time, I am incapable of giving him what he wants.

I know only one thing. One doesn't abandon family. One doesn't leave them, even in the name of love.

I left Josef that afternoon in that beautiful apartment, and arrived at my parents' home.

'What are you doing here, darling Lenka?' Father cried when he opened the door. 'You should be enjoying the day with your new husband!'

My mother took one look at my face and knew that Josef had told me about the lack of passage for them. 'Lenka,' she said, shaking her head. 'You cannot take on the sorrows of the world.'

'No, but I can take on the sorrows of my family.'

They shook their heads and Marta wrapped her thin arms around my waist. When she looked up at me, her eyes were wide and far more childlike than her teenage years would suggest. I knew in my heart, no matter the consequences of my marriage to Josef, I had made the right decision. I would never, under any circumstances, leave behind those I loved.

It was not that my parents did not try to dissuade me. Over and over again they tried to convince me to go where it was safe.

'You will go first and we will follow later,' they both said.

'Josef will go first and we will all join him later,' I replied.

They looked at me with sad, fearful eyes. My father implored me. He spoke of the comfort he would feel in knowing that even just one of his children was safe. My mother held my hands

114

clasped to her breast and told me that I must now follow my husband. It was my duty as a wife. But my sister never said a single word, and it was her silence that I heard the loudest.

17

JOSEF

Sometimes, when the children ask about our wedding day, I can see the apartment in Queens with the blue-white snow on the fire escape. The bridge table with the plates of creamed herring and baskets of sliced rye. I can hear Frank Sinatra on the radio and imagine our living room filled with a few people we knew from Café Vienna. But I still have difficulty remembering Amalia's face.

I remember that she had made the dress herself. She had spent nearly two days cutting and sewing a dress that, in the end, seemed rather unremarkable. A square collar and two bell sleeves, without a stitch of lace or ribbon. Her shoes were the same brown pumps she wore every day.

I want to be able to tell my children and grandchildren that she looked beautiful and that her face beamed clearly through the absence of a veil. But, for some reason, her face remains a mystery. Was it because she kept her eyes lowered? That her hair, braided and lifted behind her ears, was an artful distraction? Or was it because I was somewhere else, even at that moment. Somewhere that Amalia also understood. The strongest force attracting us to each other, the reason we were there holding hands.

We were not married by a rabbi, but by a judge. There was no religious ritual when we exchanged our vows. There was no cantor. I didn't even break a glass.

I simply held Amalia's small hands in mine and slid a gold ring on her finger, kissing her with a dry, careful mouth.

I did love Amalia. Those who ever doubted that are wrong. One finds love in transparency. To see wholly and without question. No one was standing there with a shucking knife trying to pry open my past. I told Amalia only once about the boat. The loosening of hands. The waters the color of coal.

But once was all that was needed.

I loved Amalia because she let me be. Who else could just let me stare out the window and not get annoyed by my silence? Who else would not mind the stack of books on my nightstand, and the lonely nights when I was at the hospital?

I tell my children I can remember Amalia's face most clearly on the days she gave birth to them. To my daughter, who wriggled into this world with a cry that struck me straight to the heart, I tell her that her mother was like a dreaming angel during her birth. I see Amalia with a cone of ether over her mouth. She is in a twilight sleep. Her face like a doll's, her eyes closed, her blond lashes pale against even paler skin.

She is so peaceful as the forceps bring our

daughter kicking and screaming into this world. Hours later, Amalia will hold her, nurse her, and look into her baby's eyes and see her own mother reflected there. She names our daughter Rebekkah after her mother, her middle name Zora, after her sister. She dangles the locket with the photo over her newborn head and says the kaddish.

I kiss both of their foreheads and I pray with her for the first time in years.

18

JOSEF

My sister and I had barely spoken since the wedding. Initially she was furious that neither Lenka nor I had told her about our courtship. And now she was furious that I had agreed to leave my new bride behind. Věruška's silence sliced through me like a saw to the bone.

The truth was, Lenka's father always knew that mine could not secure enough visas for the rest of her family. We had a distant cousin who was sponsoring us and the U.S. State Department had told our cousin he could sponsor no more. I had come to her father before our wedding and told him so.

I had assured her father that we would have one visa for Lenka, and he seemed to breathe easier knowing at least she would get out of Czechoslovakia soon.

'It will be good that you all get abroad first,' he had said, trying to sound hopeful. 'You can get things settled and then send for us.' He shook my hand. 'I am entrusting my daughter to you and your family. Promise me you will always take care of her.'

It was his idea that I not tell Lenka until after

119

the wedding, thinking that it would only upset her on what would otherwise be a beautiful, sacred day.

'Let's not disturb her joy,' he said. He embraced me as we parted.

I had been conflicted by this suggestion. I certainly did not want to spoil our wedding day, but I thought it only fair to enter into this already rushed matrimony with Lenka knowing the truth.

But that afternoon, when I saw her radiant with the thought of our impending nuptials, I just didn't have the heart to say anything.

Was I a coward? Probably. But, like her father, I thought I had her best interests at heart. Was I selfish? That was certain. But I wanted to look into her eyes after her veil was lifted, and only see tears of joy.

And so it was that I held the news from her. As I bathed the afternoon before the ceremony, I imagined her doing the same. Her white body deep in the warm and scented water. Her skin soft and awaiting my touch. I had memorized every feature of her face, every small line, as if committing it to part of me.

I shaved carefully with my face turned up to the mirror, a warm towel around my neck. As the sun began to set, I walked over to my bed and got dressed. My darkest wool suit, my whitest shirt, and my cuffs clasped with the links my father had given me when I entered university.

From my room, I could hear my mother and sister talking softly. They had spent three days packing our apartment, and their arguing had temporarily ceased only because I was to be wed that evening.

As I walked into our living room, I hardly recognized it. The bookshelves were empty, and mother's treasures were no longer on display. All that remained were the walls and the furniture. If someone were to enter, they would have thought we had already gone abroad.

Father had sold so much in order to pay for our passports and passage to America. My mother had no particular attachment to clothes, and parted easily with what she had brought into the marriage years earlier. Her mother's china and silver were sold for a fraction of their worth. How many Jewish families had already sold all their valuables in the same way? Czechoslovakia was already flooded with so many abandoned china services and cut crystal, the entire Vltava couldn't have washed them all.

My family was dressed in what finery they still had left for the occasion. Věruška was dressed in a red gown, and her hair was pulled up and tucked with two beautiful combs.

They all turned to congratulate me.

'Josef,' my mother said quietly. 'You look so much older today. How can that happen in just one day?'

I smiled and walked over to her and kissed her on her soft, powdered cheek. She was wearing a long black dress and a string of white pearls.

Father was smoking a pipe and his eyes, through his silver round spectacles, seemed to be taking every inch of me in.

'Mazel tov,' he said as he shook my hand and

handed me one of the four remaining snifters of brandy.

'Have you told her?' he asked. I swallowed, and my belly filled with warmth and a false sense of calm.

'No,' I said, shaking my head.

'Josef!' Vêruška let out a small cry. 'You must tell her!'

'Let the boy have his wedding, Vêruška,' Papa said sternly. 'We can have all the tears tomorrow.'

'It was her father's idea,' I offered as an excuse.

She shook her head and turned from me. 'To start out a marriage like this . . . I don't even know what to say.'

'Then say nothing,' Father snapped. He took another strong swallow of brandy.

'Everybody's saying nothing now. But — ' Father cut her off again.

'Enough talk already, Vêruška, we need to go now, or we'll be late!'

She looked at me with an expression of such disapproval it could have broken glass. My sister did not like to be silenced. Smart as she was, she now let her eyes speak for her.

Under a descending sun, we walked to the synagogue. I remember looking at every building, every lamplight, and trying to force them into my memory. I didn't know when we would return to Prague, and I wanted to remember its beauty on the eve of my new life.

I will remember her always in her long white dress, her veil an airy gauze over her strong, chiseled face. I can see her tapered fingers reaching to grasp mine, and feel the delicate weight of her soft rosebud kiss. Lenka, beautiful, my bride.

I do not remember the words of the ceremony, or the signing of our wedding *ketubah*. But at night, I can take myself back to that evening, when the chandeliers were lit with a warm orange light and the ancient stone floor was pitted and cold. The air damp, and the bricks so gray they appeared almost blue.

The rabbi was the same one who had officiated at my Bar Mitzvah more than ten years earlier. He was an imposing figure, with ice-blue eyes and a long silver beard that grazed his prayer book. As he began the incantation of the seven blessings, he took my tallis and wrapped Lenka and me in it together.

I remember the look in the rabbi's eyes as he pronounced us man and wife. He looked at our hurried, anxious faces, and did not have the calm that I remembered as a young boy.

'Remember the tears when the synagogue in Jerusalem was destroyed,' he said as my foot broke the glass. 'Remember as a Jew there is always some sadness, even on your happiest day.'

Looking around at the faces gazing at Lenka and me on the bimah, I knew none of us needed any reminding of that. We all wore our fears as visibly as our wedding finery.

At her parents' apartment, we drank wine from glasses rimmed in gold. Her mother had made a wedding soup with dumplings. There were small trays with delicate pastries and a honey cake with a small violet flower placed at the center.

Marta played the piano and Lucie's child, Eliška, livened up the modest festivities by clapping her hands and twirling her skirt. Vêruška was in the corner, her eyes glassy, her fingers twitching at her side. When I looked to her for a smile, she turned her face from me and shuttered her eyes.

We left after a few hours to spend our wedding night in a friend's apartment. My sister had helped me prepare the room. In another time, I would have brought Lenka to the Hotel Europa. I would have laid her down on a bed of white cotton, pulled a coverlet of down over our naked shoulders, and wrapped myself around her until dawn.

But my colleague Miloš had volunteered his flat on Sokolská Street. He was away visiting a cousin in Brno, and I seized the opportunity to avoid having to spend our wedding night under the same roof as my in-laws.

Vêruška had taken the sheets that Lenka's mother had set aside for her dowry. They were white and embroidered years earlier by Lucie; we had pulled them tight over the mattress and Vêruška had sprayed a mist of rose water from an atomizer her friend Elsa had given her specifically for this occasion.

'Will you tell her before or after?' Vêruška asked me after the apartment had been cleaned, the bed made to perfection, and the vases stuffed with flowers.

'I will tell her before,' I told her. 'I promise.'

She shook her head and looked at the bed. In happier times, my little sister would have jumped on it and giggled, kicking her feet up in the shadow of her sisterly destruction. But now she stood solemnly before me, her face white as an egret. 'She isn't going to come with you, you know. I know how she feels about her family.'

I was now the one shaking my head. 'She will, Vêruška. She will. We are her family now, too.'

My sister then looked at me as if she were the elder sibling and I the child. She took my hand and held it. With her eyes closed, she said not another word and only shook her head.

We drove to Miloš's apartment in my family's car, which Father still hoped to sell in the few days before we were to set sail. As we entered the flat, Lenka held her skirt in one hand and a bouquet of violets in the other. Glass globes were lit with candles, and the room smelled of the rose-scented linen and the crisp of the night air.

'I have something to tell you,' I said. The door to the bedroom was ajar, and the majestic sight of our wedding bed caught her eye.

'It can wait,' she said as she pressed a finger to my lips.

'No, it can't,' I tried to protest.

But she had already pressed herself against me.

'Whatever it is can wait until morning.'

Her perfume smelled of the delicate flowers one collects in the spring. She untucked her hairpins, her dark hair falling to her shoulders.

She whispered for me to come to the bed.

So I let her lead me to that mound of white, leaving the shadow of my failure at the door. I let her turn her back to me, revealing the strip of ivory buttons down her back, and I unbuttoned her. I slipped my hands under the silk, and felt the smoothness of her skin and the sharpness of her shoulder blades.

She turned to face me, her nakedness, for the first time, revealed. I stood there for a second and could barely breathe. Her body, in all its whiteness, was a beauty that I could not believe was now mine to touch, to taste, to kiss. I cupped my hands around her. I closed my eyes. I wanted to feel her before seeing her. I would spend the whole night never taking my eyes off her, that much I was certain. I would memorize her. I would make a mental map of her, trace my finger around her heart, chart every bone. Lenka in my hands. I grasped her. I held her to my heart. My fingers felt the taper of her thin torso, the small circle of her waist, the reassuring curves of her hips.

Her dress was still at her knees and she stepped over it like a puddle of spilled milk. She now loosened in my arms and I allowed her to undress me: my waistcoat, my white shirt, the buckle of my belt, and finally my trousers. We fell into that bed, two warm bodies wrapping and searching for each other. I inhaled every inch of her naked skin, as if hoping I could keep her inside me forever. Like air trapped in my lungs. In those fleeting moments until dawn, we pushed the covers back. We were swimming into each other, each of us clinging to the other, as if we were the other's life raft.

19

JOSEF

As much as the evening was white and pure, the morning was dark and haunting.

She took the news with such devastation, it was as if I had witnessed the birth and death of my wife in a matter of hours.

I told her that my father had been unable to get exit visas for her family. 'Not yet,' I told her, 'but hopefully, soon.' It was my intention to soften the news with the implication that there was still hope.

'Your father already knows.'

She was wrapped in a satin robe, her nightdress peeking out from beneath her hem. She sat down to eat the small breakfast I had prepared. Her cup of steaming coffee remained untouched. She did not reach for her roll.

'When did you find this out?' she finally managed to whisper.

'The night before last. I went to see your father, and he implored me not to tell you until after the wedding. He wants you to go anyway, and once we're settled, we'll send for the others.'

She shook her head no.

'Josef, I thought you'd know me better than that.'

'I do know you, as does your father. We both thought you'd refuse. But now we're married and you and I must live as one.'

She eyed me sharply, her gaze like a hot iron.

'Twenty years with my family does not equal one night with you.'

'Lenka. Lenka.' I said her name over and over. 'Please listen to me . . . '

She did not answer me; she was looking out the window. I stood up and went to retrieve our papers from my briefcase.

'Your family wants you to come with me. You may wish to disregard my wishes, but surely you will not disobey theirs also, will you?'

She shook her head again.

'I will come when you have done what you promised. When there are five passports in your hand, not just two.'

'The German army is on the march. They will be in Czechoslovakia any day now. We need to leave, Lenka! We need to leave now.'

I was loud and impatient. Lenka did not flinch, even when I shouted, even when I knelt down at her knees and implored her to come.

When I could tolerate her silence no longer, I rose from the ground and walked to the bedroom in a trance. I sat on the bed, whose white sheets resembled a deflated sail, and with my head in my palms I began to sob.

20

LENKA

Father's eyes are filled with fury and desperation now. Two cups of cold tea sit between us. He is exhausted from trying to reason with me.

'You must go. You must go. You must go.' He says it over and over again, as if he uttered it enough times, I'd be hypnotized and finally agree.

'I will not leave you and Mother,' I tell him. 'I will not leave Marta. I will go when Josef does what he has promised. When all our visas are in his hand.'

Father is pulling at his hair. The white of his temples looks like polished bone.

'There will not be enough time to get all five visas!' Father's fist hits the table. 'Don't you understand how quickly things have already turned for the worse?' He was shaking. In his anger, he was almost unrecognizable to me.

'Lenka, Josef's family tried their best . . . '

'How could the two of you not have told me the truth?'

'We both love you, Lenka.' His voice was cracking. 'One day you will understand when you have your own children.' He had composed

130

himself enough to stare me straight in the eyes.

'But, Papa, you have *two* children.' I was crying like a two-year-old now. 'And how do you expect me to live with the fact that I went to America and left Marta?'

The weight between us was crushing. He raised his head to the ceiling, and the sound of his sigh was more a release of anguish than an act of breathing.

'What can I do to convince you?'

'You can say or do nothing, Papa,' I said through tears.

'Lenka.' His hand is balled into a fist, like a heart torn out. 'Lenka,' he weeps in despair. 'Lenka.'

But finally he releases me.

'I have said all I can say. The decision is yours, Lenka.'

There is a momentary silence between us.

'Thank you,' I say, cutting through the quiet. I go over to embrace him. He is shaking in my arms.

'You'll see, Papa,' I said, taking his hand to my lips. 'In the end, Josef will come through for all of us.'

'You will see.' I believed those words as if they were a singular truth. A commandment that I was willing to write in stone.

21

LENKA

The week before Josef and his family left was agony for me. I wanted to be a good and loving wife, but it was difficult to be close to him when I knew he would be leaving in only a few days.

Josef insisted he would not go with his family either, and this created a terrible argument between him and his parents. They had spent everything they had to secure their passage, passports, and documents to allow them — and me — to leave Czechoslovakia, and they simply were not leaving without their only son.

His parents were furious with my decision. They had gone to great lengths to include me in their plans, and now Dr. Kohn and his wife believed their beloved son had married a fool.

Vêruška, however, understood my decision. 'They should have told you before the wedding,' she said, shaking her head. 'They should have told you the truth.'

I smiled and reached for her hand, squeezing her slender fingers in mine. 'Everything is so rushed . . . I want to be mad at my father and Josef, but there doesn't even seem like there's time for that . . . Does that seem silly?'

She smiled weakly. 'I want you to come with us . . .'

'I know,' I told her. 'I just can't leave my family . . . I just can't.'

'I understand,' she said, though I could hear the sadness and regret in her voice.

She adjusted the red scarf around her throat. Her eyes were glazed with tears.

'Part of me thinks we should all wait here until we can go together,' she said. 'Honestly, what has this world come to? Everything has turned upside down.'

I tried to soothe her, even though it was I who wanted to cry. I took her small fingers and held them. 'We'll go shopping in New York soon. You'll be wearing a new red dress and shoes with silk ribbons. We'll drink cocoa in the afternoon, and go dancing together at night.'

'You promise?'

'Yes, of course,' I said. My voice was now close to breaking. I didn't think I had the strength anymore to maintain this facade of bravery for her — for Josef — for my parents. My own emotions remained behind floodgates that I feared would collapse at any moment. I did not want to think about Josef's betrayal, my father's complicity in not telling me. I remained steadfast in my decision to stay in Prague. I did this because it was what my conscience told me to do. But inside, I felt that my entire world was crumbling.

I held Věruška for several seconds. When I opened my eyes, I saw Josef standing at the doorway. He had wrongly hoped his sister could persuade me to join them. I saw him stare at the two of us, then shake his head and go to another room.

'We will see each other soon.'

'Yes,' I said. 'Very soon.'

She rose from her seat and kissed me on both cheeks. 'I always wanted a sister, but now that I have one, I'm leaving her behind.' She shook her head and dabbed her tears.

'I am coming,' I whispered through my tears. 'Just not now.'

In the end, I was the one who convinced Josef to go without me.

'You will be the scout,' I told him like a general giving orders. 'You'll go and make a home for us. You will take English classes so you can start medical school there. You'll get the American government to support my family's application for asylum, and then we will all be together. There's simply no other way.'

I said it as if it were written in stone. Clearly. Strongly. So ultimately, he believed he was doing the right thing for all of us until my family and I could join him.

Two days before they were to leave, however, Josef came home waving a letter. 'I have good news,' he told me, kissing me on the lips.

'We are going to stay in England through the summer. Papa just heard there's a Czech doctor running a clinic in Suffolk who needs obstetricians. He's been able to rearrange our passage with the ship company, so we're now booked to depart from Liverpool in September, first for Canada and then on to New York. This will buy us some more time to work on passage for your family.'

'That's wonderful!' I cried, and let him wrap me in his arms.

'I'll tell Papa that I will stay here with you until the end of the summer, and then join them in London before the boat leaves.'

I looked at him with such sweetness. 'Josef, leave with your family now and don't cause them any more stress. I've already complicated things enough. Hopefully, we can get visas for my family over the summer and we'll all join you in England and board the boat together.'

I kissed him again. The letter fluttered against my back.

The day soon arrived for their departure to England. Josef and I were still using Miloš's apartment. We woke up early and made love one last time.

I remember that he cried in my arms before he got dressed; his face was sealed to my breast as my fingers touched his curls.

'There's nothing to cry about,' I lied. 'We will see each other soon.'

My voice was flat and the words practiced. I had rehearsed them in my head while I had lain underneath him, my head staring at the ceiling. I had not slept the entire night. Josef had fallen asleep on my chest; his cheek was warm against me, his fingers laced through mine. In his slumber, he had looked like a sleeping child, an image that both filled my heart and wounded it at the same time. As I watched the clock, counting the hours we still had between us, I had marveled at his capacity to dream.

I would never tell him what I was secretly thinking — that I was tired of having to pretend to be stoic. I did not doubt my decision because I truly believed that Josef and I would eventually be reunited. But I was still secretly heartbroken that I was forced to make a choice between the man I loved and my family. It seemed terribly unfair and, again, I was afraid that if I let myself cry, I would never be able to stop.

Josef packed little to take on the journey so he could help his parents carry their trunks and valises. We had little as a married couple. Even our wedding portrait, taken by my mother with a family camera, had yet to be framed.

I had carefully placed it in a piece of folded brown paper. I wrote on it in pen, our names and the date of our wedding.

'You take it,' I told him. I bit my lip. I was forcing back my tears. 'Place it by your bed in England, and when we're finally in the States we'll have it framed.'

He took it from me and placed it not in his suitcase, but in the breast pocket of his jacket.

We ate breakfast in a reverent silence, gazing at each other over steaming cups.

When we dressed, we stole greedy glances at each other, as if trying to store the sight for the months ahead. The entire time I felt as though I were holding my breath. A sob felt only seconds away. Again, I told myself, our separation was only temporary. We would see each other soon.

At the door, before we were to leave for the station, I stood next to him, my cheek pressed to his lapel.

When I pulled back in an effort to compose myself, I noticed a stray hair — a solitary brown string — dangling to the fiber of his coat. I took my finger to pull it away, but Josef caught my wrist.

'No. Don't, Lenka.'

'Don't what?'

'Leave it be.'

I can still see the glassiness of his eyes. Staring at me. Holding my wrist.

'Let me bring that little bit of you with me,' he said.

That little stray hair. He cupped his hand over it, as if it were a shield.

At the station, we met his family at the track. They were wrapped in heavy coats, a stack of suitcases on the cart. Vêruška looked grave.

I went up to them and greeted them, taking their hands and warming them with my own. I looked at their faces and tried to press them into my memory. I pulled each of them close and kissed them on both cheeks.

'Good-bye, Lenka,' each one said to me. 'We will see you soon.'

I nodded and tried to push back the tears.

Josef's mother and father were stoic, but Vêruška could hardly look at me, there were so many tears rolling down her face.

When the train pulled into the track, his parents and sister boarded first so that Josef and I could have some privacy in our last moments together.

We no longer spoke of my decision to remain behind. He understood my reasons by now.

And perhaps that was the beauty of our farewell. The unspoken understanding between us.

He stood before me and reached out to kiss me. I placed my mouth over his and felt his breath within my own. He placed both of his hands over my head and caressed my hair.

'Lenka . . . '

I pulled back and lifted my head to his. I was fighting back tears.

'Please just hurry and send for us.'

He nodded. I took a step back to look at him one last time. Then, just as the train whistle began to sound, Josef reached into his breast pocket and retrieved a small package. 'This was my mother's,' he said, placing what felt like a miniature box wrapped in brown paper in my hand.

'She wanted me to give it to you. Open it when you get home.'

He placed his finger beneath my chin and lifted me one last time to his mouth.

'I love you,' he whispered. And then I let go of him and stood at the platform as the train pulled away from the station.

The box contained a small cameo, carved from a smooth, pink carnelian stone, the face in white relief.

I could hear his voice telling me the face resembled mine. The long, narrow eyes. The full waves of hair.

I knew this was a conciliatory gift from his mother. A thank-you for convincing Josef not to stay with me.

I knew their travel plans by heart. First the train through Germany and Holland, and then a ferry from Calais in France that would bring them to England. There my beloved Josef would write me daily, and we would begin the countdown until we were together again.

It seemed as if the moment Josef left, events turned even bleaker.

On March 14, just two weeks after my wedding, with my husband already in England, Hitler gave the Czech government an ultimatum to surrender. Later the same day, the German army rolled its tanks across the Czech border. By morning, the Germans were in Prague. Slovakia declared its independence, calling itself the Slovak Republic, and what was left of our country was annexed to the Reich and renamed the Protectorate of Bohemia and Moravia.

I stood at the long windows of our apartment watching the motorcades and tanks driving down the streets. The roads were lined with onlookers. There were a few cheers, but mostly the other Czechs watched with sadness as our city was taken over.

Within days, Hacha, the newly imposed president, abolished the parliament and all political parties, and also vocally condemned the 'Jewish influence' in Czechoslovakia. As the Germans marched into Prague to the cheers of the German-speaking Czechs, he closed the borders and initiated the Nuremburg laws.

Konstantin von Neurath was soon appointed Reichsprotektor of all of Bohemia and Moravia. Already, we began to see our freedom evaporating before us.

He instituted German laws to control the press, crack down on student protestors, and abolish any conflicting political parties or unions.

That spring, I continued to receive letters from Josef. He spoke of the warm, generous family they were boarding with in Suffolk, and of the tall oak trees that were beginning to grow fat with green. He wrote how his father had delivered nine babies since his arrival, and how the English were bracing themselves for a second world war. He wrote that he worried about me and that every night he had a recurring dream.

In his dream, the two of us are near a foxhole in the middle of a forest. In Czech folklore, the foxhole is a magical place where children secretly placed pieces of paper inscribed with wishes. In his dream, we jointly stick our folded paper into the foxhole, and when we withdraw our hands, we are holding a small baby.

140

I laughed when I read this because every night I go to sleep I remember our wedding night, his long body stretching and pressing into mine.

By early April, I sensed that I was pregnant, but I delayed telling my mother or sister until the start of May. By that time, my breasts were so tender and swollen that I had begun to undo the buttons on my shirt at night when everyone was asleep. I was barely eating breakfast in the morning, and I was spending most of each afternoon only wanting to sleep.

I suspect my mother also knew I was pregnant. She looked at me as if she suspected something, but kept her words to a minimum during those first few months of the German occupation. Finally, as I began to worry that I should consult a doctor and after my second period never appeared, I burst into tears as I helped prepare the afternoon tea.

'Mama,' I whimpered into her thin arms. 'I'm pregnant.' I began to cry as she tightened her arms. I didn't tell her that I feared I would never see Josef again, or that I felt ill-prepared to bring a child into a world when a war was becoming more likely each day.

'I know you're scared, my love. But you will be fine, Lenka. Even if you have to raise the child without Josef for a little while, you will have us. You will never be alone.'

My heart flooded with love for her. I was right

not to leave my family. Never would I want my parents or sister to think that they were ever alone.

I wrote to Josef that I was expecting and he returned my letter saying that he was overjoyed, but sick over the fact he couldn't be with me. He included the name of the doctor who had taken over his father's practice and told me I should visit him immediately. There, I would receive the best care. At this point Jewish doctors were no longer on the Czech national insurance policy, so all patients who went to Jewish doctors had to pay cash. Dr. Silberstein saw me free of charge. He was a kind, middle-aged man who felt my abdomen with gentle hands and reassured me that I was in perfect health and would deliver without difficulty.

My abdomen thickened by my fourth month. Mother helped let out the waistbands of my skirts and she began to unpack the baby clothes that had once been Marta's and mine. I had welcomed my pregnancy even though things were so difficult for us. It was wonderful to feel that there was life swelling inside me and that that life was created with Josef. With the baby growing every day, our connection deepened in my mind. Life in Prague, however, had become increasingly difficult. We always thought the worst was behind us, until the next week when there was a new law passed and our freedom was restricted even further. We seldom left home unless it was necessary. That June, von Neurath issued a decree excluding all Jews from economic life and ordering them to register their assets. Jewish companies were officially taken over by the German Treuhand who would oversee their sale or 'Aryanization.' The day after this order was decreed, Adolf Eichmann arrived in Prague and set up house in a confiscated Jewish villa in Steřešovice.

By August, Jews were segregated in restaurants and prohibited from public bathrooms and swimming pools. A curfew was initiated that forbade us to be out after sunset, and even our radios were confiscated. My belly was now noticeably bigger and I tried to tell myself that the restrictions were not so bad, that I should welcome the opportunity to rest and keep off my feet. Once the baby arrived, I knew I would be busy and tired. I only hoped that things would improve by then and I would be able to take the baby for fresh air and walks.

I tried to remain as positive as I could, although at times it seemed almost impossible to be happy with so much tension and fear surrounding my family and our situation. I imagined the baby was a boy and thought I would call him Tomáš, after my grandfather who had died when I was three. At night, I'd lie in bed and try to remember our wedding night, the sensation of Josef's arms around me. The moonlight pouring through the window, and our naked bodies entwined.

When I felt the first kicks of life, I was bursting with happiness. No matter how bleak our circumstances had become, those first move-ments made me feel that life was continuing.

Marta, however, had grown restless from the curfew and the loss of freedom. She seldom saw her friends. I could sense her increasing frustration. She said little to our parents and had no interest in talking to me about my pregnancy, but occasionally I would catch her eye and see how miserable she was. Her long red hair was a mane of unruly curls, defiant and glorious as it rolled down her back. She refused to braid it even though her school demanded it. It was the only protest she was allowed.

I tried to remain optimistic, hoping a letter would arrive from Josef telling me he had secured our visas to England and that our exit stamp from the Gestapo had been arranged. But that letter never arrived. Instead, Josef's letters became more frantic and steeped in frustration. War was now almost certain, and the borders were closed. We both knew he was going to have to go to the United States without me and then hope he could somehow arrange for passage for me and my family later.

I accepted this with little protest. I lacked the strength for such a strenuous trip and I feared giving birth in a foreign city.

I placed my hands on my belly each night and closed my eyes. I welcomed each kick as though it were a knock heralding a better life, one in which Josef and I were together, our baby rolling on the floor to the sounds of laughter, rather than sirens and warplanes overhead.

Josef's family would leave on the SS *Athenia* from Liverpool on September 1, arrive in Canada a few weeks later, and then travel on to New York. Josef promised to send a telegram as soon as they had arrived safely.

The newspapers, however, were the ones who informed me of his status. The SS *Athenia* was torpedoed off the coast of Ireland by a German U-boat, the first civilian casualty of the war. Although most of the passengers were saved from the sinking ship, the Kohn family was listed among the ninety-eight dead.

22

JOSEF

On the deck, the sky was black as ink. I remember not a single star, only pale light from the moon. We stood in the cold, the wind lashing our faces. My mother was wearing her fur coat. She had sewn her remaining jewelry and Czech crowns in its lining. My sister was still in her favorite red dress from dinner. She had been dancing with a boy from Krakow, and the color that had flushed her cheeks over cordials was now erased to an unearthly white.

When they called for the women and children, my father pushed Věruška and Mama ahead of us. I had just said good-bye to Lenka months earlier, and now my mother and sister were clinging to the lapels of my dinner jacket, their soft, damp faces pressing against mine for the last time.

Věruška's final words were like an absolution to me. 'She was right not to come.' I watched speechless as she took my aging mother toward the lifeboats.

She turned to look back at me one last time as one of the deck-hands helped her and Mother into the boat. As the pulleys lowered them down into the sea, her dress was like a plume of red smoke rising against the darkened sky.

A half hour later, Papa and I were still waiting to be put onto one of the last lifeboats. I stood there thinking that those who remained would now drown together. I looked at the faces around me. There was a boy next to me, no older than seventeen, with a small white face and a thick head of black hair. In one of his blue hands, he held his bow; in the other, he held his violin. The instrument dangled like a wounded appendage. I had made up my mind that I would not ask him his name. I did not want to know the names of the ghosts who would be sharing my tomb, but Papa reached and put his arm around him. The boy shook at Papa's touch.

'Is your family already on another boat?' Papa asked him.

The boy shuddered. 'No, I am alone.'

'I am Dr. Jacob Kohn and this is my son, Josef,' Papa said, pointing to me.

'I'm Isaac Kirsch.' He clumsily switched his bow to the same hand that held his violin and shook Papa's and my hand. Later I would learn he had been practicing on the deck when the torpedo hit. He said his violin case had been thrown into the water during the impact.

This was a hasty introduction against a backdrop of chaos and death. Women were screaming from down below as the crew frantically rushed around the deck. They were boys who were not navy men but simply 'extra' sons who needed a job and found themselves on a cruise ship bound for Canada.

147

There were still hundreds of people on deck as we were pushed to an available lifeboat. What happened next haunts me to this day. I have relived it in my head so many times. Second by second.

Papa pushes Isaac and me ahead of him. 'The young before the old,' he says. 'I'll take the next boat.'

I say, 'No, Papa.' He reaches for my cheek. I feel the warmth of his palm. And in that rushed second, I am that shuddering bird of my childhood, cupped in a single hand. 'Papa,' I say, but he has already decided. He pushes me away and forces me and Isaac to climb into the lifeboat alone. We are lowered into the water, a pool of black. As the stern of the enormous ship begins to dip lower and lower, I see bodies jumping from the deck. In the chaos of our lifeboat, Isaac manages to hold on to his violin but drops his bow.

The rescue ship, the *Knute Nelson*, has come to help us. But its propeller accidentally tears into one of the bobbing lifeboats. I hear the screams, witness the carnage of blood spilling into the sea illuminated by the rescue ship's floodlights. Red silk spreading over the water like a parachute. I see my sister falling into the water like a drowning rose.

23

JOSEF

When Isaac plays the violin at my thirtieth birthday party years later, he is the one person who knows me for the man I really am. He plays the music that I am partial to. The melancholy music of Brahms, or the second movement of Dvořák's *American* string quartet. The melody played by the first violin makes me cry every time I hear it.

He is seven years younger than I. He is now a violinist in the New York Philharmonic. He eats Amalia's dry cakes and drinks sweet wine.

I like to think we are cut from the same cloth. We each arrived here with no one. I carry the weight of my wife and baby trapped in Europe; he carries his violin as if it could serenade his ghosts.

He tells me he plays for his mother, who loved the folk music of her village outside Brno. He plays for his father, who loved the simplicity of Mendelssohn, for his little brother, who hated the sound of the violin and cried every time he played a single note.

My Amalia sits in her kitchen listening to him. She folds her hands and closes her eyes.

Sometimes when he plays, I watch her, her face transported to someplace far away.

The three of us eat around our modest table, the basket of bread passed between us. The flowers that Isaac brought are placed in a glass milk bottle that Amalia had saved.

And our lives quietly continue in peace and safety.

I learn the comfort of a good glass of whiskey. I find solace as I clean the corridors of a sticky primary school, and teach myself English by reading the books that are kept in desks by children fifteen years younger than I am. These are the things I do as I put myself through medical school.

The letters I had written to Lenka to tell her I am safe and working to get her out of Prague are all returned unopened and placed in a box under my bed that also contains my first wedding photograph. Next to the wooden toys and miniature airplane I had bought nearly a decade earlier in London, in the giddy anticipation of the birth of my son.

24

LENKA

My world went black after I knew of Josef's ship's sinking. I became consumed with grief.

It was my mother who told me I had lost all color in my face. You must go to the doctor, she urged as she wrapped me in not one coat but two. It was the end of September and we were now officially at war. Two long lapels dripped from my chest; my belly made it impossible for either coat to close.

Dr. Silberstein took his stethoscope from his bag and held it over the stretched skin of my abdomen.

'When was the last time you felt movement?' he asked. My eyes were full of tears. I could not answer him; since the minute I read of the sinking of the *Athenia*, I had lost track of everything.

'I can't remember,' I told him. 'Is it the baby?' I felt the floor sliding out from me.

He had me lie down again and struggled to find the heartbeat. 'I can't find it,' he told me, 'but it could just be the position. Go home and we will find out in a few days.'

I woke up to a rush of blood the following

evening. Everything was sliding out from me. My husband was dead, and my baby was now a jelly of blood on the sheets.

All I wanted was to join them.

My mother bathed me and cared for me, and the doctor was kind enough to give me some precious morphine so that I could sleep.

I slept and slept as if I were sleeping into my own death. I dreamed of nothing. I dreamed black. No images, no memories, no thoughts of the future. When you dream of darkness, you are all but dead.

In the months that followed, my mother took care of me as if I were a newborn child. She washed me, fed me, and read to me as I lay like my own stillborn baby. Lifeless, with eyes like frosted glass, in my own childhood bed.

As I struggled to come to terms with my loss, things only worsened for my family and our community around us. Freedoms we once never considered freedoms were taken from us. We could no longer drive, own a pet, or even listen to the radio. We were given two days to surrender our radios and I remember foggily as Father bundled up the radio he had bought for Mother years before and turned it over to the authorities.

Lucie seemed like the only person we could count on as our former life crumbled around us. She appeared every Monday, arriving like an angel, with fresh eggs and milk from Petr's brother's farm. These visits were mother's lifeline to the world outside the apartment. The tables had clearly turned; instead of offering Lucie decadently sumptuous Saturday meals and gifts commissioned from the seamstress, Gizela, we were reduced to humbly accepting whatever was in her basket that week.

Lucie's daughter, Eliška, was now speaking her first sentences, and her chubby legs and doll-like face made Mama and Marta temporarily forget their unhappiness. I, however, could not bear to look at the child. I would see Lucie smiling as Eliška twirled around in her pinafore or nibbled on a crust of bread and I would be filled with an envy that made me loathe myself even more. It was terrible to be jealous of another person's child, especially someone you loved so much. But I felt so empty that all I could think of was craving a replacement for what I had lost.

Still, it was Lucie who saved me from my grief. She arrived one afternoon with her basket of food but also with a little package just for me. She brought the present, wrapped in brown paper and twine, to my bed.

'Lenka,' she ordered. 'I want you to open it now . . . not later.'

My hands were weak from lack of use. They trembled slightly as they went to undo the string and remove the paper. Inside was a little tin of pastels and a small sketchpad.

'Remember how we used to draw together?'

I nodded.

'Start again.' She moved the curtains beside

my bed. 'What other family still has such a view of the Vltava?'

I had wanted nothing more than to forget the emptiness in my belly, the ache for something that was no longer there. But it had remained like a wound that had no salve, a stifled wail that had no release.

Lucie had given me a gift — a reminder that I still had my sight and my hands. That afternoon I began sketching again.

At first, I struggled to get my hand back. My fingers gripped the pencil, the tip pointed to the page, but I could not connect my hand with my head. But slowly, things returned to me, and I began to regain my focus. I started by sketching small objects in my room. Just looking at things that I had not noticed for so many months was nourishing to me. The glass birds on my desk, the wooden whistle from my childhood, and the porcelain doll that had been a birthday gift.

Every week, Lucie would return with more supplies, and I found that a tin of charcoal and a stiff pad of paper went a long way toward soothing my wounds. I was like a painting that had been rendered in black and white. But after several days I was able to add the first strokes of color.

My grief still had its own ebb and flow. When I looked out the window and saw the Gentile women taking strolls with their shiny black prams, the sunshine hitting their babies' caps, I still wanted to curl up into a ball and cry.

Other times, when I lay at night in my bed, I would feel such an ache in my womb that I wasn't even sure if it was the miscarriage — for I had never even seen this child's eyes, felt the grasp of its finger — or the loss of the possibility that I would ever have a child with Josef. He was gone now and so was any connection I was ever to have with him. I had barely grieved for him when I received news of his death because the miscarriage had arrived so swiftly — but now the finality of his death swept over me.

As the weeks passed, however, my bouts of crying lessened and I was able to distract myself more and more with my drawings. I remembered how I used to lock myself in the same room that first year and study my legs or the flexed tendons in my hand, and I was comforted by knowing that there were some things that could not be taken from me.

I began to curl myself on the window seat of my bedroom with my pad atop my knees and sketch the roofline of the castle, the bridge outside our apartment, and the young girl who skipped along the edge of the Vltava as I myself had done so many times as a child. I sketched until my fingers were numb, the apron of my dress dusty with pastel.

My mother would often knock on my door and ask me to come and join her in our parlor for a cup of tea and a few biscuits if Lucie had managed to bring some butter that week. The parlor was now a shadow of what it once was. Weeks before, we were forced to bring what little remained of our valuables and turn them over to the Protectorate of Bohemia and Moravia. Marta and I took our heirloom silver candlesticks, the

155

few remaining china figurines and ornaments to the storage center at the Spanish synagogue, where they were registered and then sent on to the Reich.

I believe one of the reasons I was so content to just stay in my childhood room sketching was that I could sequester myself from the loneliness and emptiness of the rest of our apartment. Sitting in an empty room that had once been filled with so much color and life was now unbearable. It wasn't that I longed for the full shelves of glass and decorations themselves. It was the sense of emptiness that permeated the walls, a sense that was intensified by the scene of Mother sitting against a now-worn sofa, with her two girls trying so hard to act as if a single cookie was an extravagance neither of them deserved.

For most of that year, I passed each day by drawing. I even set up a small easel by my window. The scarcity of oil pigments made me more focused than I had been at the Academy. I would find myself first applying each brushstroke in my head, imagining it on the canvas even before I put it there to make sure it was just right. For I knew how precious each inch of color was.

That autumn of 1941, all Jews were ordered to wear yellow Stars of David.

I remember the afternoon in September we registered at the Gestapo office and were given our stars. The four of us returned home to find Lucie and Eliška already there. Lucie had her own key and had let herself in, and had begun making pancakes from the flour and eggs she had brought.

We had stuffed the yellow felt stars into our pockets and sat down at the table to eat with Lucie and Eliška. Our faces were strained. I could see the tears filling Mother's eyes as she looked at her namesake's rosy, sweet face. Papa sat straight in his chair looking at the grandfather clock, and Marta and I tried to forget the burning stars in our pocket and simply enjoy Lucie's delicious pancakes that we had grown fat on in our own childhood.

It was Mother's star that slipped to the ground as Lucie hugged her good-bye. I stood behind the two of them and saw the star fall to the carpet, its silent descent more powerful than the loudest cry. Mama carefully picked it up and put it back in her pocket, placing a palm over it as if to shield it from Lucie's little girl. But Eliška had noticed. 'Look, Mama, Aunt Liska has stars in her pocket. She's so lucky, Mama!'

My mother knelt down and kissed her on the forehead. 'Stars belong in the sky, dear. Remember that.' Lucie's eyes were full of tears as she came over to Mother. Lucie took her daughter's hand in hers and kissed it. I so wanted her to hold mine, too, for I remembered the safe feeling of that hand. The warm padding of her palm as it held me close, the reassuring security it gave me as a child as we walked down the street. The memory of my own childhood when the only stars were just as Mother said, those burning in the midnight sky.

One afternoon, I went to get what little groceries I could with my ration coupons. There were only a few hours each day during which Jews could shop. The lines were long and there was hardly anything on the shelves to be bought. On this day, however, I was lucky enough to get a little flour and butter, a few radishes, and two apples.

Walking home, I ran into a girl who was in the class above me at the Academy, Dina Gottliebová. She was not wearing a yellow star and I was surprised when she stopped to talk to me.

'I've just come from seeing *Snow White*,' she said. 'I took my star off to see it.'

I was shocked. I would never have imagined taking such a risk.

'You cannot imagine the drawings that made this film possible.' She was brimming over with excitement. 'The characters were so lifelike . . . the colors so saturated. I want to race home and draw all night.'

For a few seconds I had forgotten about the star on my coat, and my hungry parents and sister waiting for me in the apartment. There I was enraptured by the sight and voice of my old classmate waxing enthusiastic about a film.

We talked for a few more minutes, before the sight of a German officer walking in our direction frightened me from continuing the conversation.

How I wanted to remain there with her. Her energy was infectious and I admired her bravery, but she was the one now with the yellow star in her pocket, while mine was clearly sewn on my lapel. The two of us talking openly could only ignite trouble.

'Dina.' I touched her arm gently. 'I am so happy to have seen you, but I must go home and get these groceries — what little there is of them — home to my mother.'

She nodded and smiled in a way that communicated that she understood why I had become nervous. 'Let's hope we see each other soon,' she said, and then we parted ways.

That night, over a watery soup of flour dumplings and two quartered apples, I imagined what it might feel like to sit in a dark theater and watch an animated film. To laugh at the lively images dancing on the screen, with the light from the projector illuminating my hair, and my yellow star buried deep in my pocket.

25

JOSEF

At night, I sometimes wake up from a dream in which I am sitting in that lifeboat, with Isaac sitting next to me, his violin on his lap, his black eyes scanning the water, searching for the exact place where he dropped his bow.

In the dream, I am not watching as the *Athenia* raises its nose to the starry sky. I am not focusing on the horror of the mangled lifeboat or the blood staining the waters red.

I am staring at all the empty seats in the boat. The places where my family might have sat, and my life would have been wholly different. I have heard other survivors speak of this guilt — the boat that could have held one more, the family that could have been persuaded to hide one more child, or the wife that should never have been left behind.

If I am feeling particularly low, I try and imagine Lenka there beside me. I wiggle my old bottom to the side of my mattress and make room for her on the wooden seat. I place my hand on a stretch of white sheet to warm it for her, to search for her fingers, to wait for the grasp of her hand. Sixty years later, and I still can remember the sensation of Lenka's hand.

I tell nearly all my patients the same thing when I come to check on them after their delivery. They are almost always sitting up in bed in their robes. The baby is slightly unwrapped from its hospital blanket, its face peeking toward its mother's breast, its fingers threaded into hers.

There are two sensations of skin you will always remember in your lifetime: the first time you fall in love — and that person holds your hand — and the first time your child grasps your finger. In each of those times, you are sealed to the other for eternity.

Lenka's hand was the whitest I have ever known. The fingers long and elegantly tapered. The first time she took my hand, my heart beat so fast I could hardly breathe. She never smelled like turpentine or chalk dust even after a day of painting or drawing. I would press my lips to her smooth knuckles, and inhale the scent of rose and geranium. I could fall into the memory like a soft-cushioned chair. I could smell a lifetime of happiness. I could close my eyes and see us growing old together, our hands knotted together wrinkled and brown.

The day at the station when we parted, I honestly did not think it would be the last time. But to this day, I can still feel those fluttering hands against my cheeks. I can feel her fingertips over my eyelids, inhale the scent of flowers, and recall the flash of her white skin.

When my daughter, Rebekkah, was born — that grasp of two infant fingers over my single one — was equally powerful. And when my son

161

was born and I cradled him in my arms, the sensation was just as profound.

When Amalia was dying, lying in a bed with tubes threaded through her nose, one taped to her arm, I would take her hand and talk to her.

That hand, small with delicate fingers and pale, moon-shaped nails. My daughter's hand, but older. Liver spots and skin as fragile as rice paper. I would kiss her hand. I would find myself crying when her eyes were sealed closed. I would wipe my tears with the back of her palm and I would squeeze it as if trying to communicate with her through Morse code.

But in my heart, I knew that even in the best years of our marriage, the sensation of Amalia's hand never gave me the same thrill or comfort as Lenka's. But when Amalia's heart stopped beating and her hand grew cold, I ached, yearning for that fleeting sense of warmth and comfort, all the same.

26

LENKA

We were informed by letter that our family would be transported to Terezín in December 1942.

We were not the first to receive notice of their transport. Dina and her mother had been sent earlier in the year, and Elsa that October with her parents. By the time we heard that we were to be sent, we were almost looking forward to it. We hoped to be reunited with so many of the people from our circle who had already been sent. 'It will be a place of only Jews,' Father told us. Oddly enough, that sounded like a relief to us at that time.

Every transport was assigned a letter of the alphabet, and we were *Ez*. We were instructed to bring a total of fifty kilos that could fit into one suitcase, a rucksack, and a roll of bedding. Marta and I went through our clothes and packed three outfits each. One pair of pants, a dress, and two skirts and blouses. Stockings. Shoes. Underwear. Papa said Marta and I could each pack one book, but I chose to bring two sketchpads, along with one tin of vine charcoal and one small box of oil pastels.

When we learned we would be sent to Terezín,

163

Mother took the news so silently, so inwardly, that it was impossible to gauge her feelings. She worked like a machine, efficiently and without emotion, reading the guidelines and then making the necessary preparations. She saved two sausages over the course of three weeks. Then, as the transport got closer, she cooked milk and sugar for a long time until it turned brown, and then packed it in paper containers. She also made a roux of butter and flour and rolled it in wax paper. She baked small cookies and one cake, and several loaves of bread. She packed most of this between her and father's rucksack, packing little else for them but two sets of clothes and underwear. No extra shoes. Not a single book.

She took our sheets and pillowcases and boiled them the color of coffee so they would not look dirty when they eventually became worn. Marta gave her the pillowcase that Lucie had embroidered so many years before and asked her to boil that in coffee, too. 'I want to bring it,' she had said. Mother took the pillowcase, already fragile from being on Marta's bed for so many years, and boiled it.

After Marta and I had packed our suitcases, mother checked what we had packed and refolded the clothes, as if she needed the ritual of preparing the things for each of her children's journey. We were no longer young children — even Marta was now sixteen — yet, in her eyes, we were ever still in need of her care.

Father used a thick black pen to mark our suitcases and rucksack with our transport numbers. I was 4704Ez, Marta 4703Ez, Mother 4702Ez, and Father 4701Ez. We also were given identification tags with the same numbers that we were required to wear around our necks.

The night before we were to leave, Lucie came to our apartment. She was solemn. Her black hair was pinned behind her ears and her face was tense. That beautiful white skin of hers — which only a few years ago had looked like porcelain — was now showing the first whispers of age. The fear on her face was so visible that I felt a chill down my spine. I could not look her straight in the eyes.

And so I focused on my mother. I watched as she took Lucie's capelet and smiled as she glanced over the fine navy gabardine that looked as good as the day she'd given it to her. She reached to touch Lucie's shoulder, and Lucie responded by opening her arms and enveloping Mother in such a tight embrace that I saw the fabric of Mother's dress gather into the grasp of Lucie's fingers.

When I saw the two of them, Mother bending to embrace Lucie, her chin resting on Lucie's shoulder, I thought of the history between these two women. How each of them had loved me through my childhood, and had mothered me in her own way. But watching them together now, it was clear that their connection was more like the bond between Marta and me. They did not say a single word, but each movement, each gesture, was like a pantomime of worry and reassurance, of fear and of the other extending comfort. All expressed without the utterance of any sound.

Lucie sat next to my mother at the dining room table. She watched as my mother opened three velvet boxes. As required by the Germans, my parents had turned in their other valuables weeks ago. The shelves in the basement of the Spanish synagogue — a designated collecting station for the German authorities — were filled with silver candelabra, mother-of-pearl gramophones, sets of sterling, as well as paintings and jewelry. All of these things, now considered extravagant luxuries, would be sent abroad to enrich the senior members of the Reich. We had stood in line for hours to hand over our watches, Father's cuff links, Mother's strands of pearls, Marta's earrings with the faceted stones, and my favorite garnet ring. But Mother's engagement ring from Father, the gold choker with the seed pearls that Grandmother gave her on the eve of her wedding, and the small ring Father gave her when I was born, those things she had kept hidden.

I can still see it so distinctly as she pushes them over to Lucie, who quietly wraps them in old scarves and places them in her basket.

'I will keep them safe,' Lucie says just by lowering her eyes. She knows how much it means for Mother to be entrusting her with these things. Their significance lies not in the monetary value of the stones or the weight of the gold, but in the different milestones in her life that each marked.

Mother stands and Lucie embraces her one

last time, rising on her tiptoes to reach her. A single tear falls across Mother's cheek. My beloved Lucie kisses not the dry cheek but the wet one, and Mother nods before pulling away, pointing over to her two children, who are not children at all now, but two young women.

Lucie comes over to Marta and me, and we each stand to hug her as we say good-bye. She holds her basket tightly to her, and we know she is signaling to us that the jewelry will be safe with her. That she will never sell it. Her eyes are fierce and defiant, a look I have never seen before.

'I will see you girls when this is over,' she says, trying her best to smile. 'And your mother can decide which of these you can wear.'

I look at her and I know that my eyes are frightened. The tears, the emotion of saying good-bye to her, is almost too difficult to bear. 'Lucie,' I say. 'Take this, too.' I unpin the cameo that Josef gave me that last day at the station. I also wiggle off my gold wedding band, the one I promised to myself that I would never take off as long as I lived.

'Keep these safe, too.'

Lucie reaches to embrace me, and tells me she will do as I asked and not to worry. I try to thank her, but the tears are coming and she shushes me the way she did when I was a little girl.

She holds me tight to her chest, kisses me, and then Marta once more, before she rises and walks quietly out the door.

The next morning, we left our apartment with our suitcases and rucksacks. We had slept little, and now spoke only a few words because we were anxious and had no idea what to expect. Our deportation cards informed us that we were to report to a local school where we would remain for three days until our transport to Terezín. When we arrived, the school was already teeming with hundreds of people. Marta found one of her former classmates immediately, but I recognized no one. We slept on the floor with our sheets and blanket. The air was stagnant with the smell of sausages and warm milk. It was an awful, rancid odor, one that made me sick. I remember reaching for my pillowcase to inhale the scent of the coffee mother had boiled them in. My stomach ached, not yet from hunger but out of a sense of dread. A fog of nervousness and fear hung over all of us. Every pair of eyes seemed scared. Even the toddlers who roamed about with their little stocking-clad feet and rounded faces appeared tense. I looked at them with sympathy. My own childhood had been so carefree. Long walks with Lucie and Marta, painting watercolors by the Vltava, and slices of rich chocolate cake. I had not yet let myself feel thankful that I had lost my baby; that would come much later, but it pained me to see the child who was looking longingly at other people's food, the one who already needed a bath, or the one whose parents had lacked the room in their suitcase to pack a single toy.

There was one little boy whom I befriended the first night at the school. His name was Hans and he had turned three the month before. I had left my parents and Marta by our makeshift beds and gone for a walk alongside the perimeter of the auditorium. Out of habit, I took my tin of charcoal and sketchpad out of my rucksack, and hoped to find something of interest to draw. I found a quiet corner and made myself as comfortable as I could.

But before I had the chance to settle in, Hans found me. He was wearing a white shirt that was already stained with what looked like jam, and a pair of brown trousers. His dark hair was thick and curly. His eyes were bottle green.

I'm not sure why he chose to sit next to me. I didn't have a cookie to offer him or even a stick to play with, but he settled by my feet and smiled at me. I showed him my sketchpad and asked if he minded if I drew him for a little bit. He nodded and smiled. I felt such a pang in my heart as I looked at his curls and the color of his eyes. I wondered if my baby would have looked like him at three.

'Hans,' I whispered. 'Look at the shadows on the glass.' High above, the gymnasium windows were filled with the reflections of the trees outside. Almost like large puppets, they swayed back and forth. One branch resembled the neck of a giraffe; its cluster of leaves on the top could have been the animal's bobbing head. Another tree had a long sweep of boughs that looked like a dangling jellyfish. Hans giggled, and I began drawing him in profile.

Over the next two days, we became fast friends. I met his parents, Ilona and Benjamin, who were close to the same age as Josef and me. I sketched them holding hands, with Ilona gazing past her husband's face, past her son drumming on the floor. She was already trying to envision where we were headed, a mother's worried anticipation of the unknown written all over her face.

Before Terezín I wrote at the bottom of the page. One could scan the room at every other mother, the gaze was the same. Where were they sending us?

The name Terezín meant nothing to me at the time. I did not know of extermination camps or work camps, or even really the concept of a ghetto. I had never heard a whisper about a concentration camp.

We had heard we would only be with Jews, which was a relief to us. To be in a place where we were all the same, and not have to live next to others who would be permitted their freedom while we were saddled with one restriction after another. We knew there would be SS and that there would be work for us to do. But did we know what else truly lay in store for us? No. We did not. Absolutely. No.

We were loaded into the train, over one hundred of us herded inside a space that would have been overcrowded with less than half that. I stood next to Marta and Mother. Papa was pushed away from us as we were forced deeper and deeper into the car. Once the doors were closed, I looked for him. There was only a faint line of sunlight in the car, coming from a narrow window above, but I could see a glimmer of his profile in the back of the train. Every time I tried to look over in his direction, he was staring straight ahead.

The train crawled over the tracks. Babies cried and people tried not to complain, but we were terribly uncomfortable and there was no place to sit. The air was stifling and ripe with the smells of everyone's provisions. I looked to find Hans, just so I could lift him for a second and smell his unwashed hair.

By late afternoon, the train came to a halt and the door of the car was finally opened. We had arrived at the small train station of Bohušovice, which was about three kilometers outside Terezín. We were told by the Czech police to carry our suitcases and rucksacks for the remainder of the journey.

There was already quite a lot of snow on the ground. The white drifts were piled high against the road, and a light mist had begun to fall as our transport headed in the direction of Terezín. I remember looking at the sight of snowflakes on Mother's and Marta's hair. The two of them already looked so tired, and their black coats no longer seemed elegant after such a long journey. But in the fading sunlight, they looked almost like fairies, with their coils of red hair now adorned with snow. Little crystal beads that sparkled for a second before disappearing.

Later on as we walked, we finally saw the ramparts of Terezín on the horizon. I noticed

171

Mother ahead of me, fumbling in her pocket, then bowing her head, her gait slowing for a moment. Later on, when we were standing and being counted, I noticed that she looked different, that the color in her face was almost revived. When I looked more closely, I realized what had caused the change. She had secretly applied some lipstick.

Most of us did not know anything about the town of Terezín. We had no reason to, given our previously comfortable lives back in Prague. I eventually learned that at the orders of the Emperor Josef II, Terezín had been built as a Baroque fortress in the late eighteenth century. In the beginning, it served as a political prison for the Hapsburgs, with an addition of a small town to house the garrisons and soldiers. So do not imagine Auschwitz or Treblinka when I tell you what follows next in my story. There was no chimney of smoking, burning ash to greet us when we arrived. There were no brown, split-beam barracks. It resembled a small town — with buildings, dirty and dusty. Façades once painted Maria Theresa yellow, were now faded and peeling; the church was boarded up. But it was also the perfect place to prevent any escape: the town was surrounded by a moat, its perimeters lined by ramparts, and all exits and entrances marked by iron gates.

Upon our arrival, we were led to the Schleusse — the arrival hall — where we were registered, our bodies searched, and our luggage expertly checked by a special detachment of German women. For several days after our processing, we were kept in the Schleusse until we were assigned our housing by the *Raumwirtschaft* — a special department of the Jewish self-administration. The men and women in this department had been notified and had already prepared the bunks for the new arrivals in our transport. Luckily, Mother, Marta, and I were all placed in the Dresden barracks, and Father was assigned to live in the Sudeten. Most of the barracks, we soon discovered, were named after German towns.

As we were about to make our way to our barracks, I saw Ilona standing in a corner, holding Hans close to her. His legs were wrapped around her waist, and his head was nestled against her shoulder. I tried to look over in his direction and get him to smile, but he was lethargic from the journey and the lack of food. I made a shadow puppet with my hand and saw a little smile cross his lips. Ilona told me that she and Benjamin had yet to receive their barracks designation, and I told her I hoped she would be with us. That way, we could all look out for each other and maybe also care for Hans, who was still too young to be taken from her and put in the children's barracks.

She nodded, but already seemed as though she were in a dream. Her eyes were cloudy and her hair not pinned back. How quickly our appearances had changed without the luxury of clean clothes, a bath, and a mirror.

My family and I said good-bye to the people we had befriended over the course of our few days in the Schleusse, and began to make our way deeper into the ghetto.

While heading to the barracks, I searched for the gaze of someone we passed on the road who might somehow reassure me that Terezín would not be a terrible place to live during the war. I, like so many other Jews, could not then conceive that there was a master plan to exterminate us, but only to segregate us. But as I walked through Terezín that first afternoon, it was clear that this was a place of great deprivation. The roads were filled with half-starved prisoners, their cheeks hollow and their clothes threadbare. Men as thin as skeletons pulled old funeral carts loaded with suitcases or supplies. There was no color or vitality to be seen. Even the park in the center was fenced off.

Already another transport was arriving from Bohušovice, and I will never forget the sight of the people it contained. Men with long white beards, some wearing top hats and tails. Women in long dresses, fur coats, a few even walking with parasols that were bending from the snow. Later we would learn that this was a transport of German Jews — distinguished war veterans, intellectuals, and men of culture — who had paid thousands for supposed contracts that falsely promised them a privileged resettlement during the war.

I was craning my neck to watch them as they headed down the path to the Schleusse, when Marta tapped me on the shoulder. 'Have we underdressed?' It was the first time I had laughed in several days, and I wanted to reach out and hug her. Our whole lives it was I, the

174

older sister, who had tried to be strong and make Marta smile, so it was a strange feeling to see her trying to be so brave when inside I knew she was just as afraid as I was. 'If we have, it will be the first time,' I answered her.

Our parents had not heard us. They were walking solemnly in front of us like two people who were already resigned to following orders. Their pace slackened when the others in front of them slowed down. They did not talk between themselves. They looked not at each other, but straight ahead.

We had already been told that the men would live separately, so Marta, Mother, and I did our best to give Father a brave good-bye when the group stopped in front of our assigned barracks.

Papa kissed each of us on the forehead. He had been carrying Mother's rucksack, and I could see him inwardly struggle as he handed it over to her. It pained him not to be able to help her anymore.

'It's fine,' I heard Mother whisper. She extended her arm to take the bag from him. 'It's not heavy,' she said.

Father's arm was shaking. A strong arm trembling through a woolen coat sleeve.

'I will look for my girls at the curfew tonight.' He touched Mother's wrist.

Mother nodded.

'Yes, Papa,' we both said as we reached to help our mother with her bag. We saw Mother look back one more time at Father, her face straining to remain composed.

We climbed the stairs, our hearts sinking as we were greeted immediately by a gut-wrenching stench. The smell of dirty latrines and unwashed bodies laced the air. Marta had walked ahead of Mother and me. She turned to us with a frightened look in her eyes.

'Lenka,' she whispered. 'Where have they taken us?'

I quietly mouthed, 'It will be fine . . . just don't stop . . . keep moving.'

Eventually, we got to our room. Imagine hundreds of people crammed into a space the size of a small classroom. With three-tiered bunk beds laid out in blocks. With dimensions so narrow and small that one could not have turned over in the night without touching another person in the next bed. The people in the lower and middle bunks could not sit up on their straw mattresses without hitting their heads. Even though it was midafternoon, the room was cast in an eerie twilight. A small incandescent light dangled from the ceiling, a single lightbulb on a crooked wire.

Suitcases were stacked either in an available corner or on a shelf above a bunk. Clothes were strung everywhere, and the foul smell that had initially greeted us had grown even more intense. It was freezing cold, as the only source of heat was a small stove with a coal scuttle. There was a single sink and one latrine for every hundred people.

Standing in what now would be our room,

Mother turned to Marta and me, tears rolling down her cheeks. Both Marta and I were rendered speechless. Our always proud mother, her mouth frozen for a second from the shock, touched my arm and I heard her whisper the words 'Children, I'm so sorry.'

The thought that she felt the need to apologize to us still makes me want to cry. That and the image of my sister trying to sleep that night — spreading the pillowcase that Lucie had embroidered for her so many years ago over a 'pillow' made of hay.

'Education?' he asked me. I stood in front of a desk at the office of the Council of Elders, and nervously informed the man with the gray-stubbled head that I had been a student at the Art Academy in Prague.

The Council of Elders was a group of elected Jewish representatives who worked out of the Magdeburg barracks and oversaw every branch of activity of the ghetto. Terezín, we would all later learn, was an experiment within the Reich. A 'model ghetto' that was created to show the world that the Jews were not being exterminated and that in fact was largely run by the Jews. There were Czech gendarmes and SS officers within Terezín, but the Council of Elders oversaw the logistics of daily life. Like a small government, it organized the housing and work assignments, the water and power of the ghetto, the welfare programs for children, the running of the infirmary, and was even responsible for maintaining the amount of people who were on the next transport 'east.'

I stood in front of the men who were in charge of deciding my work assignment. Two bald men, whose eyes barely glanced over me, before one of them asked my age, my education, and any particular talents I might have.

'I'm Lenka Maizel Kohn,' I said strongly, as if I already needed to remind myself who I was. Behind me, there was the rustle of a mother trying to soothe her fussing baby.

'Two and half years at the Prague Academy of Arts,' I said. 'I studied life drawing and painting.'

The older of the two men raised his head and now squinted at me. Something I said had piqued his interest.

'You're an artist?'

'Yes,' I answered.

'You have a good, steady hand?'

'Yes, I do.'

The man whispered to his colleague who then nodded.

He then reached for a small piece of paper from his desk on which he scribbled the words *Lautscher Werkstätte*.

The room number was marked at the bottom. He didn't bother to look up from his desk, he just told me to go and report there at once.

I walked with my papers to the Lautscher Werkstätte, a small room in the Magdeburg barracks. When I arrived, the door was open and there were already ten artists working at a large table.

To my relief, I was greeted by the comforting smells and colors of my days at the Prague Academy: the piercing scent of turpentine, the oily perfume of linseed oil, and the rich, fatty smell of the blended pigments. Large canvases of Old Master paintings, created either as forgeries or as decorative copies, rested along the perimeter of the room. On a countertop, I could see small, postcard-size watercolors of cheery, pastoral scenes and a few of small children.

I was approached by a woman who looked close to my age. She was petite with short blond hair. Although she was wearing a Jewish star on her smock, she had the face of a Slav. Broad cheekbones, a small flat nose, and wide green eyes. She was razor thin.

'I'm Lenka,' I said, and showed her my work assignment. 'I was told to come here and work.'

She smiled. 'So I assume you have some artistic experience?'

'Yes, a little over two years at the Academy in Prague.'

'Good,' she said, and smiled again. 'You can call me Rita. I think you'll be happy to be here. We're a bunch of painters, primarily unsupervised, save for an occasional German soldier who comes at the end of the week to give us our assignments and to ship off the works that we've completed.'

I looked around the room wide-eyed. I was

179

confused by what I saw. Every surface was occupied with drying paintings. Some were landscapes, but others were copies of well-known paintings. 'Who's ordering all this?' I was incredulous.

'It's all requests from the Reich. Some of the postcards are to be sold in Germany. The enamels and decorative pieces will most probably be given out as gifts within the SS, and the Old Masters will be sold for a lot of money because they're flawless copies . . . Theresa over there is a genius.'

She pointed to a thin girl of no more then eighteen who was standing by an easel. She painted without a smock; her palette was nothing more than an old piece of cut plywood with the paint clustered around the edge.

'No one can do a Rembrandt as perfectly as Theresa. Perhaps not even Rembrandt himself.'

I looked over at the copy of *The Man with the Golden Helmet* that the girl was working on, and could not believe my eyes. The painting was an exact replica of the original. The tight, solemn-looking mouth, the downcast eyes. Even the figure's armor was perfectly rendered — its heavy weight draping over his shoulders.

The embossed scrolling on the brass helmet was painted with such precision that it seemed to be bursting from the canvas. But it was the reflection of the metal itself that took my breath away.

'Are you given any gold leaf to work with?' I asked. I knew how rare and costly gold had been even before the war, and couldn't believe that the artists working in Lautscher would have access to it.

'No, we aren't,' Rita answered. 'We have no idea how she does it.'

I walked closer to Theresa and studied the painting. How, I marveled, was she able to create the reflection in the helmet without gold leaf? The girl must have layered fifteen pigments to achieve such an effect. She used a tool to scrape some of the paint away, changing the surface and altering the play of light on the surface.

There were four other 'Rembrandts' drying to the left of her, each an exact duplicate of the other. Every helmet, every feathered plume, every single line within the pensive face, was done with the same factorylike precision.

'Unless you have Theresa's remarkable talent, you should probably start on postcards first.' Rita pointed to the central table. 'They're easy and fast to do. The Germans come and collect on Friday, and you should try to have a hundred done by then.' I raised an eyebrow. A hundred postcards in a week seemed like an impossible quota.

'Lenka, take this . . . ' She handed me a book of landscapes. 'Many of the girls like to work from this. Keep the colors light and cheerful. And try not to make mistakes. The less paper we waste with errors, the more we have to use ourselves for something else.'

She paused for a moment and squinted at me. 'Do you have a child here with you?'

'No.' I went silent for a moment. 'I have no children.'

She shook her head. 'Perhaps that's for the best, the heartache of seeing them crammed into such filthy barracks . . . can you even imagine?' She clicked her tongue with disgust. 'I guess we all try our best under these conditions. A lot of the girls here have been saving our scrap supplies. We take a strip or two of paper, some paints, or whatever else we can find back to the children's barracks so they can use them there . . . it makes them so happy, and there's a wonderful teacher who appreciates whatever we can sneak out to give them.'

The memory and the wonder of my mother giving me my first set of paints and sketchpad came back to me. I could not help but smile that there were still people, even here, taking on great risk just so this magic could continue.

And so I began painting in Terezín. I woke up each morning with the other women in my barracks, drank the miserable coffee, which really wasn't coffee at all but lukewarm water with ersatz grounds floating on top, and ate a scrap of moldy or stale bread. But I was luckier then most. I did not expend much energy painting in a small studio, compared with the others, who worked in the fields or tended to the sick.

Though Marta, Mother, and I remained healthy, the bedbugs and fleas were a problem that needed constant vigilance. Every night we looked over each other's bodies for any little black spot, and removed it with two pinched fingernails.

The barracks was a crowded place, teeming with restless, hungry women whose misery and agitation seemed to increase with each passing day. There was too little space for everyone and people grew irritated with each other at the slightest thing. One woman would start yelling at another if she was holding up the line for the latrine. Another woman might accuse someone falsely of stealing, when it was far more likely that the culprit was one of the female Czech gendarmes who pounced on what little possessions we still had.

One evening, a girl named Hanka slit her wrists with a piece of broken glass. She had done it without making the faintest sound, slicing through her veins when the room was still filled with fifty other women just returning from work. Someone by the name of Fanny was the first to discover her.

'She's bleeding to death!' Fanny cried out. We all rushed to see the sight of Hanka, her tiny pale body curled at the edge of a lower bunk. One arm dangled to the floor. Beneath it was a puddle of blood, whose edges were spreading rapidly over the dirty, wooden floor.

One woman ripped her pillowcase and tied a tourniquet around Hanka's wrist while Fanny and I lifted her into our arms. We then ran as fast as we could, her featherlight body bobbing in our arms as we rushed her to the infirmary. Two days later, having miraculously survived, Hanka returned to our barracks. But not all of us had showed her an act of kindness. For when she returned from the infirmary, all the possessions she had brought from home were stolen. Everything from her toothbrush to her wool coat had vanished. Everyone in the barracks claimed they had no idea where her things had gone.

27

LENKA

The incident with Hanka had taught me that there was no one in our barracks whom I could completely trust. No one except Mother and Marta. Many of the other girls continued to socialize with each other, some even inviting me to walk with them before curfew or gossip outside, but I always refrained.

My job at the Lautscher Werkstätte became my escape. It was also the only time I had any control regarding my life in Terezín. When I sat in front of that white rectangle of paper, paintbrush in hand, I could select the composition, the colors, and the lines I chose to draw. No one dictated how I arranged the scene. If I chose to put the windmill on the left or to paint a sky full of clouds, it was my decision alone.

This eased the strain of my everyday life. My stomach ached from hunger, but I was thankful for the access to the art supplies. And although I mostly painted small watercolors — images of cherubic babies or landscapes to appeal to the German masses — who would buy them to use as greeting cards — it still gave sustenance to my spirit. And the sight of Theresa, who was one of the few people given the opportunity to work on the canvases or use the oil paints, gave me a bit of joy. Looking at her over in the corner, scrutinizing each brushstroke and applying layer after layer of pigment, reminded me of my school friends back in Prague.

The others in my family tried to make the best of their work assignments. Father's job was to deliver coal to the different buildings in Terezín. Marta was assigned to cleaning the soup vats in the kitchen. Mother worked in the children's barracks with two other women. The three of them had begun to teach the children art, and I smuggled as much as I could to them every few days.

At night, Mother told me about the Austrian woman with whom she was working at the children's barracks, by the name of Friedl Brandeis. She was trying to give the children some release from their oppressive surroundings.

'She wants the children to close their eyes and put on paper what they are feeling,' Mother told us. 'The younger children's paintings and collages are of their fantasies and hopes, but the older children portray the hardship of living here,' she told us. 'It's a marvel to see what would otherwise be trapped inside them.'

'You're doing such a good thing, Mama,' I whispered. She was on one side of me, and Marta on the other. Marta had fallen asleep, and as Mother too began to drift off, I found myself staring at my sister's neck and braids. Although her neck was bitten from lice, her braids dirty, they still gave me comfort.

But on the nights when the memory of Josef crept into my head, it was impossible to get my mind to rest. I would imagine the ship sinking in the ocean, his limbs swollen with salt water, his black hair tangled like seaweed. Like a slow water leak, the sorrow still found a way of entering me, and it was often more than I could bear. On some other nights the hollow of my belly would ache for the baby I had lost. When these awful images snuck up on me, I tried to counter them with thoughts of our family before the war, to force away the heartbreak of seeing Mother as she now was — rolled on her side, tightly packed against Marta, her red hair twisted like frayed rope, and her body covered in a veil of dirt. Instead, I would shut my eyes tight and try to conjure up her image, resplendent as she was the day of Lucie's wedding. In her sea-glass gown, her white throat encircled in pearls.

At the Lautscher Werkstätte, Rita and I became close friends. I was continually learning from her the ins and outs of the system. Sometimes a German or Czech soldier would appear and bring a photograph and order us to do a portrait for him. Rita would always ask him if, by any chance, he had any extra food on him. 'Of course not!' he would bark. But then a few days later, when he would reappear to claim his portrait, he would slide a small bar of chocolate into her hands or an extra gram of sugar. Those two things were coveted more than gold.

Rita also showed me the art of smuggling out some of the art supplies. At the end of our work shift, she showed me how she took near-finished tubes of oil paint and placed them in her brassiere so she could paint on her own late at night or save them for the children. The stealing of supplies and the creation of art other than for the Reich were punishable offenses, but she took the risks without hesitation.

'What more do I have to lose?' she said when I looked at her. 'If they take away my ability to see, to record . . . I am already dead . . . And if we can get some of the paint and materials into the children's hands, then even better.'

I knew what she meant. Aside from the joy it brought me to get supplies to the children, I also had an unyielding desire to channel what I was feeling. I had not felt such an overwhelming surge to capture what was around me since those first few months when Josef and I were falling in love, and all I wanted to do was paint in a palette of red and orange.

But I was not allowed to paint what I was feeling. Had I been given that freedom, I would have used a palette of black and dark blue. Instead, I was forced to paint these inane caricatures of bouncy, rosy babies with captions that read *Congratulations on the birth of your little angelic boy*, when the Jewish children all around me were getting sick from typhus, or their bellies starving for more than a piece of stale, moldy bread.

I looked at my palette of soft colors: the

carnelian red, the pale yellow and powder blue, and remembered the colors of the Old Town Square with a bittersweet wistfulness. How many years before had I sat in the café with Father and looked up at the great Orloj clock. If I closed my eyes, I could almost taste the pastry, sticky on my fingers, with Father sipping his coffee with steam rolling off the white porcelain cup. Now, outside, there was only melting brown snow, black smoke from the chimneys, and skeletal men walking in half-torn clothes. Or women with hollow eyes, and children to whom a glass of milk and a chocolate biscuit would be heaven.

Our daily rations were one hundred grams of bread and a bowl of soup. The bread was not baked with flour, but with wood shavings that gave all of us the most terrible digestive problems. Children were given a weekly ration of a quarter liter of milk. The elderly and sick received even less than the amount of bread we were given because they were not working. The old sat huddled on their beds, cramped next to one another, coughing and wheezing. Their eyes as cloudy as dirty dishwater.

And although I was lucky enough to remain healthy, my former life seemed so far away to me. I had been married, lost a child, become a widow, and transferred to Terezín all within two years. My dark hair was already beginning to see the first threads of gray even though I was only twenty-three years old. Sometimes an SS guard who was in his early twenties would come to pack up our paintings, and I would catch him stealing a look at Rita or me. And as strange as it might seem, that fleeting look of interest in his eyes would allow me to remember that I was still young and perhaps even a little bit attractive. But on most days I felt a thousand years old.

At night, I would return to the barracks and sit with Marta and Mother and hear about their day. Marta would steal some fruit from the kitchen, and we would share a precious apple or pear. She would always try to bring a little something to Hans, whom Mother was able to care for during the day.

He had become so thin in the months since we arrived. His once-chubby cheeks were now sunken, his thighs half the size they were at the time of our transport.

I continued to bring back scraps of discarded paper or small nubs of pastel or charcoal for Mother to give to the children.

'They have nothing, these children,' Mother would tell us, 'and yet somehow during the day they still manage to laugh or create a game among themselves.'

Marta would shake her head. I could see how depressed she was growing with each passing day. But I was thankful she at least got some fresh air and sunshine when she was in the fields, or else I didn't think she would survive.

We all had at least something that was good for our spirit. Mother had the children, I had the art, and Marta now had a job outdoors. But Father was not as fortunate.

We could steal a few hours before our 8 P.M. curfew and see him outside his barracks. The hard labor already had aged him terribly. He looked weakened, and his skin was always covered with soot. The first time I saw him in his work clothes, he looked like a chimney sweep — black from head to toe.

He tried to laugh when the three of us stood outside the door to his barracks.

'Eliška, how about a kiss for your handsome husband?' he chided her.

She blushed. I could read her face. She wanted to kiss him, but if the dirt got on her, would she ever get it off?

'Papa,' I said, stepping close to him, 'I'll kiss you right now!'

Both Marta and I kissed him on both cheeks and our lips and faces instantly were smudged with soot.

'Look, now we've made him all clean for you, Mother,' we chided.

She managed to smile and then walked closer to him. I can see the image of the two of them so clearly in my mind's eye now — as if cast in eternal slow motion. Mother walks up to her once-elegant husband, who is now dressed in an old flannel coat that I have never seen. The white of his eyes shining out from coal-dusted skin. His black mustache erased from his face. And his once-full cheeks now sunken to two empty wells.

But it is Father's hands that I remember most clearly. How they trembled as they took hold of Mother's narrow shoulders. How he kissed her on the top of her head so not to leave a smudge of dirt on her beautiful face.

'*Milačku,*' he whispers.

'*Lasko Moje,*' she whispers back.

He closes his eyes as he kisses her again, as if he were wishing something that was now impossible. That, instead of being in the cold outside the Dresden barracks, he had transported my mother and him to the street of their first kiss, or to our apartment with its view of the Vltava.

In the cold, I think of the story Father had told us of how when the swans were frozen and trapped in the river, the men and women of Prague cut them out to free them. And yet not a single one, when we were all rounded up for our transport, had come to help us.

28

LENKA

Several months after we arrived at Terezín, a warm breeze finally replaced the mounds of snow. Marta told us she saw fields of flowers across from the orchard where she worked, which lifted her spirit a bit, though we could not see anything within the walls of the ghetto. There were few birds, and one never saw the scampering of a squirrel or the wings of a butterfly. We had insects, of course, the mosquitoes, the fleas, and lice. The smarter creatures knew enough to stay away, while those who feasted on filth and squalor were more than happy to join us.

I carried on painting my postcards. Theresa still created her enviable copies of Old Master paintings, and my beloved Rita continued to make me laugh with the faces she made as she churned out her innocuous landscapes one by one.

'It's too bad we can't send secret messages through our work,' she whispered to me one day. I watched as she dipped her brush into a glass pot of watery blue paint and then drew a small Star of David in the center of the page where a pond would soon be.

'Think of how da Vinci would paint one thing, and then cover it with an entirely different painting. One image buried under a layer of paint purely for the painter's benefit, and another one created for his audience.'

I sighed. The postcard I was working on was of a water mill with a mountainscape in the background. No secret messages were encrypted inside, that much was certain.

Rita moved closer to me, her eyes alive with an idea. 'What if I told you that I've heard rumors that a handful of artists are trying to document what's really going on here. Some men in the studio next door are doing their own paintings . . . that some are being hidden within the ghetto. Someone even told me they have contacts with sympathetic Gentiles on the outside who want to publish them abroad.'

I looked at her with disbelief. 'I don't believe you. That's suicidal.'

Only three weeks earlier, an entire barracks had been raided because a letter had been intercepted that contained one forbidden line: *I'm starving*.

'Imagine what they'd do if they found drawings of, say, the wooden beds filled with half-skeletal men and women, the piles of corpses we see each day,' I said skeptically. Just that morning, I had sidestepped a dead woman outside the doorway of our barracks. When someone died during the evening, they were placed outside the door to be carted away.

'You wouldn't take the risk, Lenka?' Rita

raised one of her eyebrows at me. 'I know I would. There would be no doubt in my mind.'

I looked around the studio. Theresa was busy working on yet another canvas of *The Man with the Golden Helmet*. In front of me, I had painted over twenty postcards of a Bavarian windmill. And yet outside, I could hear the faint sound of a horse's hooves as it pulled the funeral cart loaded with the dead.

I stared at my friend.

I had never been one to take risks in my life. I remembered how my schoolmate Dina had placed herself in danger just to be able to see the movie *Snow White*, while I had trembled at the thought of breaking any rule. Yet now I felt there was little more that could be taken from me. I wasn't even sure, with the rate of starvation and disease that flooded the ghetto, that I would live another year. What did I really have to lose at this point? And didn't I want to make an impact during what time I had left?

And so I found myself nodding to her. 'Yes, Rita,' I said with more enthusiasm than I knew was inside of me. 'I would.'

At night, the thought now became all-consuming. I could think of little else but this secret resistance movement within Terezín. I imagined myself receiving an assignment to memorialize the conditions. The filth. The squalor. The ravaged bodies. The sunken eyes.

I confided to Rita that I couldn't get the

thought out of my head. 'This resistance movement would give my life here purpose . . . ' I told her. 'I have no husband or child to consider. I know if only given the chance to help them, I would.'

'Tell me about it,' Rita said. 'I think about it every day, too.'

She let out a deep sigh and I watched as she dipped her brush into a jar of water, swirling it until it rinsed clean.

'I haven't been able to find out any information about it, as much as I've tried. There is an artist who works in the technical department, by the name of Petr Kien. My friend Leah said she saw him drawing one of the old men who are hidden away upstairs in one of the attic rooms.' Rita turned her head away from me, her gaze now focused on one of the studio's windows that had been boarded up with wood.

'Did you know that they keep the old in these attic rooms with no air, no windows. There are too many people and too little space, so the Council of Elders assigns these rooms to the people who they know won't survive very long.'

I was, in fact, all too aware of this. On the top of our barracks, there was a room that housed six women who all looked like grandmothers. Not only did they have no windows or light, they were allotted half the amount of food rations as those of us who were young enough to work. Mother sometimes went up there and gave them a piece of fruit that Marta had smuggled from the orchard.

'This boy, Petr, is certainly part of the

196

resistance . . . Leah tried to get more information from him, but he clammed up immediately. He told her he was drawing it for himself to keep up his artistic skills.' Rita was now shaking her head. 'But even she knew better.'

Nearly a month later, much to Rita's and my excitement, one of the men from the Jewish Organizing Committee came and asked for a volunteer to go work in the technical department.

'They need someone who has a good hand for drafting,' the man said.

Both Rita and I raised a hand. We were like two schoolgirls, desperate to be chosen. In both our minds we were imagining that once we got through the doorway and stepped into the drafting department, we'd be part of an underground movement that wielded brushes instead of swords.

'Please pick both of us,' I whispered under my breath. I did not want to lose my friendship with Rita over this, as badly as I wanted it.

'You with the pale eyes,' the man said, pointing to me. 'What's your name?'

'Lenka Kohn.'

'Go report now. Tell them I sent you.'

I looked quickly over at Rita, hoping she'd give me a sign that she wasn't mad at me. I had made up my mind that if she looked upset, I would forfeit my new assignment. But Rita was not one to hold a grudge. She immediately smiled at me and mouthed the words 'good luck' as I stood to follow the man out the door.

I met Bedřich Fritta that afternoon. I walked into the studio, which was also housed in the Magdeburg barracks, and was immediately greeted by a tall thin man who appeared to be in his midthirties.

'Are you the new recruit?' he asked. There was a trace of warmth in his voice, but mostly I heard a curiosity for more information.

'Yes, sir. I was told to come here immediately.'

'What's your background?'

'Two and a half years at the Prague Academy.'

'Just like our young Petr Kien over there . . .' Now he smiled. I watched as he lifted his hand to point to a man in his twenties with thick black curly hair. I recognized the name as that of the man Rita had mentioned. I also now realized I had seen him before, walking through the camp prior to curfew. We all had. He was the only one who risked walking around with a sketchpad in one hand and a bottle of ink in the other. Mother had shaken her head, thinking he would end up imprisoned in the small fortress for his brazen disregard for the rules, but I had been envious of his courage.

'I'll need to see you draw something freehand,' Fritta said, sliding a piece of paper and handing me a cartouche pen. 'Here, sit down. I want to see the line of your hand . . . It will be important to know where to place you.'

I surveyed the room to decide what to draw, and chose to do a quick profile of Petr. Something about him resonated with me. Was it the thick, tempestuous hair? The fleshy mouth — lips so full they seemed to belong more on a woman than on a man — that reminded me of Josef? Or was it something else? I could feel my eyes running over the contour of his face. I noticed the thin blue vein pulsing from his temple. The curled fist resting against his cheek. His other hand with its fingers wrapped tightly around his pen. He was so completely absorbed in his work, he had neither heard Fritta mention his name to me nor realized that I had already taken my paper and pen and begun to sketch him.

I imagined I was the same way when I worked, my focus whittled to a sharp nib. A thread running between my eyes, my mind, and my hand. The artist's sacred trinity.

I sat at the drawing board, and within a few seconds I had recorded an enviable likeness of Petr. I drew the sharp angles of his face, the length of his fingers pressed onto his paper, and his arched back as he huddled over his work. It was the sort of fast drawing I knew that Fritta, one of the preeminent satirists back in Prague, renowned for his political caricatures, would like, for it was a method he himself often used.

'Excellent,' Fritta said as he studied my drawing. 'We will make good use of you here.'

I remember I looked not at Fritta when he said this, but at Petr. He was still completely focused on his drawing, and not for a single second had he lifted his gaze.

29

LENKA

Few people are sensitive to the sound of paper being torn from a sketchpad or the scrape of a pen nib that is thirsty for ink. But to me they are like the sound of a razor or a scythe slicing through the air. These were the sounds of the technical department: sharp and unflinching, and I heard them every morning when I walked through the door.

Unlike my time in Lautscher, there were no piles of insipid postcards or thick, oily canvases sent on trucks to decorate the interiors of German villas. Here, there was a sense of efficiency and urgency.

'We are responsible for many things here, Lenka,' Fritta explained. 'There are architects who are preparing blueprints for Terezín's expansion. We need new roads for the increased population. Drawings for new barracks. The train tracks from Bohušovice into Terezín need to be extended. The camp's antiquated sewer system needs to be updated. All of these things need to be drawn up by architects and engineers working in this office, and artists like yourself will help them with that.'

As he spoke, he moved across the room with a quiet authority. I noticed everyone was working — a line of backs arched over drawing boards — a few people were clustered in groups, a pile of supplies placed in the center of a shared table. Everyone's head was down. I did not see a single face.

'We have deadlines that we have to meet, Lenka. So when I tell you I need something in three days, try and get it done in two.'

I nodded.

'Do not waste our supplies. They are our most precious asset.'

Again, I nodded.

As Fritta talked to me, his eyes scanned the room. His physical presence sent a signal to everyone that order had to be maintained in the drawing room at all times. Fritta was the commander here, and the rest of us were his troops. But why, I wondered, were we working — and working so hard — for an army whose objective was to corral us into a ghetto of disease and starvation? Where was the resistance? I wanted to ask Fritta. I looked around the room, past the dozens of men and women who looked like mechanical drones, and shuddered. I could not sense any sort of resistance at all.

'Lenka, meet Otto Ungar.'

Fritta and I stood next to a desk where a frail man was hunched over a book of illustrations.

When he stood up, I saw that his face was

201

chiseled. He gave the appearance of someone sculpted from clay, deep tunnels fingered out from underneath his eye sockets.

'I'm Otto.' He stood up and extended his hand. His smile was warm, but his fingers were ice cold.

'I'm Lenka Kohn,' I said.

'Lenka?' He said my name like a question. 'It's a beautiful name. You're the first Lenka I've met in Terezín.'

I blushed.

'No flirting here old man.' Fritta wagged a finger at him. It was the first break for levity I had experienced since I had walked into the room. I smiled.

'Since when is forty-two old?' Otto teased. I shook my head; the harsh conditions had clearly made him appear older than his years. It would only be a matter of time before the same thing happened to me.

'Otto, I want Lenka to work on the workbook detailing the progress of the railroad tracks from Bohušovice into the camp. Show her the format you used with the drawing for the sewer system. She should model her illustrations on them.'

'No problem, sir. Yes, right away.

'Let's get you started here.' Something about Otto reminded me of my father. He had wide dark eyes, a narrow face, and a gentle way of speaking. He pulled out a chair for me and handed me a stack of technical drawings. 'These are the engineer's drawings,' he began. 'You will need to do some illustrations that will supplement the book. Your drawings should show men working on the construction of the railroad lines into Terezín and the new buildings that surround it. We will send it to the Germans who have requested detailed information on Terezín's expansion.'

I nodded that I understood the assignment.

'We have gouache and watercolor pigments on the shelves, as well as brushes and pen and ink. Choose whatever medium you think is best, but please try not to make mistakes.'

'Yes, I know.' I smiled. Seeing how hard Mother was working to get supplies to her students, I was sensitive to the importance of these materials.

He smiled back at me. It was a warm, paternal smile and it made me miss Father.

'Very well, then.' He knotted his hands in front of him. 'I'll let you get to work, Lenka.' He returned to his chair and reached for his pen and pad.

Otto's face was the color of wax. He always looked melancholy when he drew, while the others in the room hardly had any expression at all. I watched him sometimes out of the corner of my eye. He always wet his paper with water before applying his pigment. This made the painting more difficult, because the colors could bleed. The borders could blur. I wondered if he did this for the challenge. He had to work that much quicker to get everything into the drawing.

Occasionally, he would glance over at my work.

'I like the expression on the soldier's face . . .' he said, and he appeared slightly amused.

I looked at the tiny figure I had drawn next to the men working to lay the tracks, and I noticed that I had given him an almost maniacal expression.

I laughed for a second. 'I hadn't even realized that I did it. Perhaps I need to start over.'

Otto shook his head. 'No, keep it. It's accurate. They tell us they want us to represent everything with complete accuracy, and you have.

'They're all little shits,' he whispered to me. 'I hate this. I loathe working for them.' He pressed his pen to the paper with such pressure that the ink began to pool. The drawing would have to be scrapped.

I looked at the ruined drawing and shuddered. What would Fritta do if he saw that ball of crumpled paper? It wasn't Fritta who had the temper, but his second-in-command, an artist by the name of Leo Haas. He rarely spoke to any of us. He spoke only to Fritta.

But Otto didn't throw the paper into the waste bin. Of course not. He waited for it to dry and he then folded it into a little flat square and hid it in his pocket.

Otto and I begin to spend more time with each other. Part of me, unrealistically, hopes that he will reveal to me that he is part of the artistic resistance. But he says very little except that he hates being forced to draw for men who want him and his family dead.

We eat our bread slowly together at lunchtime, chewing slowly, pretending that it is something else.

'I'm eating dumplings and pickled cabbage today. Mountains of it,' he tells me. Otto breaks a morsel of his stale bread. I watch him close his eyes as he attempts to use all his powers of imagination to transform a single bite into something far more satisfying.

'I'm eating chocolate cake,' I tell him. The bread is sawdust in my mouth. Yet I still cup one hand underneath my ration as I eat. I will not let a single crumb escape.

When Otto laughs, his eyes fill with tears.

Our fifteen-minute lunch break is nearly over.

'Fritta is a great man. We are lucky, Lenka. We are better off than the others,' he says as if he needs to remind himself or remind me.

'Yes, I know.' I nod. There are two pieces of paper folded against my brassiere. 'Otto, I know.'

Every day I learn a little more about the technical department and our boss from my new friend Otto. I learn that Fritta was one of the initial arrivals at Terezín in November 1941 — the *Aufkommando*. They were a select group of 350 or so highly skilled Jewish engineers, draftsmen, mechanics, and construction workers who volunteered to leave Prague to help enlarge the infrastructure within Terezín to prepare for the influx of Jews who would soon be arriving by transport. These men volunteered to work at Terezín early, with the promise that neither they nor their families would be sent 'east.'

I learned that many of my colleagues at the technical department were like Fritta and had helped with the initial plans for the camp. An engineer by the name of Jiří had created drawings for the entire septic system, and another man, Beck, had drafted the original plans that were used to build the ghetto. These men had knowledge of the infrastructure of the camp that even the SS was not aware of, and later that knowledge would prove to be invaluable. If you wanted to hide something so no one would know where to find it, these would be the men to ask.

My fifteen minutes every day with Otto are my lifeline to information.

One day I dare to be bold.

'I've heard Fritta and Haas are working to get their drawings to the outside,' I whisper.

Otto doesn't answer me. He chews more slowly. He closes his eyes as if he is pretending he didn't hear what I just said.

'Otto?' I repeat my question. Still, he doesn't answer me.

'Otto?' My voice is now a bit firmer.

'I heard you the first time, Lenka,' he says. He

wipes his mouth with a handkerchief that is the color of dirty dishwater.

'Did you know I have a wife and five-year-old daughter?' he says changing the subject. 'Her name is Zuzanna.'

I am shocked. It is the first time he has mentioned their existence.

'I don't see them as much as I want to. At night, I miss them so much I close my eyes and try to imagine that I am digging a tunnel between my barracks and theirs.'

'I'm so sorry, Otto,' I say. 'I had no idea.'

'It's a terrible thing to go to sleep dreaming that you are clawing at the earth.'

I say nothing. I nod my head.

'It's as though you're buried all the time. Suffocating.'

Again I nod.

'No,' he tells me, 'I know nothing of any resistance.'

He looks at me and his eyes are full of warning. The irises look like stop signs instructing me to halt.

'Lenka,' he says, reaching for my hand. 'It's time for us to go inside.'

❦

I watched in amazement as Otto started on a watercolor of the Terezín ramparts. He worked quickly, first doing the dark lines of the brick walls, then filling them in with bleeding colors of soft browns and yellow. With a nimble hand he painted the soft, cloudy haze of the mountains beyond and patches of watery green. The next day, after he must have secretly stored the painting so that it could dry, he took a brush with pen and ink and painted the roping barbed wire like a knife blade cutting through the page.

I knew the Nazis had forbidden any kind of illustrations that depicted them unfavorably. We had been told that anyone caught doing so would be either imprisoned in the small fortress or put on the next transport east. Thus, it was no surprise to me that I had not yet seen any depictions of the atrocities that were ongoing within the camp. If these paintings existed, they could only be made in secret, either at night in the barracks or in crowded places where no one would be watching. Still, I would be lying if I did not say that I sensed a secret language flowing between Fritta and Haas while we all worked.

'Write this down!' they'd occasionally bark to each other over their desks. It was as though they were telling each other what they were recording.

Fritta and Haas left us alone as long as we met our deadlines. I'm sure they knew many of us were pilfering the supplies for our own work in our rooms. Otto was even bold enough to work on some of his own paintings during the day. He taught me how to keep my sketchpad filled with my illustrations for the Germans, and my own personal work hidden between the pages. If an SS officer surprised us at the studio, we could just pull down one of the pages in the sketchpad to cover what we were really painting.

I had yet to become friends with Petr Kien. There were times when I saw him secretly sketching program covers announcing an opera or a play that was going to be performed before curfew. We would later see these posters nailed to a post by one of the barracks, and we would all congregate to watch that evening's entertainment.

As I look back on it now, it's hard to believe how much artistic activity we managed to make time for in Terezín. Although the Germans turned a blind eye to the performances as long as they were not critical of the Reich, there was always some inevitable cruelty. How many times would we see German soldiers watching one of our performances, clapping at the tenor's wonderful range, or the soprano's mesmerizing aria, and the very next day ordering those same singers on the next transport east.

I would often see Rita at one of these performances. She loved the singing, she told me, and she had started seeing a man named Oskar, who had a good voice and was often chosen as one of the leads.

They were a handsome couple, with her high cheekbones and cropped blond hair, and his broad shoulders and almond-shaped brown eyes. When he sang for the others, he would always take his hand and place it over his heart, as if he were coaxing out each note in the name of his beloved. Of course, that was Rita, who stood in the corner with her radiant smile and shining eyes. In the few moments before curfew

209

sounded, I often saw them sneaking behind doors and other hidden places within the camp to steal a kiss, and I would smile, happy that they had both discovered a bit of romance under such misery.

As crowded and disease-ridden as Terezín was, romances like Rita and Oskar's somehow did bloom. I heard lots of the girls in the barracks talking of boyfriends and secret meetings. I saw how they tried to groom themselves with nothing but their bare, dirty fingers and a spot of saliva on their palm. I saw how they pinched their cheeks and bit their lips so the tiny droplets of blood would bring a semblance of color to them.

But I did not have anyone, just the ghost of Josef in my heart. In the nights I was able to dream, I dreamed only of him.

30

JOSEF

There were countless times over the years when I swore I saw Lenka. I'd be on the subway and see someone who could have been her. I'd be on vacation with Amalia and the children and think I saw Lenka walking away from the pool. At other times I'd be on a bus, and swear I had seen the back of a head that was the same shape as hers, the hair the same color. I would hold my breath until the woman turned her head and I could see it was not her.

This is what Amalia referred to as a 'ghost day.' When you saw those you've been looking for in the shadow of another. Isaac once called it a 'projection of your longing,' but I preferred the simplicity of Amalia's term. She had coined it early on in our marriage. All she had to do when I came home tired from the office was to say she'd had one of those days, and no further words were needed.

When she had one, I'd simply nod to her, my eyes sincere with understanding. I'd try to smile, and squeeze her hand.

After she died, I sometimes let myself wonder what her ghost days had been like compared

with mine. I was looking for a wife, a lover I had
left behind. She was searching for a mother, a
father, and a sister who was supposed to have
joined her on her journey. Mine was lost love,
hers was lost family. But loss was loss, wasn't it?
Cold and white. Blue and dark. Cut a vein and it
bleeds.

I am in love with a shadow. I look for her in
the darkness of the hallway. I search for her
in the eyes of the old women crossing the street.
My second wife, whom I used to spoon every
morning as we lay in bed, was not the saddle for
my sleep; it was Lenka, who visited me in my
dreams. She still haunts me like a lioness, a cat
with piercing eyes. Over sixty years have passed
and her shadow still walks beside me. Her
shadow stretching long and black — waiting for
me to reach for her — waiting for me to extend
my hand.

In my old age, I have come to believe that love is
not a noun but a verb. An action. Like water, it
flows to its own current. If you were to corner it
in a dam, true love is so bountiful it would flow
over. Even in separation, even in death, it moves
and changes. It lives within memory, in the
haunting of a touch, the transience of a smell, or
the nuance of a sigh. It seeks to leave a trace like
a fossil in the sand, a leaf burned into baking
asphalt. I never stopped loving Lenka, even when
my letters were returned and the newspapers
revealed the deaths of millions of Jews who had

been incinerated into a ceaseless cloud of black smoke.

I told my daughter, the first time she fell in love, not to hold it too close. Think of yourself in a warm, summer pool, I told her, concentric circles rippling all around you. Golden beams of sunlight flooding your hair, striking your face. Inhale it. Breathe it. It will not leave you. If you place sunlight in your palms, it will turn to shadow. If you put fireflies in a jar, they will die. But if you love with wings on, you will always feel the exhilaration of being suspended in flight.

She fell in love with a boy in college who proposed to her the night before graduation. He was tall and dark like I was. He was quiet and loved books. I liked Benjamin. I saw how he sat at the table with Amalia and me, looking at us with a reverent gaze, a trace of confusion in what he saw.

It was the confusion that made me think he was the right man for Rebekkah. He looked at the quiet between Amalia and me, the careful, almost cautious compassion, and I could read his mind: *Let this never be me.*

And that is what bound me to him. Yes, let this not be you. Kiss my daughter and feel the warm breeze in your face, the warmth of the sun on your eyelids. Embrace the fluttering of butterflies in your stomach. If I give you my blessing, marry her and make love to her as if you were the king and queen of your own kingdom. Feel the beating of her heart on top of yours. Seal yourself to each other.

But betray her and I will burn your eyes out.

Love her purely and do not let her go. May the two of you be rewarded with the songs of angels in your ears.

When he finished his dessert and reached for her hand, placing his on top of hers, I saw the confirmation I needed. I saw how his eyelids closed, as if he were slipping into her. As fluid as honey. As strong as a current of waves.

And I, too, closed my eyes.

31

JOSEF

My grandson was born five years later. I stood in the waiting room with Benjamin and Amalia. The doctor handling the delivery was a protégé of mine. I knew his hands at the sight of them. They were large and strong. He had delivered over three hundred babies and I trusted him implicitly. His cesareans were flawless, and his sutures were seamless and healed without the faintest trace of scarring.

Rebekkah had never been more beautiful than when she was pregnant. Her long hair grew thick and glossy, her pale skin glowed.

Amalia sewed her maternity dresses. Benjamin brought her milk shakes and bouquets of lily of the valley on his way home from the office. He had grown wiry after law school, and the two of them looked like one of the medieval paintings I remembered in the churches back in Prague, my daughter, the Madonna with her swollen belly, and Benjamin one of the wise men bearing her gifts.

When Rebekkah went into labor, Amalia and I walked from our apartment to Lenox Hill Hospital. I knew the walk by heart. I had done it for twenty years: seventeen minutes if we made every light. Twenty-one if we missed more than three.

Amalia was fifty-two and I was fifty-six. We were already gray. I had a bit of a paunch but Amalia was still thin as a reed; only the skin on her arms betrayed her age.

I could see in her eyes how nervous she was on the way to the hospital. 'She'll be fine,' I told her, and I squeezed her hand and then put my arm around her shoulders. The bones of her back shivered as I held her close.

At the nurses' station, I was welcomed like a king. 'Congratulations, Dr. Kohn,' they all chirped, even before the birth was over. 'She's doing great. Four centimeters already.'

Benjamin was sitting on one of the vinyl couches, his face white from lack of sleep.

'Dad,' he said, standing up. 'So glad you're finally here.'

I loved Benjamin like a son, and every time he called me Dad it was like an extra shot of paternal love straight into my heart. 'Don't worry,' I said, and hugged him. I was like a general comforting my troops.

I brought them coffee — black for Amalia, lots of milk and sugar for Benjamin — and then went to check on Rebekkah.

She was lying on her side, the pain clearly visible on her face.

'Hello, sweetheart,' I whispered.

She smiled, though I could see how forced it was. A doctor can measure a patient's pain just by looking at her, and Rebekkah's was escalating. I could also see the fear in her eyes.

I took her hand. Oh, that hand of my daughter. Her grip took hold of my heart, threads of warmth soaking into my fingers.

'Where's Dr. Liep?' I asked softly.

'He just checked on me a few minutes ago and said I still have to wait.'

'Hurry up, already! Motherhood is waiting,' I joked, patting her leg through the thin hospital sheet. It was a line I had used many times before.

But my Rebekkah didn't laugh, which was unusual for her, because Rebekkah always laughed when I tried to be silly with her. That was the kindness of my daughter; she laughed even when I wasn't funny. She laughed with me so I wouldn't feel alone.

'I'll go look for him,' I reassured her. 'Are you comfortable?'

'Yes,' she said bravely. But I knew she wasn't. She had told us she didn't want any Demerol because she was going to go through labor without drugs, not in a twilight sleep. She was going to give birth with her wits about her and her eyes wide open.

'With your wits about you?' I remember Benjamin shaking his head in our living room. 'Dad, how many natural deliveries have you seen where the women still had their wits about them?'

'Not many. Not many at all,' I said with a laugh. 'But Rebekkah can handle it.'

'Great,' Benjamin said. 'We'll know just what to do if things get a little rough in there.'

217

I smiled and recalled the sight of Rebekkah only a few days before, sitting on the couch, her stomach round as a watermelon, her slender arms defiantly folded on top.

I remember thinking, here I was, an obstetrician looking at my own daughter about to give birth, and I was still capable of being amazed by her.

Under the fluorescent lights of the doctors' lounge, I find Dr. Liep looking over a folder of papers.

He looked up when he heard my footsteps. 'She's fine, Josef. Another five centimeters, and we're there.'

I knew I had looked over thousands of papers while my patients lay in their beds and nature took its course, but I would be lying if I said I didn't expect Dr. Liep to be in the room with Rebekkah for the majority of her labor.

I escorted him back to her room but left when he went to check her. My daughter wanted me to respect her privacy, and I wanted to keep that promise.

If she was now at five centimeters, I estimated that she would start full labor in three to four hours.

I went back to the waiting room. 'We'll be here for some time,' I told them. 'Benjamin, why don't you and Amalia go and get a bite to eat downstairs, and I'll man the fort up here.'

They agreed, and I settled into one of the

hospital chairs. It was such a strange thing for me to now be on the side of the family awaiting the good news — that the baby was healthy, that the mother was doing just fine, and to tell the family whether they now had a new baby boy or girl.

I had to admit, I didn't like the loss of control. I wanted to be in the room with Rebekkah, with her chart in my hand and my gloves on in case there was an emergency.

But even I knew that wasn't a good idea. I think in my heart I thought everything would go smoothly. So when Susan, one of my favorite nurses, appeared and told me the baby's shoulder had gotten caught in the birth canal, she and another nurse had to hold me back from racing to the room.

Shoulder dystocia is every obstetrician's worst nightmare. There is nothing worse than seeing a head and watching it turn blue.

A cesarean was almost always impossible because the baby was typically trapped too far down.

As I struggled to break myself free, Susan put both of her hands on my shoulders.

'Phillip thinks it is better if you stay out here, Doc.'

I knew I would have given the same instructions were our situations in reverse. No one wants to bring familial emotions into the operating room. But the thought of Rebekkah suffering and frightened in the delivery room, the thought of my grandchild possibly not making it or having a limp arm for the rest of his or her life — a very possible complication of a dystocia delivery — terrified me.

Susan took my arm. 'C'mon, Dr. Kohn. Let's take a walk.'

'You need to have someone waiting here to keep Amalia and Benjamin calm when they return,' I told her. 'Have one of the nurses say there is a complication but everything is going to be fine.'

'Absolutely,' she told me. 'Consider it done.'

She guided me down the corridor. I had walked this length of linoleum a thousand times, but this time fear nearly froze me in my tracks.

My grandson was born blue. I have often returned to that image of him, a limp nine-pound boy on the warming table, his skin mottled like a plum. Rebekkah told me his first cry sounded like he had been lost to water, a gurgled wail from the bottom of an ocean.

'He fought his way out of the womb,' the doctor said. 'A little warrior, he is.'

'McRoberts position failed, but suprapubic pressure worked like a charm.' He was smiling at me but I could read his face perfectly: he had been terrified. The exhaustion and fear were still just behind his eyes, and if I hadn't been so drained at the time, I would have hugged him and told him how thankful I was that he had delivered my grandson healthy.

'We're calling him Jason, Dad,' Rebekkah told me. 'After Benjamin's grandfather, Joshua.'

'A fine name,' I told them.

I held Jason in my arms and wept. My daughter's son. My grandson, with my blood running through his. Another life in this world to love, to sing, to do all sorts of good. My heart leaped at the thought of him traveling through life and all the milestones he would eventually reach: his first words, his first steps.

His first love.

I read his features like a map. I looked at his high forehead and the curve of his lip and saw my daughter. The strong brow framing two scallop-shaped eyelids were my son-in-law's, and the small chin was Amalia's. I did not see myself until he opened his eyes later that evening. In the watery gaze of newborn indigo, I saw myself reflecting in his gaze. As dark as my memory, as deep as the sea, I loved that boy from the moment he was born.

I have skipped the story of my son, Jakob. My little boy with his chubby limbs, his deep thoughts, and his quiet way.

After his bris, Isaac serenaded him with the melodies of Brahms and Dvořák, and years later when I brought him to the doctor, I wondered if it was on that eighth day that all of our sadness had been saturated into his little soul.

Of course, how could our child not have grown up sad and quiet with the two of us as parents? Rebekkah somehow was blessed with a fire within her, like my sister, her spirit bathed in red.

But Jakob's eyes were sad from the moment we held him. Amalia spoke of it before I did.

'His is different,' she told me when he was less than two weeks old. 'I can hear it.'

I told her she was imagining it. 'He is perfectly fine,' I told her. 'He is healthy and strong.'

'His isn't a cry of hunger or for sleep,' she said. 'It is crying for the sake of crying.'

'Babies cry,' I told her. 'They can't speak yet.'

'I feel it in my bones,' she said. 'It is a cry of sadness.'

My son needed to be held. In the months following his birth, we took turns cradling him at night. Amalia sang him the songs her mother had sung to her. Her quiet, lilting voice would temporarily soothe him — as if the melodies were as familiar to him as they were to her. When it was my turn, I would take him to my office that was adjacent to our bedroom. We'd sit at my desk, with his little face turned toward my chest, and I'd read to him. I probably should have read him a children's book like *Babar* or *Benjamin Bunny* instead of the novels I preferred, but he always quieted when we were together.

At preschool, they said he was unusually bright and that he could work with puzzles all day long. He didn't enjoy playing with the other children, but who could blame him? I thought. He is a deep thinker, the teacher told us, exquisitely sensitive. He had noticed that the rain fell against the windowpane like tears, that the linoleum titles were speckled with amber freckles. To this, Amalia and I smiled. A three-year-old who gazes out the window, who prefers solitude to playing with others on the jungle gym or in the sandbox. I told myself to take my son as he was.

When Rebekkah was born, it only emphasized Jakob's difference. She was a ball of constant energy, and her eyes danced when you held her. She giggled. She only cried when she was hungry or overtired, but Amalia was right in what she had sensed about our son. Rebekkah's cry had a definitive beginning and end. It wasn't a long, mournful wail like Jakob's.

What do you do with a child who has no interest in making friends? Who instead invents imaginary playmates when he is alone in his room, with the blocks piled high, and the LEGO towers color-coordinated, and who only wants to wear the color blue?

Blue T-shirt. Blue pants. Blue socks.

'He likes the color blue, so he's decisive. He is passionate about what he likes,' I tell Amalia.

She shakes her head. 'No. There is something wrong.'

I'm the doctor, I want to tell her. *He is a little strange, yes, but he's ours and he's fine.*

But a mother's intuition is always right. Shouldn't I have known that? How many times have I seen a woman come to my office saying she sensed something was wrong with her pregnancy, and she turned out to be right?

As Jakob entered elementary school, it became

clear he couldn't function in the structure of a classroom. His dark brown hair was often in his eyes, and his once-chubby body had now lengthened and thinned. He reminded me of a sickly colt, floundering as he tries to get himself up on his legs. Noises bothered him, any adjustment the teacher made to the schedule sent him into a tantrum, and he could not bear to have anyone but Amalia or me touch him. It was as if his skin burned if someone else even grazed him.

We took him to specialist after specialist. He perplexed everyone with his intelligence scores, but he seemed unable to function outside his own bubble.

The Yeshiva school in Brooklyn was the only one that would take him, and he seemed to blossom under the care of its teachers. He loved the Hebrew language, taking to it as if it were a mystery he needed to decode. The schedule was rigid and the children there were obedient and left him alone.

He embraced the uniform; although it was black and white rather than blue, he liked the consistency of having to wear it every day and the material didn't irritate him like so many other things did.

He liked the little brick building and the benches in the schoolyard, and that no one bothered him if he played by himself or simply watched from the side. When he rocked back and forth or flapped his arms, the teachers told the children it was Jakob's own method of prayer.

My adult life is cursed with a constant duality. It is as if someone came and took a cleaver to my existence so that I cannot enjoy one thing without seeing the sadness on the other side. I married Amalia, but couldn't stop thinking about what my life would have been like with Lenka. I saw my beautiful daughter grow into the woman she is, while I saw my son barely able to eke out an existence with all his various limitations.

Those years, when Jakob and Rebekkah were teenagers, our daughter would dress up in her corduroy skirt and turtleneck and meet friends for a hamburger or milk shake down the street, while Jakob joined Amalia and me in front of the television. I cleared the plates of Amalia's over-boiled vegetables and overcooked meat, scraping them quietly into the dustbin as I heard my son answering every answer correctly on one of the quiz shows before any of the contestants even had a chance to respond.

And I watched Amalia and Jakob's heads staring at the screen. I wanted my wife to look at me, but she continued to gaze ahead. I know she must have heard Jakob calling out the answers, but she did not smile with any pride. Nor did she cry. She simply ate her food that had no taste and looked at a TV show that, for her, had no meaning, and never said a word.

Rebekkah is now a wife and mother. Married to a lawyer with a son. My son, now fifty, still lives with me at home. He is competent enough to live by himself, but has always refused the opportunity.

'Why, Dad? I'm happy . . . I'm happy here with you.' His speech is careful and deliberate, as if he is weighing each word in his head before he articulates it.

I raise my eyebrows and stare at my son's wan complexion, the pale of his eyes like cracked ice. The nervous hands. Part of me wants to raise my hand to him, to release so many years of frustration at seeing my brilliant child cocooned in his own silken shell. But I don't have the will.

He reads my mind. He reads my sadness. He reads my anger. It flashes across my retinas like lightning in a storm.

And then it's gone.

32

JOSEF

At Amalia's funeral, Isaac played the Kol Nidre. He looked ancient to me now. He was entirely gray, his once-black hair now looked like a heap of curling leaves dusted in snow. But his thin body was still elegant and straight. He was dressed in a tasteful black suit, the one he wore when Amalia and I went to hear him play at Carnegie Hall years earlier. When the rabbi called his name, he rose from the pew behind me and reverently walked to the bimah. His violin at his side as he walked down the stairs; he held his bow carefully to his heart.

There was complete silence as he stood still, the gilded ark behind him and the scrolls of the Ten Commandments flanking him on either side. There were only a handful of mourners around us, those few people who had become friends over the years, Benjamin's family, my two children, my grandson, and a few patients I had become close with.

He stood there for what seemed like several seconds, looking out beyond the pews as if trying to catch someone he hoped in vain was still there. I sat with my hands folded, watching as he took a deep breath and closed his eyes. He finally raised the instrument to his shoulder and he settled his chin. Then he lifted his bow.

He played more beautifully than I had ever heard him play. The music resonating like a heart torn wide open, each note released onto golden wings. The skin of his cheeks shuddered as he played; the lashes of his eyelids sealed his gaze. But it was clear to me as I watched him — almost an epiphany as I heard him play — that he had always been in love with Amalia. That all those years when he sat in our little kitchen quietly watching us, he had been there to be around her.

Rebekkah wept as he played. Her body shivering and quaking, her thin frame unable to contain her grief. My son stared ahead, his clear eyes ethereal in his mourning. A single tear streaking his face.

And my tears eventually came, too, as the music, slow and mournful and then rising and falling, came like waves in the sea. I cried because yes, I missed Amalia. But also because it was all too clear to me that my best friend had loved my wife in a way that I never could.

The kaddish he played consisted of the notes that came from my heart, my yearning for a love eternally lost. But not for a woman who now lay in a pine coffin before me. It was for a woman I left forty-five years ago in a crowded train station in Prague, who had never been given a proper funeral. And had I played the violin, my sorrow for having lost her would have sounded exactly like Isaac's did for Amalia. Each note played hauntingly in the fullness of its sorrow, each chord emphasizing the loneliness that she was gone.

33

JOSEF

We sit shiva in our apartment, Rebekkah with her young family, me and my lethargic son. As custom dictates, we cover the mirrors with cloth. We rip our clothes. We sit unshaven on low stools.

My grandson reads a book in my office. He is in high school now, and loves books as much as I did when I was his age. His mother chides him so he will sit with her and her brother, but I tell her it's fine. He is young. He is vital. Let him not sit in a dark room with us and receive visitors he couldn't even name.

Another plate of rugelach and a platter of bagels with smoked fish arrive from one of my daughter's friends. She writes down each arrival on a small pad so she can write them thank-you notes afterward.

The sofa is covered in the slipcovers that Amalia had sewn herself. The curtains are drawn so there is no sunlight. Outside on Third Avenue, the taxis honk their horns and mothers call out to their children as they get out of school. Inside, the containers in the cabinets are still marked with labels in Amalia's careful hand: *Flour,*

Sugar, and *Salt*. The phone numbers she had written for the hospital, the fire station, and the police are still taped to the wall.

Already, I can barely remember the sound of her voice. A week in the ICU after a stroke, a long sleep, and then a wordless good-bye. I know, in the weeks that will follow, I will look for her in the simple cotton dresses that hang in the closet, in the tube of hand cream by her nightstand, or in the round of rye bread that will go stale without another mouth to share it.

I don't imagine Amalia will now visit me as a ghost. She will be busy elsewhere, searching the heavens for her family, flying to the arms of her mother and father and beseeching forgiveness from her sister, who will tell her she should have forgotten long ago.

Her ghost will finally be at home now. Because that's what happens when we eventually return to the ones we loved but left behind. To the ones we never forgot. We slide into them like two perfect hands. We fall into them like two cotton-filled clouds.

Isaac attends Amalia's burial but doesn't come to pay his respects at the house. For seven days I expect him to walk in the door or call. But he doesn't. I finally hear from him the following week, when he tells me he is sorry. He tells me that he had a bad cold and was in bed all week. He also mentions in passing how he seemed to have dropped his bow somewhere and so now must buy a new one.

But something in his voice reveals that he is not telling me the truth about either thing. I suddenly imagine him burying the bow alongside Amalia. And as soon as I think it, I know in my heart it's true. While my children and I were walking to the limousine, I looked back and saw him standing there alone beside her grave, his head tipped solemnly down.

I imagine he placed it there in the earth, when no one was looking, to be buried beside her. Quietly. Just as she was quiet. A single note hanging in a crowded sky.

'It's okay,' I tell him. 'I understand. You'll just have to get a new one.'

'Yes,' he says. 'A new one.'

I think of the two bows Isaac has lost over the years. One dropped in the sea where I lost my parents and sister, and one placed with my wife of thirty-eight years. Each of my own losses marked by a single slip of his hand.

34

LENKA

My mother had grown even thinner that summer in 1943. I could see the ligaments under her skin, her collarbone protruding in such high relief that it reminded me of a scythe. Her cheekbones so sharp they reminded me of the bladelike facets in the glass drops of a crystal chandelier.

The *Jugenfursorge*, the welfare initiative started by the Council of Elders, had set up a schedule for the children, ensuring that they had some schooling in secret and some exposure to poetry, drama, and music. Mother would come home from the children's barracks bleary-eyed but invigorated. It was strange to see Mother's much younger artistic self now resurrected in Terezín. The woman I had imagined so many years ago that afternoon in the cellar with Lucie, her long-stored-away paintings executed in a palette of aubergine and mottled plums, was now appearing before me. She was burning with excitement from her work with the children.

Mother said there would soon be an exhibit in the basement of one of the children's quarters. The children were all working on collages and paintings, so I continued to steal what supplies I could from the technical department for them.

I was now an expert in stealth. Every few days I would take a colored pencil or a small tube of paint that was nearly finished but could still be squeezed to bring forth a few drops of pigment. Theresa and Rita also hid things for me to pass to Mother, as they were just as adamant as I that not a single piece of art supplies be wasted. Theresa was so quiet, saying almost nothing as she pulled out two squares of torn canvas from her skirt. Rita would look defiant as she pressed crumbs of charcoal or pastel in my hand.

When I was able to visit Hans, he always asked if I could draw him. I would joke with him and say, 'Well then, you must draw me, too.' I would take a small piece of sketchpad paper from its hiding place in my blouse and break a piece of charcoal in two.

'Here,' I would say. 'You try.'

He would look at the paper and then at me, squinting his large green eyes, and begin drawing. A lopsided circle would appear on the page. Two dots for eyes and a line for a mouth. But he was only four, and I knew this was a milestone for a child so small.

The best part of it all was knowing that something that could have easily occurred outside the walls of Terezín could still be achieved within them.

I reached over and put my arm on his little shoulder.

'Lenka,' he said quietly. 'I love you.'

'I love you, too,' I whispered.

But before I could begin to cry, he reached for my hand and pressed it down on the paper.

'Now it's your turn,' he said.

'Yes, my turn,' I said with a smile.

And I began to draw.

The exhibition of the children's art was an amazing feat. Mother, Friedl, and the other teachers had spent countless hours with the children, and now their beautiful collages and paintings hung on the walls.

Marta and I walked through the exhibit with our fingers raised to our mouths, so moved were we by the sight of the work, and of its breadth. There were images of trees and butterflies. Some children had drawn pictures of their families, their old pets, and memories of their lives before Terezín. But the most moving of the images were those that tried to document their current situation. One child had drawn his memories of his arrival in Terezín. Seven figures in a line, each with their identification numbers written on their rucksacks, the face of each person sad and fearful. Another child had drawn a bunk bed in a barracks — a dream image floating above the sleeping figure's head — clouds filled with bars of chocolate and jars of candy.

I was transported by the children's images. I could close my eyes and remember my own childhood watercolors, the sensation of first seeing paint drip from my brush, the rivers of inky colors bleeding onto the page.

I was so proud of my mother that evening. She was standing in a dark basement, her students' drawings tacked on the walls, in the same simple dress she had worn the afternoon of our transport. It was now stained with paint, sections were threadbare, and it hung on her bones like an old sack thrown over a scarecrow. But Mother stood there with her arms crossed in front of her and her eyes beaming, in a way that reminded me of the way she had been before the war. She had a smile of satisfaction that lit up the whole room.

35

JOSEF

Among Amalia's possessions I half expect to find love letters from Isaac. I go through her belongings wondering if I will discover a secret life. I look over the shelves for tapes of classical music, a program from Carnegie Hall, a hidden photograph, or a lock of salt-and-pepper hair. If I died first, would she do the same? Would she find the photograph Lenka packed of our wedding day, the only thing I had on me when I was lowered to safety in the lifeboat? Would she finally see the face of my ghost, the one I had never shown her, whose eyes pulled at me from deep within her nameless grave? Would she finally reach under the bed and uncover my box of returned letters? Or would she, as I suspect she would, respect the sanctity of the past and keep the letters within their box, the lid tightly closed?

Her closet is half empty, the ample space between the hangers telling more about her than the clothes themselves. The coat she wore in the winter reminds me of her, with its checkered fabric and knotted belt. I look down at her three pairs of shoes and see the faint scuffs, the imprint of her feet on the insoles, and the leather straps. worn thin. On her vanity, I reach for her brush and notice a few wisps of hair. I unwind a half-used lipstick, the color so pale it reminds me of sand.

I pull memories of us and they appear before my eyes like negatives of film. I see her cradling Rebekkah in her arms, I see her running her fingers through our son's hair. I see her with her back turned to me, warming my dinner after I've returned home late from the hospital.

So that night, as I go to sleep, I don't dream of Lenka, as usual, but of Amalia. I let her finally go back to her family. I say good-bye to her, and I see her as I did the first day I met her, a cotton dress and wispy blond hair. I see her beside me at Café Vienna, a cloud of steam rising over her cup of hot chocolate, her brown eyes cloudy with tears.

36

LENKA

The Terezín children were staging a repeat performance of *Brundibár*, an opera written by Hans Krása with scenery created under the direction of one of Prague's most famous theatrical designers, František Zelenka. The set consisted of a makeshift fence constructed of scrap boards and three posters: one each of a dog, a cat, and a sparrow. Each poster was hung on the fence; a circle was cut out in the center so that the child assigned to the role could insert his or her face and be put immediately into character. The painted image thus eliminated the need for a sewn costume. The set was amazingly convincing. *How many people in my office and in Lautscher have been secretly feeding supplies so that this can take place?* I thought to myself. The children squealed with delight in their transformation, distracted for a moment from their hunger and deprivation. We all applauded as they took to the stage.

The opera is about two children, Little Annette and Joe, who set out to buy milk for their sick mother. On the street they encounter an organ grinder by the name of Brundibár.

They sing a song for him in the hope of getting some of his coins, but he only chases them away. That night, the children fall asleep under the painted posters of the dog, cat, and sparrow. When they awaken, the animals have come to life and they all join forces to fight Brundibár. They sing a beautiful song and the villagers throw coins at them, but Brundibár is not yet vanquished. He returns to the stage and steals the coins. The opera ends with the animals and children victorious over the organ grinder, their caps overflowing with coins as they return home with milk for their mother.

Almost all of us in Terezín loved this opera. For the children, in their performance, had created a message of resistance all their own. As they triumphed over the evil Brundibár, the metaphor of the opera was lost on no one.

That evening, when I saw Rita carefully untacking the posters from the fence, I immediately sensed that she was pregnant. Although she was still rail thin, her breasts appeared fuller and noticeably rounder. Even her face looked slightly different. Despite the dark circles under her eyes, she looked more beautiful then ever, a tiny yet ethereal figure.

Later that night, after the exhilaration of the children's performance, I was able to corner her without Oskar's presence.

'Rita,' I told her. 'You and Zelenka did a fantastic job on the scenery. But you look tired.'

I touched her arm. 'Are you all right?'

She moved me to a corner of the set where no one was around us.

'I thought I was just late, but, Lenka, I'm pregnant.' She reached for my hand and squeezed it. She looked down at herself and touched her belly with a cupped hand. She lifted her tattered dress and showed me the soft swelling of her abdomen. She placed her hand on her stomach as if cupping a secret.

'Rita,' I said quietly. 'What are you going to do?' We both knew what it was like to be pregnant in Terezín. In the past few months, we had heard rumors about women who'd become pregnant within the ghetto being put on the next transport east.

She looked at me with tears in her eyes. 'What can I do, Lenka?'

I had heard whispers of women who went to the infirmary, where one of the Jewish doctors would make the issue go away. It was a terrible thought, but Terezín was no place to bring a child into this world. To be placed on a cattle car, pregnant and forced to a work camp, was an even worse thought.

I had personally known only one woman who had become pregnant in Terezín. Her name was Elsie, and she was in my barracks. I had seen her crying on her bed one night. She was whispering to one of her friends, who was working as a nurse in the infirmary. I could hear the friend say that she would take Elsie to see Dr. Roth.

Later, I would learn from Rita that Dr. Roth had performed several abortions in Terezín. He did it in secret and only when the girls begged him, sacrificing the unborn fetus to save the mother's life.

Oskar told Rita there would be time to have children after the war, but not now. She told me this through tears, wringing her thin white hands.

'He loves me,' she said through her crying. 'He even says he wants the Council of Elders to marry us, but he thinks they are sending pregnant girls to their deaths.'

'And what if he is right?' I said.

'How? How could anyone believe that? Because it might just be a camp with facilities more suited for mothers, after they can no longer work.' She paused. 'Why would they let women on the trains with their prams if there weren't places for the children?'

I shook my head. I didn't know the answer. All I knew was what existed or didn't exist within Terezín, and everything about the transports east seemed like one big black hole.

'But what if he is right, Rita?' I whispered to her. 'Is it worth the risk? Now you have a safe assignment at Lautscher and Oskar's job as an engineer gives you some added security within the camp. Take him up on his offer to get married now, and start your family later.'

I could not believe I was actually telling my friend to end her pregnancy, especially one involving two people who wanted to spend the rest of their lives together. I knew that if anyone had made such a suggestion to me when Josef left for England, I would have despised that person with every ounce of my being. But since our transport nearly a year before, I had witnessed the roundups for the trains 'east.' I saw how the majority of those sent away were sick, old, or pregnant. And now when a new transport arrived, even some healthy prisoners were shipped off. It was clear to me that wherever the Nazis were sending these people, it was bound to be a place far worse than Terezín.

I could only imagine the horror and betrayal Rita must have felt at hearing me tell her this. I'm sure she expected me to support her, to tell her that I would speak to Oskar and convince him that he was wrong.

'I suppose it's that you have no idea what it's like to have a baby growing within you, Lenka.' She looked at me with eyes like a cornered animal. 'If you did, you would never tell me what you just did.'

'Rita,' I said, my voice cracking even though I spoke in the faintest whisper. 'I do know what it's like to be pregnant.'

I did not elaborate about my miscarriage, of the sadness of losing my only connection to my husband, who had drowned in a freezing ocean. There was already too much sadness around us. I just reached to squeeze her hand.

For the next two weeks, I watch Rita struggle, caught between Oskar's fear for her safety and her desire to preserve the life growing inside her. In this barren ghetto, where no sapling or flower grows, the capacity to create life was still a miracle. How many women had I heard say they no longer got their periods and believed their emaciated bodies were now incapable of conceiving anything during a hurried, unromantic encounter with their boyfriends?

Rita shows me her decision without speaking directly of it. When she sits, she now folds her hands over her belly as if the two flat palms can protect what grows secretly inside.

When she talks, she does not look straight ahead, but toward her lap.

'Oskar is sick with worry,' she tells me. 'The only way I can silence him is by putting his hand here.' She unfolds her hands and pats her stomach. She is four months along now, yet still not even the slightest bump shows. 'I feel flutters,' she says, and her face is flushed with happiness. 'I know I don't look pregnant, but I still feel it.' I look at Rita and try to push away the fear and enjoy the sight of my friend so alive, so full of life.

Oskar tells her he wants them to marry before the baby is born. He fashions a makeshift engagement ring out of some twisted electrical wire and proposes to her on bended knee, just after she has finished her day's work at Lautscher.

There are no extended engagements in

Terezín. Within days they are married in the chamber of the Council of Elders. The night before her wedding, the girls in Rita's barracks all got together to wash her hair. They placed a large bucket under the spigot in the wash sink, where it remained for several hours, collecting the droplets of water until there was enough to bathe Rita's head. Her hair is short and cropped around her sharp face, but two girls stand and fuss over her and use their fingers to arrange it as best they can.

Rita wears an old brown dress with a frayed hem and a worn collar. She is solemn-looking, a bride without adornment. There is no veil, not even a single flower for her white fingers to clasp.

Theresa appears and quietly tells Rita she has brought something for her to wear.

She hands Rita a small package wrapped in old newsprint. The parcel, which seems almost weightless as it is placed in Rita's hands, seems suddenly to become heavy and worthy of reverence as Rita slowly unwraps it.

We all watch awestruck as she peels off the layers of newsprint to reveal a small corsage constructed from strips of painted canvas, sewn together with a yellow felted center, a blooming flower made from nothing but scraps.

'It's for your hair,' Theresa says quietly.

She withdraws a small piece of metal wire from the pocket of her dress. 'Here. You can use this to twist it around some of the strands, perhaps just above your ear.'

Rita touches her face to fight back the tears. 'Thank you, Theresa. Thank you.' Her fingers now reach to cup the girl's face. She kisses her cheeks. 'Only you could make something so beautiful out of nothing.'

Theresa blushes from embarrassment. 'It's really nothing . . . I — I . . . ' She is stammering from all the attention her gift has brought her. 'I just wanted you to have a flower.'

It is true, Rita holds no wedding bouquet. Yet she is beautiful with her handmade corsage pinned to her hair, her hands folded protectively over her slightly swollen belly. Oskar's four friends hold up wooden sticks, a white sheet making the marital canopy over their heads. We all gaze at them as the chief rabbi of the ghetto evokes the seven blessings. An old glass bottle is placed in a napkin and Oskar smashes it beneath his boot.

'*Ani L'Dodi v'Dodi Li,*' the rabbi tells them to say to each other. '*You are my beloved and my beloved is mine.*'

I think of those words and remember my own wedding day. It seems so far away and yet like yesterday at the same time. I try to hold back my tears at the memory.

The other girls all clap to congratulate the couple, and I see them absentmindedly touching their fingers to their hair. We are all wishing for another time, where there could be an abundance of flowers — or even just a handful — so we all could have one to tuck behind our own ears.

Rita's belly grows no bigger than a loaf of bread. She wears the same baggy dress she has always worn. She learns to walk even straighter so that the little bit of new weight is even less noticeable. I take fewer bites of bread for myself, and pour half of my soup into a watering can. I bring both the half-bitten morsel of bread and the watery soup with a single piece of turnip to her barracks.

'Eat,' I tell her.

She refuses my ration. 'I don't need any more than I have,' she insists. 'Please don't save your food for me, Lenka. You need to eat, too.'

'You'll need it when the baby comes,' I say.

I leave the food, despite Rita's pleas. Later, when I run into Oskar, I notice how thin he looks. 'I try to give her my ration, too,' he says. 'She refuses it, but I won't leave for the evening until I see her eat it.'

'You need to keep your strength up, too,' I tell him, and touch his elbow in a sympathetic gesture.

The next time I go to bring Rita food, she uses a stronger voice with me.

'Lenka, you *must* stop this. I am serious.'

'I don't understand,' I tell her. 'You need to eat more, for you and the baby.'

'I don't want to eat more! I can't get any bigger than this, or they'll figure out I'm pregnant and send me away!'

I looked at her, her wide green eyes now filled with a wild fear.

'But the baby needs nourishment, Rita.' I could barely force out the words.

'The baby will take what it needs from me. I just want it to be born in Terezín . . . ' She began to weep. 'I am too afraid to go anywhere else.'

I understood now what she was saying. So I did the only thing I could think of: I took Rita in my arms, just as I remembered my own mother doing to me when I was scared and pregnant back in Prague. Hoping that the warmth of my embrace gave her at least half as much comfort as I remembered Mother's giving me.

37

JOSEF

One of my earliest gifts from my grandson Jason was a paperweight he made when he was three. It was a stone he had painted blue, with two black-and-white eyes and an orange felt nose. It still sits on my desk alongside my papers, adjacent to the photographs of my family members, all now grown.

I love that paperweight. Every time I place it atop a pile of bills or a notepad, I remember the day he brought it home from preschool.

He called me 'Gampa' back then, the closest thing to 'grandpa' he could manage. He pulled it out of his little red knapsack and handed it to me.

'For you. Gampa.'

I held it in my hand and smiled. The stone was wrapped in wax paper, its opaque paint still a bit wet; the felt nose was off center, and the two plastic eyes wobbled back and forth.

'I'll cherish it,' I told him. We went to the kitchen and placed it to dry on a paper napkin. Then we washed our hands together, the water running blue.

I close my eyes and remember my grandson

when he was small. The first time I took him somewhere, just the two of us, we went to the Metropolitan Museum of Art and I led him through the Temple of Dendur, explaining the history of the Egyptians, the magic of hieroglyphics, and the curse rendered on those who had excavated the tombs. There was the joy of his first visit to the Central Park Zoo, the sweetness of his first frozen hot chocolate at Serendipity, and the wonder of our first visit to the Hayden Planetarium, when he asked me if every star represented a person who had died.

His comment rendered me speechless. Wasn't it a wonderful thought, to imagine every soul alight in the darkened sky? I reached for his hand and held it close to mine. As the projection of planets and stars filled the black dome, I saw the look of awe spread over his face, and I just wanted to watch him forever. I wanted to witness how he experienced the world, how he learned to navigate his way through it. And as I watched him grow, I mourned what I had missed with my own son. Jakob kept me at a distance, or perhaps I was the one who had created the distance. I would never truly know.

But what I did know was that I wanted to glue my grandson and me to those seats in the planetarium and count every star alongside him. And how I wanted his thought to be true! That, in death, I'd become a star. Suspended from above, burning brightly over him. Protecting him with a pure white light.

His wife-to-be is beautiful, elegant, and refined. Her red hair reminds me of Lenka's mother's and sister's.

I had met a handful of his girlfriends over the years. The brunette he met at Brown his freshman year, the one who did not shave her legs and supported animal rights so fervently it seemed as though it were her religion. The curvy Italian girl in his sophomore year, whose breasts were so full I kept thinking she'd begin lactating at the table, and the twin who had one brown eye and one blue, her face all angles and her body all curves.

Then there was the British girl he met during his junior year abroad, who had the most lovely laugh I had ever heard and who charmed me even though I was now nearly eighty-five and a widower for almost ten years.

His visits to me began to decrease around the time he entered law school. He was busier, so I understood. There were his studies, the pressure of getting good grades, plus the pull of alcohol and music in the New Haven bars.

He had not dated Eleanor more than a year when they announced their engagement, and at that time I had only met her once, at Rebekkah's apartment on the evening of Rosh Hashanah. She was quiet and polite. I could tell she was intelligent by her careful choice of words and her interest in the books that lined my daughter's shelves.

I had brought my son with me that evening,

and it was Eleanor's gentle kindness to him that fully won me over. She sat next to him and tried to coax him out of his shell. My son was now fifty, with a gray beard and a receding hairline that accentuated the shine of his taut, red skin.

She asked him what he was reading and he rambled off a list so long I was sure her head was spinning. Yet minutes later, I heard them talking about one title at length, and I saw a faint glimmer of light in his eyes. I wanted to go over and kiss her, so happy was I that Jakob had finally connected with someone.

I saw how Jason beamed in her company. How when she was standing, he couldn't help but gravitate toward her. I was an insatiable observer that evening, also watching my own daughter, with the first sprouts of gray running through her wiry curls, cutting bagels and making sure there was enough cream cheese and lox for everyone. I watched how Benjamin, now deep in the throes of middle age, still seemed to be in love with her. And that gaze warmed me, because they would soon be celebrating thirty-three years of marriage, and it was no small feat to keep the embers of love aflame for so long.

That night, my son and I stayed up late together and watched television. The gentle hum reminded me of the quiet times between his mother and me. I couldn't help but be sad that Amalia would not see Jason's wedding, and share the joy of meeting his beautiful new bride. But then I thought of my grandson's comment nearly twenty years earlier, at the planetarium, and hoped that he was right. That she would be there, watching in her own quiet way, one of many stars beaming down.

38

LENKA

By her own reckoning, Rita was now six months along. Whenever I stopped by the Lautscher workshop, she was almost always sitting, still painting postcards. The completed, dried ones were stacked in piles to her right. The wet ones were set in front of her.

Her hand was still steady. I noticed the scenes of the horses and the bales of hay, the mother with the child sitting on her lap, the Nativity scene that she had painted in abundance even though it was only September.

Theresa was standing in the corner by the easel, painting a copy of Rembrandt's *Jewish Bride*. Had the SS commissioned this as a sadistic form of irony, or was it Theresa's quiet form of defiance? I looked quickly at the canvas and saw the gold and red of the bride's dress executed in Theresa's delicate brushstrokes.

'It's beautiful,' I told her.

'I'm hoping they don't know the title,' she said. 'They just told me to do another Rembrandt.'

I smiled at her and she looked at me directly.

'You know they say Rembrandt's wife was a Jew.'

I nodded and each of us smiled at the other with satisfaction.

As I turned to face Rita, however, I noticed how pale she was.

'How are you?' I asked, touching her shoulder.

She was quiet for a moment.

'I'm tired, but I'm better than so many others here.'

I knew the truth of what she was saying. There had been an out-break of typhus and the infirmary was flooded. The dreaded roundups continued. Those inmates who were lagging were sent east to Poland.

We saw the smoke rising from the ghetto's crematorium, its two chimneys burning with the bodies of those who had died in the infirmary or at work. And while the only executions were rare hangings of those who had tried to escape, two gallows remained in the center of the ghetto as a stark warning to all of us.

And still, new trains arrived weekly with more and more Jews.

On some days, we would hear whispers from someone who had overheard some information coming from within the Council of Elders that a thousand would be arriving from Brno; on another day there might be fifty from Berlin, a week later another thousand from Vienna or a few hundred from Munich or Kladno. We saw the new arrivals walking down the street from the windows of our workplaces: women holding their babies in one arm and a suitcase in the other. There were the young and single always walking in front, the elderly and unaccompanied lagging behind.

It reminded me of a funeral procession, these men, women, and children walking with the look of death and defeat on their faces. I couldn't imagine how the ghetto, which was already overflowing with people, could accommodate a single person more.

One evening, just before curfew, Rita confided to me that she had seen Fritta in her barracks the night before. He had come to draw the woman who was known as the Fortune-Teller, an ancient woman who always wore a tattered shawl.

Rita lived in one of the attic dormitories, where, because of the pitch of the roofline, there were no three-tiered bunks. There were only mattresses and straw on the floor, and a few low wooden beds.

Fritta found the Fortune-Teller in a corner, sitting next to a window lined with metal pots and pans. 'He drew her quickly in pen and ink,' Rita told me. Her white hair tied with a rag, her spectacles, her slackened jaw, and her toothless mouth.

'He said nothing as I watched him draw,' she said. 'It was an amazing thing to see.' Within seconds, he had exaggerated the weight of her head on a narrow body, the length of her spindly arms, her two enormous eyes.

She described how he drew the window where she was sitting as if it had been flung open, even though it remained firmly shut. He drew the brick wall that was next door as if it were broken down the middle. He drew the side of a rampart, an old sparse tree in the courtyard, and an iron gate on an ancient wall. Sweeping from one corner of the paper were three squares of laundry on a clothesline, dangling like white flags.

'It took him less than an hour,' Rita whispered. 'The Fortune-Teller asked if he wanted her to read his cards.'

'And what did he say?' I was now riveted by the story.

'He said that sadly, he already knew what lay in store for him.'

I shook my head.

Rita closed her eyes as if she, too, knew her fate. 'The Fortune-Teller did not disagree.'

I continued to hear whispers of the many paintings and drawings that Fritta and his colleague Leo Haas were doing in secret, but I saw only two of them, and that was by accident. One morning I had come to our drafting room early, as I had wanted to collect some materials for Mother before the others arrived.

When I got there, the room was still dark. A single incandescent light was lit at the back. I moved closer, only to see a single figure hunched over the wash sink. It was Fritta.

'Sir?' My voice sounded far louder than I had intended. At the sound of it, Fritta swung back. One of his hands must have jerked to the side, as a glass jar came crashing to the ground.

'Lenka?' he cried as he whirled around. 'You scared me!'

'I'm so sorry, I'm so sorry, sir . . . ' I must have sounded like a nervous child as I tried to apologize. I immediately rushed to the floor where the glass had shattered and tried to collect the mess with my hands.

'Don't, Lenka. Don't.' He put up a hand to stop me. 'You'll injure yourself and what use will you be for me then?' He quickly went to the corner of the room to retrieve a short broom and knelt to clean up the shards of glass.

'You should know better than to sneak up on someone before work hours.' He looked more perplexed than angry with me. 'And why are you here so early? What if someone caught you?'

He worked quickly and efficiently as he spoke to me, pushing the glass shards onto a piece of cardboard then dumping them in a waste bin near his desk.

I followed him as he walked.

'I'm sorry, sir. I should have known better.' I avoided his gaze. My words were caught in my throat as I struggled to come up with an explanation for my early arrival. 'I . . . I just wanted to get a head start on those illustrations of the pipeline for the SS,' I lied. As I stood next to him, I could not help but see two fresh pen-and-ink drawings on his desk.

The first was a drawing of a transport arriving. The second was of the old people's dormitory in Kavalier. Three skeletal bodies, again sketched in pen and ink, were painted as seen through the bars of an arched window. Their bodies were ravaged by starvation — hollow eyes, sunken cheeks, and elongated

258

necks, twisting underneath the flimsy blankets of their bunks.

'You needn't get here early, Lenka. The hours you already put in for the Germans are more than enough.'

I nodded and looked again at the sketches on his desk. Fritta must have noticed this, for his eyes suddenly met mine and held my gaze, as if to say, *Don't question me about those drawings.*

He quickly spun around and flipped the drawings upside down.

A second later, we heard the sound of footsteps. We both turned to look. It was Haas.

'What the hell is she doing here?' he demanded when he caught sight of me.

'I'm sorry . . . ' I started to stammer the same excuse I had given Fritta, but Haas lifted his hand to stop me. He clearly had no use for my excuses.

'Kish,' he barked. Kish was his nickname for Fritta. 'We said no others.'

I looked over to Fritta, who was staring straight into Haas's eyes.

'Lenka is so diligent, she wanted to get an early start on her work.' His eyes now widened as if to signal to Haas to stop.

For a few seconds a silent exchange ensued between them. Haas raised one of his dark eyebrows, then Fritta nodded. They ended their silent dialogue with each of them staring intently at the other. Haas seemed to understand that the only crime I was guilty of was my arriving at an inauspicious moment.

'Very well.' It was Fritta who ended the

259

standoff. 'I think Lenka now understands she shouldn't get to work any earlier than she is expected.'

'Yes, sir.'

'We don't want the Germans to know we were here, so let's the three of us make a pact not to mention this again.'

'Yes, sir.' I nodded. I looked over at Haas, who was now looking around the room for something.

'Now let's get you back to your barracks, Lenka.' He quickly lifted the book off the covered drawings and rolled them into a paper tube so quickly that I could barely see anything other than the swift movements of his hands.

'Let's not mention any of this again.'

I nodded.

Fritta turned to Haas. 'I will be back in an hour when the others arrive,' he said.

Haas was already at his desk, his back to us. He nodded.

Fritta tucked the tube with his drawings under one armpit, and the two of us walked silently and briskly out the door.

39

LENKA

Rita is now in her seventh month. I look at her body through her dress, her stomach resembling a small melon. She is severely undernourished and no one would suspect that she is with child.

She is exhausted. You can see that just by looking at her face. When I visit her this time at Lautscher, I see that her hands are shaking when she paints.

Theresa looks sideways to me from her easel and shakes her head gravely. I nod. Rita does not look well.

'I think we should go to the infirmary,' I tell her.

She shakes her head no. She continues her painting as I talk to her. Her small, wispy strokes of watercolor are bleeding all over the page.

'We won't tell anyone you're pregnant. We'll say you're just unwell.'

'I would rather stay here than risk getting typhus, or worse,' she says, turning to me. She places her paintbrush down. 'I have already told Oskar. So please just let me finish my work, Lenka.'

The severity of her tone surprises me, but I try

not to take offense.

I watch as she presses her palms to the table where she's working, her back slightly hunched forward, the small outline of her stomach against the cloth of her dress.

And then I hear Theresa gasp.

Beneath the low wooden stool, between Rita's legs, is a swelling puddle of water.

40

LENKA

Theresa runs for Oskar. He and I carry Rita to the infirmary. There, the baby is born two months early amid the sick and the wretched. Rita's baby boy pulled out of her, his body no bigger than a newborn pup.

He is alive, but barely. He is blue, and he is no bigger than my hand. When she lifts him to her breast, there is no milk.

I will never forget the sound of his cry. A whimper, but so low it was almost imperceptible. But in its faintness, in the child's desperation to live, it was thundering.

Oskar is at Rita's bedside. His skin is ashen and reminds me of the color of a seagull. His brown eyes are wet with tears.

They call one of the rabbis, who suggests they call the baby 'Adi,' which in Hebrew means 'my witness.' Rita holds him to her breast, convinced that his suckling might bring forth her milk.

I leave to afford them privacy. But within the

hour I see a friend of Oskar's standing in front of me.

'They want you to do a drawing of the baby,' he says. He is breathless from having run to find me.

'*It is urgent,*' he says. '*There isn't much time.*'

I go to my barracks and find a scrap of paper. It is my largest one, but still no bigger than a dinner plate. Its edges are jagged, but it is clean and without any markings. In my pocket, I stuff two nubs of charcoal. I have nothing else, as I have given everything to Mother for Friedl and the children.

When I get to the infirmary the baby is at her empty breast. 'I have no milk,' she says, weeping. I put my sketchpad down and go over to embrace her. I kiss the top of her forehead, then Adi's. I sit down and look at the two of them. My beautiful Rita, with her blond hair wet from perspiration, her cheeks flushed, her eyes cloudy with tears. The child's features, without the padding of baby fat, are Rita's in sharp relief. The high planed forehead, the sharp, upturned nose, and the sickle-shaped cheekbones. Rita's face is bowed to Adi's, her eyes fastened to him, his tiny body cradled in her shaking arms.

The child's face is exquisite and delicate; his skin is still rosy from what nourishment Rita was able to give him within the womb. But with each passing minute, the color in his little body begins to fade. The blue first appears at his fingertips, then spreads to his limbs, then to his face. I can see Rita's face stiffen with pain as she tries to draw him closer to her, to warm him.

'He's turning blue!' she cries. 'Oskar, he's so cold! Don't we have anything to warm him with?' she cries like a frightened animal.

Oskar takes off his dirty shirt and tries to lay it on the baby. I see Rita wince. The dirt on the shirt is evident, and probably the smell is, too. There are no embroidered receiving blankets like I remember Marta being swaddled in. This wretched piece of cloth will be the first and perhaps the last thing to touch the child's skin.

Rita is now beyond grief as the baby's breath becomes more labored, his color now no longer blue but china white.

I start to sketch them. I see the first lines give way to an image of mother and child, their faces emerging on a piece of precious, stolen paper. I sketch Rita's face nestled close to her child's, his cheek against her breast, their features one and the same. I want to capture life — by adding even the slightest bit of color to the picture, but I don't have a single stick of oil pastel or a tube of paint. The stick of vine charcoal is already dust in my hand. And then it comes to me, in an act of almost primal desperation. I look down at my ragged hands, my frayed cuticles, and pull at them. I tear the skin until the corners are leaking blood. I squeeze red droplets of blood onto various parts of the drawing: Rita's cheeks, mouth, and breast, and the child's limbs. My drawing, first intended to show the love between a mother and child, now becomes one of blazing defiance: cast in black and red.

41

JOSEF

I never told my children or grandson about Lenka. They grew up thinking their parents found each against the backdrop of a war, two misplaced people in a foreign country who married out of a shared longing to forget.

I think Rebekkah would explain it as a longing to make a new start, a new family, because both of ours had perished like a whisper of smoke, a desire so loud it thundered in our chests and clouded our judgment.

I think my son would say I married Amalia simply because it was better than being alone.

And I would tell my children, had they ever asked for the truth, that it was a little of both.

I learned when my daughter was in college that I was incorrectly listed among the dead on the SS *Athenia*. Rebekkah discovered this while scrolling through reams of microfiche one late night at her school's library.

She told me quietly during her spring break,

when we were alone in the apartment, two cups of tea between us.

The Xerox copy Rebekkah made of the newspaper now rested on the table. I glanced at it before touching it. The headline concerned Roosevelt's signing of the neutrality proclamation for the United States. Below, next to a smaller article about the French army penetrating Germany, was a photograph of the *Athenia* and an announcement that 117 were confirmed dead. My name, my father's, my mother's, and sister's were among those listed.

'Are you okay, Dad?' Rebekkah asked me. I had been looking at the paper for several seconds but was struggling to believe what I was seeing was actually true. I knew that there had been tremendous chaos when the rescue boat landed near Glasgow. I had reported my parents' and sister's deaths to a clerk and the only explanation I could come up with was that when I told him my name, he accidentally included it along with the others as one of the deceased.

'This is unbelievable,' I said. My stomach was doing somersaults and I thought I might be sick.

'It's as though you were given a second life,' she said. There was a youthful quality to her voice, and at the same time a depth of understanding far beyond her years. I remember that she reached past the cup and saucer and touched my hand.

But I was not thinking about my daughter and her compassion. My head was instead swimming with thoughts of my beloved Lenka. She would have read this in the Czech papers. She would have believed that I was dead.

I remember I excused myself and told my daughter I needed to lie down. I felt dizzy. I felt as though I might choke. Lenka. Lenka. Lenka. I saw her pregnant, dressed in widow's black, believing herself to be abandoned. Terrified. Alone.

My guilt was suffocating me. I had felt its unforgiving grasp for years. Letters to the Red Cross. Searches that led to dead ends. Letters that stated that Lenka had been sent to Auschwitz and was presumed dead.

Is this what it means to be in love? To mourn for an eternity for a mistake I foolishly made? How many times did I revisit those last hours in our apartment? I should have insisted that she come with me. I should have wrapped her in my arms and never let her go.

And my naïveté pierces like an ice pick. A painful, slow, bleeding wound.

I close the door to my bedroom while my daughter finishes her tea. I stretch out my arms, imagining Lenka. All these years and all I want is to hold her, comfort her.

Ask for her forgiveness.

But all I hear is quiet, then the sound of Rebekkah carrying our dishes to the sink.

I wrap my hands together like a knotted ball.

Air and memory. I press them deep into my heart.

42

JOSEF

After the war, I began to search for Lenka through more official channels. The Red Cross had created tracing centers across the country, so I registered at one on the Upper West Side. I would go there once a week, whether it was blustering cold or a torrential rain, to see if they had located Lenka.

I made an official request and filled out form after form.

At my first visit, the woman who was helping me urged me to be patient. 'We are working with Jewish organizations throughout Europe,' she said. 'Give us time. We will contact you immediately if we discover any news.'

But I did not wait for her to contact me. I continued to come back week after week, every Wednesday at noon. The regularity of the visits made me feel that I wasn't giving up. I never missed my weekly appointment.

Month after month.

Soon it became a year.

'Every day, the list of survivors grows,' I was told. 'We're constantly receiving new names. So there is hope.'

Over the course of the first year, I came to know nearly every person working in the office. Geraldine Dobrow became my assigned caseworker.

One afternoon in February, we began what had evolved into our typical weekly meeting. 'Mr. Kohn . . . '

'Josef,' I said. 'Please call me Josef.'

'Mr. Kohn,' she repeated.

I felt she wasn't listening to me. I wanted to scream. I had been given the same answer every time I saw her.

'I NEED YOU TO HELP ME FIND HER.' My voice was louder than it should have been. Ms. Dobrow's back straightened against her swivel chair. She wrote something on my file. I was sure she was going to recommend that I see a grief counselor, or worse, abandon my case altogether.

'Mr. Kohn,' she said firmly. 'Please. You have to listen to what I'm telling you.'

'I'm listening.' I sighed and fell back into my chair.

'I understand your frustration,' she said. 'I really do. We're trying to find her.' She cleared her throat. She pointed outside the glass window of her office to the line that snaked down the corridor. 'Everyone who comes here is looking for a loved one.'

'It's just that I need to find her.'

'I know.'

'I *have* to find her.' I realized I sounded desperate, but could not help myself. 'I made a promise to her.'

'Yes, I know. Many people made promises . . . But you have to believe me when I tell you we're doing all we can to help you. To help all the others like you.'

I wanted to believe in the kindness of this woman. But I couldn't help myself. She infuriated me.

She had no idea what it felt like to visit her office and be told no progress had been made. It was impossible for her to understand what I was going through — what those people she pointed to outside her window were going through. How could she fathom what it was like for us to search for someone who was an ocean away? Day after day, Americans were inundated with photographs of war-torn Europe. The piles of dead bodies. The mass graves. The stories emerging about what the Nazis had done to the Jews.

So, yes, on more than one occasion, I sat across from Ms. Dobrow and simply put my head in my hands. Or pounded my fist against her desk. Or swore out of frustration that her office wasn't doing enough to help me.

And most of the time, she sat quietly across from me, her hands resting on a large stack of manila folders.

'I told you from the beginning, Mr. Kohn, that it could take a long time, a very long time, to locate your wife.'

She took a deep breath.

'Europe is in a shambles right now. We are relying on the few Jewish organizations over there that are in the middle of registering the

271

living, accounting for the dead. Millions of people have been moved around in displaced persons camps. It's complete mayhem over there.' She cleared her throat. 'You will need to brace yourself for what might be a very long search. As I keep saying, you're going to need to be patient.'

She looked me straight in the eyes.

'And you need to be prepared to find that she did not survive.'

I shuddered.

'She is alive,' I told Ms. Dobrow. 'She is alive.'

She did not answer me. It was the only time I remember she lowered her eyes.

I remained undeterred. For six years, once a week, I went to that office. The tracing center continued to receive new lists from Auschwitz, Treblinka, and Dachau, as well as from other smaller camps like Sobibor and Ravensbrück. Lists of both the living and the dead.

Ms. Dobrow was replaced by a Mrs. Goldstein, then by a Ms. Markovitz. And then, one day, I was told they had found Lenka's name on a list from Auschwitz, which by then was well known as the most dreaded of the camps. Hers, along with her sister's and her parents'. There was no mention of any child.

'We believe they were all gassed the day of their arrival,' she said. 'I'm very sorry, Dr. Kohn.'

She handed me a copy of the transport list.

Lenka Maizel Kohn, it said in typed letters. I

pressed it to my lips.

'If you need to be alone,' Ms. Markovitz said, touching my shoulder. 'We have a special room . . . '

I don't remember much after that, except for a small room with several other shocked people sitting on plastic seats around me. I remember hearing two young girls reciting the kaddish. I remember seeing some people holding each other and weeping. But there were a few like me. Alone, and too stunned even to cry.

43

LENKA

I gave Rita the drawing of her and her baby as soon as I finished it. I placed it next to her small cot and hugged Oskar, who was now trembling in a tattered undershirt, his ribs rising beneath the threadbare cloth.

'Thank you, Lenka,' he said, trying to regain his composure. 'We will treasure this until our last breath.'

I nodded, unable to speak. I looked at my friend, who was still clutching her now-lifeless baby.

I went over to squeeze Rita's leg through the blanket. I still remember the sensation of touching her. That feeling that there was no flesh on her, only bone.

All I could do was embrace her, as gently as possible.

She did not look up at me. She did not even hear me. When I left, she was singing the Yiddish song 'Eine Kinderen,' into the dead child's ear.

I wish I could tell you that Rita was able to rebound after the death of her baby. But that

274

would be lying. Who *can* ever recover from such a loss? I watched as my friend grew weaker. She was unable to paint. Her hands shook too much, and she was unable to concentrate. It was as if her will to live had died with Adi.

Terezín had no tolerance for such inefficiency. It allowed you to live — and perhaps even create — within its walls, as long as your work proved valuable to the Reich. Certainly you might die in the infirmary from typhus or on your cot from starvation, but your passing would be seen merely as an inconvenience. And when you were no longer needed, or when the barracks were too full and new space was required for the next arriving transport, you were simply sent east.

Within a few weeks of Adi's death, Rita received notice of her transport. Oskar did not receive such a notice, but he volunteered to go anyway, not willing to remain in Terezín without her.

We were not permitted to walk with them as they were sent away, so I had to say my good-byes the night before.

Oskar had taken Rita to meet me outside my barracks just before curfew. He held her up with his arm. She looked the way Adi looked the first time I saw him. She was almost transparent except for the blue veins of her throat straining through her skin.

She was nothing more than a ghost now. Her pale green eyes were the milky color of apple jade, her blond hair the color of ash. She was little more than a tired, empty shroud containing sparrow-thin bones and a world of heartache. I hugged my friend. I whispered her name and told her we would see each other again after the war.

Her husband nodded to me and squeezed my hand. He reached under his shirt, where my drawing of Adi and Rita was rolled up and lodged against his waistband.

'Here,' he said. 'We're afraid to take it where we're going.' He was choking on the words. 'It is safer with you, where it won't get lost.'

I took the drawing and told him I would keep it safe. 'I will find you after the war and give it back to you then. I promise.'

Oskar placed a finger to his lips, signaling me that I needn't say another word. He knew — just as I knew Lucie would do when I gave her my most treasured possessions before the transport — that I would do anything to keep it safe.

I hid the drawing between two pieces of cardboard under my mattress. But I began to worry that the weight of three women might harm it in some way. Then I placed it in my suitcase, but soon found myself racked with fear that someone might steal it.

But, I thought, who would steal a simple drawing of a mother and child? It couldn't be used for bartering. It had no value except to me, Rita, and Oskar.

So the picture remained in my suitcase for some time, and I tried not to think of it too often. I considered myself only its temporary caretaker, whose job was to keep it safe until its rightful owners could reclaim it. Every now and then, though, I would climb the ladder in our barracks to make sure that it remained hidden and out of harm's way.

Terezín had grown even more crowded. Later, in books, I would learn the exact population. By 1943 there were over fifty-eight thousand men, women, and children within the walls of a town that was built to hold seven thousand.

And with each newly arrived transport, hundreds, sometimes a thousand at a time, were sent away.

Girls with names that were foreign to me like Luiza, Annika, and Katya began to fill the beds in my barracks that were once occupied by girls with Czech names like Hanka, Eva, Flaska, and Anna.

The fights increased within the barracks. The girls were irritated from lack of sleep and hunger, and from working so hard that the skin of their once-elegant fingers was worn to bloody tatters.

One girl steals from her own mother. Her younger sister accuses her. Their fight begins as verbal insults; then it escalates. Soon they are fighting like animals, pulling hair, one even biting the other's arm. The dorm matron tries to break them up. I watch, speechless. I have often shared what little bread I have with Mother or Marta, but I cannot help but wonder how much longer it will be before I become like them.

The stealing in the barracks has gotten out of control. Articles I would have once considered garbage — a broken comb, a single shoelace, a wooden spoon — are now commodities that can be used for bartering for something more precious: a single cigarette, a pat of margarine, a piece of chocolate. We sleep in our clothes. Some of us even in our shoes — frightened that if we leave them below our bunk, someone will steal them.

Everything is at risk for pilfering by another pair of hungry hands. And anything that isn't of use, people will think nothing of throwing onto the brazier as fuel. I think of my drawing in my suitcase and know that when winter comes, someone will find it and use it for kindling, one more discardable thing someone will decide to throw into the empty stove for an extra second of warmth.

In November 1943, a census is ordered from Berlin. The entire ghetto is summoned one morning at 7 A.M. to a large field at the outer perimeter of the ramparts. We are forced to stand without our coats, some of us without shoes, until every head is counted. We stand there through the morning, through the afternoon, and then the evening. We are given no food, no water, and are not allowed to go to the toilet. After they finish their tally, reaching a total of more than forty thousand, we are led back in the darkness to our barracks. We walk past the bodies of hundreds of people who were too weak to endure the seventeen-hour ordeal, their corpses remaining in the exact spots where they fell.

In the technical department, I continued to work on my assigned project. I completed fourteen drawings illustrating the ongoing construction of the railroad into the ghetto, and began others that showed the addition of new barracks. Fritta told me he was pleased with my work, though Leo Haas rarely looked my way. Sometimes, I would hear the two of them arguing in a corner about something. Haas would raise his arms and his face would be red with frustration.

'These are excellent,' Fritta said one afternoon as he lifted my pages to the light. 'Too bad you have to waste your energy on this nonsense.' He shook his head. 'In another time, your talents would be put to better use.'

While he is saying this, I want to interrupt him and shout, *Yes! Let's put this hand of mine to a higher purpose! Let me in on what you and Haas are working on. Let me paint pictures of the transports, or the smoke from the new crematorium . . .*

But my voice is caught in the back of my throat. I look up at him, hoping he understands that I am eager to work in any kind of underground movement that is taking shape within the concentration camp.

I think he senses what I am thinking. He takes one of his large hands and places it on my shoulder. 'Lenka,' he whispers, 'when this is over, you'll always have your brush and paper to record it all. Until then, don't do anything that might jeopardize you and your family's safety.'

I nod and take my drawings back with me to the drafting table. I put my elbows down and rest my head in my hands for a few minutes to compose myself. When I straighten up, Otto is looking over at me and I manage a smile.

One afternoon, when I am waiting on line to receive my lunch ration, I find Petr Kien standing behind me.

'What is it today, Lenka? Water soup with a slice of potato or water soup with one black turnip?'

I am surprised he knows my name.

'I think it smells like rotten cabbage.'

He laughs. 'It always smells rotten, Lenka. You must have figured that out by now.

'Where's Otto?' he asks.

I look at him. The handsome face, his shock of thick black hair that reminds me of Josef.

I am suddenly flushed. Could it be that he has been watching me?

'Otto's wife was able to have lunch with him today,' I say. I had been so happy to see the rare look of pleasure on Otto's face when he set out to see her.

Petr doesn't mention his wife, though I know

he's married. We sit on a bench outside the Magdeburg barracks, sipping our soup without tasting it.

A single cabbage leaf floats on top.

Petr was clear bright light. Otto, a melancholy slip of shadow. I loved them both. Being friends with men of such contasting personalities helped sustain me. Petr volunteered to illustrate every operatic program, every poster promoting a play or concert. He could not stop drawing even at lunch, even when we were done with our work in the technical department, even when only a few hours remained before curfew.

Although Petr took risks to paint openly, what he chose to paint was by no means controversial. He painted mostly portraits.

I watched him one evening as he worked on a study of a woman named Ilse Weber, her hand touching her cheek, her eyes dark and intelligent, her lips slightly upturned. Another time, he drew Zuzka Levitová in black ink, her large froglike eyes rendered like a caricature, her enormous bosom protruding from a checkered dress he did in quick crosshatched strokes.

'I wish I could work as quickly as you do,' I tell him one night. Just watching him brings me so much joy. He paints a watercolor of Adolf Aussenberg in a palette of rose and blue, the slender figure looking downward, his hands resting on his knees. But it is the drawing of Hana Steindlerová that is the most beguiling.

'A woman in the four stages of life,' he explains to me. First, he draws Hana as a young girl, her features in soft focus, his pencil smudging light shadows across her face. Next to this, a quick sketch of her as seductress, her hands behind her head, her hair tousled, her blouse undone, showing the faint outline of breasts, a navel, the gentle curve of hips. The largest image of her is as a wife and mother, her face now more serious, the youthfulness replaced by maternal softness, her expression one of distant thought. At the far bottom corner, the final image is a quick study of a girl with bobbed hair, her gaze downward, her smile almost impish.

'I love that,' I tell him. 'It's both the image of Hana's daughter and Hana herself as a young girl.'

'Exactly,' he says, and I can see in his eyes a sense of happiness that comes from being understood.

Every day, I see him working in the courtyard on another portrait. There is the portrait of Frantiska Edelsteinová. The portrait of Eva Winderová with her thick eyebrows and hopeful gaze. The striking rendering of Willy van Adelsberg, the young Dutchman, his long hair and ripe mouth so seductively drawn he appears as beautiful as a girl. With Petr, I am constantly awed.

Then there is Otto. My sweet, soulful Otto. He works in color. Watercolor. Gouache. He paints the images that haunt him. The crematoriums, the coffin storeroom in front of the morgue, the long queues for food, the old praying over the dead.

I see him slide his drawings between pages of his official work. He never shares them with me, but he doesn't hide them from my view either. When he leaves for the day, he tucks them into his waistband. I always pray that no one will stop him on his way to his barracks. I cannot imagine him withstanding any form of physical punishment, and I shudder at the thought of him being transported east.

After months of observing Petr work on his portraits, I finally hear him ask if he can paint me.

We are sitting on the same bench we always sit on, but now the air is pregnant with fall. I can detect the wind cooling, and smell the perfume of drying leaves. The red, dry earth is a dusty veil on my shoes.

He asks me to stay later one evening in the technical department. There is risk involved in this. The obvious risk of a German soldier discovering we've broken the rules and the risk that I will break my promise to Fritta not to come to the office after hours.

'But Fritta will want us to leave with everyone else,' I tell him. I don't want to seem cowardly in mentioning the risk of being discovered by a German. 'He doesn't like people alone there. I once made the mistake of coming early . . . I promised I never would do it again.'

'Don't worry. I'll speak with him. We have an understanding.'

I raise an eyebrow. But he is evasive, giving little other explanation.

That evening, after the others have packed away their work and headed out the door, Petr and I stay at our desks.

Otto lingers a little longer, his eyes shifting from me to Petr.

'Everything good with you, Lenka?' he asks. Again, he reminds me of my father. His sweet concern and the softness of his voice as he asks his questions, always careful not to appear too forward or direct.

I wonder if Otto thinks Petr and I are having an affair. Even though Petr is married, affairs are not out of the question here. When everyone is convinced that they are soon going to die, a warm body, a beating heart, can cause them to do things they would never have contemplated before.

Otto looks at us, then makes his way to the door. 'See you both tomorrow,' he says. His voice is sad.

'Yes, Otto.' I try to sound chipper. 'See you tomorrow.'

He gives me a slow wave and a paternal look of warning. I smile and shake my head.

Petr does not bother to say good-bye. He pulls five tubes of paint out of the drawers. His hands are strong and assured; he knows the palette he wants to employ even before he makes the first brush-stroke.

Cadmium blue. Titanium white. Burnt umber.

'Sit,' he says. I obey without thinking. I am dizzy just at the thought of his eyes fixed on me, and that he has considered me worthy enough to paint.

He squeezes out the pigment carefully, reverently. Little oily blobs on a small, tin tray. He unrolls a piece of canvas, hidden beneath a pile of drawings on his desk. It is ragged at its edges, its shape not quite a rectangle or square.

There are no stretcher boards to staple it around, so I watch as Petr flattens it with his hand and pushes two pins into the top corners to secure it to the top of his desk.

'Don't look at me, Lenka. Look at the door.'

So I do. I focus on the threshold. The wooden framing. The imagined sight of my colleagues walking in and out, the shadows of those who have come to Terezín before me and left before I knew their names.

The minutes pass. Perhaps now it's been an hour. We will soon be pressed for time, as curfew will be called. My heart is thundering in my chest. My body is laced with fear that a German soldier might come and inspect the room, and adrenaline from the excitement of watching Petr work. He is painting so quickly now. His wrist travels across the canvas with the speed of an ice skater.

My thoughts are now overtaking me. Part of me wants to leap from my seat and get my own canvas, my own palette of paints. I imagine Petr and me as mirror images, each sketching the other's reflection.

'Stand still, Lenka,' he says. 'Please.'

Now the minutes seem like hours.

I feel so thirsty. I imagine paint bleeding into dry, parched cloth.

My neck begins to ache and the thought I have been fighting to repress surfaces like a wound.

A sense of loneliness overcomes me. I haven't been touched — not touched the way I am craving to be touched at this moment with Petr's eyes hard upon me, his hands working deftly, the sound of wet pigment whisking across canvas.

'Lenka,' he says. 'Don't close your eyes.'

I redden. 'Yes . . . sorry. Sorry.' I am almost ashamed to be having these thoughts.

I look at his black hair, the angles of his face, the white of his fingers as they hold his brush. I feel a stirring within me, an urge to kiss him. I long to be close to someone. I have almost forgotten what it is like to be held.

I try to conjure up the thought of Petr's wife, Ilse. I imagine them lying side by side, the hurried passion of their lovemaking, not a feast of the senses, but the quick sating of a hunger.

'Lenka, be still. We're almost done. Yes . . . there it is, we're almost done.'

I look over at the canvas. I am a creamy-white skin, dark hair falling behind a sharp edge of shoulders. Two blue-white eyes. My gaze sharp. My focus piercing and unflinching. My face more beautiful than I believe it actually is.

44

LENKA

With the painting between us, it is as if Petr and I have become lovers who have never touched. He has looked at me, studied me; he has seen me with razor-sharp eyes. Ask anyone who has been painted and they will tell you they have never felt more vulnerable than when they were sitting for hours under the gaze of another's eyes. Clothed or unclothed, you are naked all the same.

The next day, over lunch, I ask him if he is doing secret paintings other than the portraits.

He doesn't say anything at first. He stares at his bowl of cloudy soup and remains quiet.

'Lenka,' he says at last. 'I don't want to lie to you . . . ' He looks up at me and his eyes meet mine. 'But I don't want to get you involved.'

'But I want to get involved, Petr. What else can I do? Am I supposed to do drawings of the railroad every day for a gang of Nazis who are waiting for the chance to see me dead?'

Petr pushes his bowl to the side and stares

ahead. In front of us, our colleagues are eating their rations without thinking. Hunger before taste. They remind me of an army of ants performing every motion, every task, without thinking.

'Yes, Lenka, I'm working on secret paintings, if that's what you're asking.'

He then goes on to tell me what I've been suspecting, that there is indeed an underground network of painters illustrating the atrocities. Petr is working with Fritta and Haas and a man by the name of František Strass, who has non-Jewish family members on the outside. They are working to get the paintings to people who want to expose the atrocities of the ghetto.

Strass, a shrewd businessman who had been a successful merchant with a passion for collecting Czech art, was now running his own trading house from his barracks in Terezín. With some other prisoners, he was exchanging food he received in care packages — jars of marmalade or boxes of chocolate, biscuits, and cigarettes — for things he needed in the camp. But he was also smuggling the paintings done by some of the artists working in the technical department to his Gentile relatives on the outside. Haas and Fritta, a painter named Ferdinand Bloch, and even Petr and Otto were all passing their forbidden paintings on to him.

Once he had the paintings in his hands, Strass regularly bribed two Czech brothers who were policemen in Terezín to get them out of the ghetto.

'Strass has succeeded in getting our paintings to some of his relatives and other people who are sympathetic to our cause.'

'Oh my goodness,' I say, barely able to contain my elation.

'I know, Lenka, but this has to remain a secret. Promise me. The situation is more dangerous than ever now. Strass's relatives have made contact with people in Switzerland. There is talk that they might even publish some of our paintings to show the world what is really going on.'

I tell Petr about the drawing of Rita and her baby that I've hidden in my suitcase.

We are outside the Magdeburg barracks before curfew.

'Lenka, there might be searches.' He is visibly worried for me. 'There was a raid on Strass's barracks a few weeks ago. They found paintings underneath his mattress that were, thankfully, not political. But still, the Germans are on the lookout for *Greuelpropaganda* now.'

'*Greuelpropaganda*?' I did not know the meaning of the word.

'It means work that portrays the Reich unfavorably. The literal translation is 'horror propaganda.''

'Horrific images of Terezín?' I ask Petr.

'Yes, Lenka.' He pauses for a moment and

looks me straight in the eyes. 'In other words, the truth.'

Petr and I sit with each other for what seems like hours. I am wringing my hands.

'What do I do with the painting I've done of Rita and Adi?'

He looks at me as though he is not focusing on my question, but searching for what to say. Am I the only one who feels that strange sense of hunger between us? That feeling I remember from that summer so long ago in Karlovy Nary.

There are no wedding rings in Terezín. But I try to force the image of one on Petr's hand.

I feel like I am choking as he stares at me.

Was it my hand that reached out to his first or was it his that reached out for mine?

I still can't remember, but I do know that I felt the warmth of his hand flooding through me as it first covered my knuckles, then squeezed the fingers so tightly I felt I might break from the intensity of his touch.

'Petr,' I whisper. But he interrupts the thought that is about to fall from my lips, suddenly bringing us back to the painting.

'Give it to Jiří. He'll know what to do,' he finally says.

Again he squeezes my hand. Although both of our hands are cold, I feel like I'm on fire. And I want to cry.

For months I have wanted to tell him that I, too, yearned for a chance to record the truth, to

290

send my paintings out to the world like Haas and Fritta were doing, but now those feelings are muddied with a desire for something that is even more impossible.

He does not kiss me as I imagined him doing. As I hoped he would do. He just looks into my eyes.

And when he looks, does he see a woman who is hungry for his touch? Or an artist who is nearly as hungry to use her talent for the good of her people?

I am sure he sees both. But he chooses to respond to only one.

'Give your painting to Jiří, and don't do anything else to put yourself in jeopardy,' he says. 'Things are more dangerous now than ever. The searches will continue . . . they might even intensify.' I see pain in his eyes. 'I should never have told you, Lenka.'

I feel our fingers loosen, the fire between us suddenly feels like bathwater. Petr's hand falls to his side before fumbling to retrieve a black pen from his pocket.

'Don't get involved in any of this, Lenka. Promise me.'

I nod my head.

Jiří is one of the most trusted and talented engineers in Terezín. Like Fritta, he was a member of the prestigious *Aufkommando*, ordered to draft the technical drawings for the expansion of the camp.

'I've been here since the beginning,' he tells me. 'I know every nook and cranny of this place.'

He unrolls my drawing. 'It's beautiful, Lenka.'

'Did you know Rita Meissner?' I ask him. 'It was of her and her baby son, Adi.'

'No, I'm sorry, I didn't.' He is still looking at my drawing.

'He died right after being born, and they sent Rita and Oskar East a few months later.' I paused. 'I promised her and her husband I would take care of it as best I can.'

Jiří nods. 'I know how important these drawings and paintings are. They are the only documentation future generations will have of Terezín. Don't worry, Lenka, I will hide your painting in a safe place.'

He tells me that he will make a metal canister for it and bury it in the basement of the Hamburg barracks.

'There is a small antechamber when you first come down the stairs,' he says. 'When it's time for you to reclaim it, dig there.'

He does not tell me that he has performed this task for Fritta and Haas many times already. Years later, I would learn that he had wrapped the tin canister in a piece of torn cloth like a shroud and then placed it carefully in the ground. Fritta's and Haas's works were buried elsewhere: Fritta's in the field and Haas's bricked up within the walls of one of the barracks. But my drawing was just like theirs — a time capsule of the pain of Terezín, planted in secret within the camp's own walls.

45

LENKA

There was severe hunger in Terezín. There was disease. There was exhaustion and there was overcrowding. But despite the horrific conditions and overwhelming sense of despair, we still somehow managed to create art.

The Nazis had forbidden anyone to bring musical instruments into Terezín, as they were not considered a necessity. Karel Frölich smuggled in his violin and viola, Kurt Maier an accordion. Then there was the legend of the cello: its owner, prior to his transport, carefully dismantled it into a dozen pieces; once he was inside Terezín, he put them back together. An old piano, with only one leg, was discovered. It was propped up against a wall and bolstered with some extra support and under Bernard Koff's masterful fingers, it came to life.

Eventually the musicians of Terezín grew defiant. Gossip floated around the camp that Rafael Schächter, one of the most talented and beloved conductors in the ghetto, was organizing a performance of Verdi's *Requiem*.

'A requiem is a mass for the dead,' Otto told

me, shaking his head. 'Has the man lost his mind?'

'He's being brave,' I said. 'He's standing up to the injustice of being imprisoned.'

'He's going to get a bullet in his brain. That's what he's going to get if he goes ahead with it.'

'They didn't do anything when the children staged *Brundibár*.'

'This will be different, Lenka. This is the musical equivalent of an uprising.'

I didn't know what to believe. What I did know was that the Council of Elders had gotten wind of Schächter's idea and were not keen on the idea of a Jewish choir performing a Catholic mass. 'Terezín is the only place the Nazis control where anything Jewish can still be performed,' they argued. 'They've banned it everyplace else.'

Schächter would not be deterred.

'It is one of our few remaining freedoms,' he said in his defense. 'The Germans sing their Nazi slogans, their marching song. Let us do our own requiem on our terms. Our voices rising and united.'

Schächter campaigned for the support of people within the camp. and many joined with him. His performance of *The Bartered Bride* was legendary. He had conducted the opera while standing at the half-broken piano, the instrument now supported by several stacked, wooden boxes. I was in the audience when the opera was performed, the night so freezing that water that had been left in pots froze and audience members had to cluster together to keep warm. But I remember that the performance transported us. Many people even wept, they were so grateful. Against the austerity of our surroundings, the sound of those voices evoked such a strong storm of emotion that, when I scanned the audience, I saw not only tears of joy, but tears of hope and rapture as well.

Schächter's choral singers remained fiercely loyal to him. Once he gained the approval of the Council of Elders to perform the requiem, he set out to work on what became a theatrical tour de force. It would be his own act of mutiny against the tyranny of Nazism, set to Verdi's score.

One hundred and twenty singers elected to lend their voices in support of Schächter's cause. At one rehearsal, he rallied his singers. 'You are all brave for joining me,' he told them. 'Yes, we are Jews singing a Catholic text.' He took a deep breath. 'But this is not just any requiem, this is one that will be sung in honor of all of our fallen brothers and sisters, mothers and fathers. Our friends . . . who have already perished at their hands.'

On the days leading up to the performance, Petr paints posters in black and gold ink announcing the production. I help him tack up the announcements around the camp. I am giddy with excitement to hear it.

My frail parents see this evening as a big night out. Mother does her best to enhance her appearance, biting her chapped lips for lipstick and squeezing her cheeks for rouge. But there is no gilded state theater, no velvet dress and string of pearls for Mother, no black suit and silk waistcoat for Father. Mother is in rags, and her hair has turned completely white. They are two old people, transparent shadows of what they once were.

That night, my parents, sister, and I huddle with hundreds of others around the makeshift stage. The one-legged piano is in the center of the stage and comes to life under the masterful hands of Gideon Kein. Frölich stands with his violin, caressing the strings to make it sing, rivaling even the best voice within the choir.

Even now, as an old woman, when I hear a violinist, no other musician reduces me to tears the way Karel Frölich did when he played in Terezín. As I watched him that night, the instrument cradled between his neck and bony shoulder, his eyes closed and his hollow cheek pressed against the wood, both man and violin appeared locked in an eternal embrace.

I'm sure I was not the only one who felt chills run through her body. With linked hands, those hundred and twenty singers sang more beautifully, more powerfully, than any others I had ever heard before or after.

But a few days after the performance, the underlying message was not lost on the Nazis. Every one of the singers who had participated in it was sent on the next transport east. Rafael Schäcter remained at Terezín.

Schäcter repeated the performance, and again, all one hundred and twenty singers were sent on the next transport east.

The third and last time the requiem was performed in the camp, Schäcter only managed to corral sixty singers to perform.

The irony was not lost on anyone.

Every singer who performed in the requiem was singing a mass for his or her own death.

46

JOSEF

In the years since Amalia's death, I often wake up in the middle of the night with my heart racing and my mind addled by dreams I can't understand. I imagine that I hear the sound of my beeper, or the voice from my answering service, telling me that I am late to a delivery. I hear the sound of my daughter calling out, as she so often did when she was a little girl, for a glass of water or a lost teddy bear or a simple reassurance that my wife and I are home. And then there are the panic attacks that begin late at night, when the house is quiet, when Jakob has fallen asleep to the sound of the television and I lie awake thinking, *How have I managed to grow so very old? To be so very alone?*

I push the covers back with my wrinkly feet. The hems of my pajama bottoms are frayed and parts are threadbare, but I have yet to replace them. They were a gift from Rebekkah for Father's Day years before. I can still remember the Lord & Taylor box, the long-stemmed rose with the black script writing, and the thick white bow. 'Green to match your eyes,' she said. And as I crumpled up the clouds of white tissue and placed the pajamas back in the box, I wanted to kiss my baby girl in the middle of her forehead, even though she was then nearly forty years old.

I often wonder if it's the curse of old age, to feel young in your heart while your body betrays you. I can feel the slackness of my sex, curled underneath my boxer shorts, yet I still can close my eyes and remember those few days with Lenka before my family and I left for England. I can see her lying on my bed, my torso rising above her, her eyes burning into mine.

I can see her arms reaching for me, sliding around my shoulders, her fingers clasping behind my neck. I can see the pale of her throat as she tosses her head back, that fountain of dark hair grazing the pillow. Her narrow waist held between my two hands.

I torture myself sometimes by conjuring up the weight of Lenka in my arms. I try to force myself to remember the sound of her laughter, that giggle as I playfully lay her down on the bed. The sense of bottomlessness as I enter her, travel through her. When I made love to her — was within her — there never seemed to be an end.

In my dreams, I pull up her hair. I kiss her neck, her eyelids. I kiss her shoulder, her perfect mouth.

I find her spine with my finger and trace each vertebra as she pulls herself around me. Her legs lock like she is climbing a tree, clutching my back so tightly that I am pressed into her, so hard that I feel my bones imprinted on her flesh.

And in these thoughts I am still a young man in my twenties, vital and strong. I have a head full of black hair and a chest that is not concave but robust, and a heart that needs no medicine. I am Lenka's beloved and she is mine, and in these dreams there is no threat of war, no dire need for passports and exit visas, for ships that will be torpedoed and letters that will remain unanswered. They are dreams.

Mine.

Silly. Old. Mine.

And they keep me from ever resting. Perhaps from dying.

My head full of dreams. My heart full of ghosts.

I sit up and wiggle my feet into my slippers. I adjust the tuner on the radio and fall asleep to the sounds of Duke Ellington.

And dream again. Then I wake up, wipe the drool from my lips, and slide a hand down my pajamas trousers to see if I'm still all there.

And, cruelly, I always still am.

47

LENKA

I continued my long hours at the drafting board in the technical department. Some days I could hardly see straight as I walked back to the barracks. I often had to redo many of my drawings because my hands had begun to shake. I had heard the others complain of this, too. The fatigue, the dehydration and lack of food, caused our bodies to deteriorate. Our bellies were concave, our skin yellow. We were road maps of bone and bruised skin.

Despite my physical decline, my admiration for Fritta continues to grow. I never see him doing the work that is intended for Strass, but I do see that he is creating a book to commemorate his son's third birthday. What a wonderful father, I think to myself. There is so little in Terezín to give to a child — Fritta is creating some joy just with his pen and paints. I begin to create excuses to walk past him, to watch him at work and catch a glimpse of one of his illustrations. I see him drawing the little boy as a small cartoon figure, with two black button eyes, full cheeks, and a button nose. Dimpled legs and a cowlick on his head.

One afternoon Fritta walks up to me and says, 'Lenka, it's finished.'

'Sir,' I say. 'What's finished?'

'My book for Tomáš.' He places it down on my desk. 'I know you've been peeking.'

I smile. 'I suspect I wasn't very discreet,' I say.

He chuckles. It is the first time I've heard him laugh in all the months I've worked for him. 'Tell me what you think.'

He leaves me there with the book. He must have had someone sew the binding for him, for it was bound in a coarse brown cloth.

To Tomíčkovi on your third birthday. Terezín. January 22, 1944, Fritta has inscribed on the first page.

But it is the colorful images on the pages that take my breath away. He draws the little boy standing at a window of a walled fortress, his bare feet atop a suitcase that bears the number of his transport: AAL/710. Outside the window he sees a blackbird flying against the sky, the spindle of a lone tree, and the angle of a red rooftop. The other illustrations that follow, all done in black pen and filled in with washes of watercolor, are his wishes for his son. He paints a birthday cake with three tall candles. He paints him standing with outstretched hands, clad in brightly colored mittens and a wool coat, amid a flurry of snow. He paints him as he imagines him in the future, Tomi in a checkered trench coat, and a matching cap, smoking a pipe. He asks him, in writing at the bottom of one of the pages, *Who will be your bride?* And he paints Tomi in a tuxedo and matching top hat, bringing flowers to a beautiful young girl.

The last page of the book is inscribed with a wish: *This book is the first in a long line of books that I will draw for you.*

I close the book and hand it back to Fritta.

'It's beautiful,' I say.

But it is more than beautiful. It is touching. It is heartbreaking. More precious than if one of the gift packages Fritta had drawn had come to life off the page.

I watch as Fritta's long fingers grasp the book. He gives it a small shake and smiles.

'You think he's going to like it, Lenka?' He looks down at the book. 'It's meant to be a primer, to teach him to read and write.'

Now it is Fritta who seems like the small child, giddy with a gift to give to the person he loves most.

'He's going to cherish it forever,' I say.

'Thank you, Lenka,' he says with such kindness. I'm not sure if I'm more touched by the fact that he let me alone see this beautiful gift he has prepared for his son, or that he said my name with such tenderness. It seemed he looked at me with the same expression I had seen in my own father's eyes years earlier, and for a brief moment I felt as though I were that little girl again. My father, bearing a secret gift in his pocket, his warm arms around me, and his eyes so happy to see me pleased when he gives it to me.

48

JOSEF

A few months before my grandson's wedding I made the decision to put my affairs in order. I was now eighty-five years old. My hair was gray, my skin dotted from too many years in the sun, and my hands were so wrinkled I hardly recognized them. For some time I had been thinking that it would be wrong to let my children find my old letters to Lenka. It would tarnish their feelings for me, I was sure of it. They would question my marriage to Amalia, and would despise me for loving a ghost and not the woman, their devoted mother, who served me dinner every night for thirty-eight years.

And so I took out the box containing my letters to Lenka that had been returned to me, that I had stored beneath my bed for so many years.

I pulled off the rubber band that had been wrapped around the letters, and set aside the three that she had sent me while I was in Suffolk.

The white envelopes were now yellow, but the stamp telling the post office to *Return to Sender* in German was still blood red.

The letters had not been opened for almost sixty years. It was my intention to read each one, then light the burner of the stove and set each one aflame.

I did not put the needle on the record player. I would read each letter in silence, one after the other. It would be my kaddish to Lenka, a way to perform a ritual of mourning for her that had eluded me all these years.

I turned to the first one:

Dear Lenka,

I pray you received my last letter telling you I was rescued off the coast of Ireland. The people in the village where we were taken were so kind. When our ship arrived, they greeted us with food and clothing, and offered to put us up in their homes. I waited for three days for word about Mother, Father, and Věruška, but my worst fears were confirmed when I was told by the village chaplain that their rescue boat had been sucked into the propeller of the Knute Nelson — a ship that was meant to save us. I cannot tell you how much I have wept in these past three days. They are all gone and my loneliness feels like a blackness that threatens to swallow me whole. My only solace is in knowing that you are safe. I pray our child is growing and is healthy. I close my eyes and imagine you with your rosy cheeks, your long black hair loose around your shoulders, and your belly round. It is the image I fall asleep to, my only treasure.

I am now in New York. I know many weeks have passed and that you are probably exhausted from worry. But do not waste your energy on such thoughts. I am well and I will be working on getting you and your family over here as quickly as possible. My father's cousin has helped me get a job in a school, and I need to save money so I can prove I have the means of supporting you. Trust me. I will work harder than ever.

I send you my love and my endless devotion.

Always,
J.

I turn the stove on, the blue flame rising like an orange-tipped sword. Burn.

The others were more of the same. *Lenka*, I write, though my letters are returned. Others have received letters from their loved ones in Europe, though much of the writing has been blacked out by censors. But mine continue to be returned.

I am losing hope.

Burn.

Are any of my letters reaching you?

Burn.

I am worried.

Burn.

And there was the last letter that I wrote shortly before I met Amalia. Dated August 1945.

Dearest Lenka,

I have not heard from you in almost six years. It is funny how stubborn the spirit is. I probably could write for an eternity if I thought my words might somehow reach you. You are still alive in my memory, Lenka.

There is so much regret on my part, my darling. It is so clear to me now that I should never have left you. You were so brave, but I should have insisted that you come or I should have stayed until everyone could leave. This mistake haunts me every day.

Every morning when I awaken and every evening when I bed down, I wonder if you are alive and if we have had a child together. I pray that it is healthy and strong. That it has your blue eyes, your white skin, and that mouth of yours, so perfect that even now when I close my eyes I can imagine its kiss.

You will be happy to know that after spending two years in night school, I now speak and write English well enough to be accepted to medical school. I am repeating much of what I studied back in Prague, but it is a blessing to be back in school, learning and preparing for the future, whatever that might be.

I am considering focusing on obstetrics, partly out of respect for my father and partly because the thought of bringing life into this world gives me great solace.

Darling, please let this letter find you. I am giving up hope, yet I cannot accept that I am writing to a ghost. I love you.

Always,
J.

The smell of singed paper. My fingertips nearly burning as the edges blacken and furl.

Burn.

I wished that had been the last letter. But I knew there was one more. It was the last in the pile. The envelope was still pristine. There was no stamp saying *Return to Sender, Address Unknown*. There was not even a postage stamp affixed. It had never been sent.

My beloved Lenka,

I have no address to post this letter to. But I am writing it anyway because it is the only way I can say good-bye. It has been six years since I last received word from you. Your three letters that were sent to me in England are my life's only treasure. Every night before I go to sleep I read them and try to conjure up the sound of your voice.

With each passing day, month, and year, you have never faded from my heart. But it has become harder to imagine the sound of your soft breathing next to me, the cadence of your words, or the smell of your hair.

Still, memory can also be kind. You are forever beautiful in my eyes. I can remember as clearly as ever the symmetry of your face, the pink of your mouth, the soft, gentle curve of your chin.

And if God is kind to me, you still visit me at night when I'm dreaming. I can almost touch your skin, feel the graze of your lips, the weight of your body falling into mine.

The Red Cross tells me you perished in a place called Auschwitz. They say you arrived in one of the last transports from a place called Terezín with your mother, father, and sister.

Terezín and Auschwitz are names I have seen in the papers. The images they've published are so horrific that my mind cannot believe that man could conceive of something so evil. I cannot imagine that you, my beloved Lenka, perished in such a place. I will not write on this paper that you are among the pile of dead, the windstorm of blackened ash. I will only let myself think of you as waiting for me. My bride. You, Lenka, the young girl at the train station in Prague with my mother's brooch in your outstretched hand.

I am fooling myself, I know, but it is all I can do to survive.

Always,
Josef

I had put it in an envelope and only labeled it *Lenka Kohn*.

309

Now that envelope was open and the letter fluttered in my shaking hands. Over the smoking flame, I recited the kaddish.

Yit-gadal v'yit-kadash sh'may raba
B'alma dee-v'ra che-ru-tay
Ve'yam-lich mal-chutay b'chai-yay-chon
uv'yo-may-chon
Uv-cha-yay d'chol beit Yisrael
Ba-agala u-vitze-man ka-riv, ve'imru
Amen. Y'hay sh'may raba me'varach
Le-alam uleh-almay alma-ya . . .

I drop the last letter into the burner and think of Lenka. As the ashes of the letters fly, I see her as my bride in my arms, then let her finally float up into the heavens like an angel. I try not to evoke the image of my children, as they did not need to know the heartache that preceded my years with their mother. It's mine alone to carry, to take with me to my grave. To incinerate in a single burning flame.

49

JOSEF

The week before my grandson's wedding, I find myself unable to sleep.

Insomnia is the bedroom for the restless. Roll down the covers and pull out your legs. Turn your clock to the wall and don't bother to turn on the light. For you always see your troubles more clearly in the dark.

If those we love visit us when we dream, those who torment us almost always visit us when we're still awake.

And in those nights of sleeplessness, they all appear. No, not Lenka. But my father. My mother. Vêruška.

Often I can anticipate their arrival, particularly when there is a milestone in my family: the night before my wedding to Amalia, the day before my son's bris, my children's Bar and Bat Mitzvah, Rebekkah's wedding, and now her son's.

And other times they appear without reason. Three figures who look the same as they did ten, twenty, now sixty years before.

To those who believe the dead do not visit them, I say you have cataracts in your soul. I am a man of science, yet I believe in guardian angels and the haunting by ghosts. I have experienced with my own eyes the miracle of life, the complexity of gestation, and still believe that something as perfect as a baby cannot be created without the assistance of God.

And so, when the dead come to visit me, I don't bother to try to close my eyes. I sit up and invite them in. Although my bedroom remains pitch-black, I see them as clearly as if they were in my living room, the light of a floor lamp shining on them.

Father. A gray suit. Broken glasses on his forehead. His bald head and crinkled eyes.

He holds in his perfectly smooth hands a book he read to me as a child: *The Story of Otesánek*.

Mother. She is wearing a black suit with gold buttons. Around her neck is a string of long pearls. She holds in her hands a box of photographs. It contains a photo of me as a young boy on a horse in Karlovy Vary and the one at my Bar Mitzvah. I always wondered if she had ever placed the one of Lenka and me after our wedding with the other ones of our family in that box.

Vêruška. Wrapped in scarlet taffeta. Her eyes dark and shining. She is always carrying something I can't quite place. There are markings on the paper, and I can't tell if it is writing or images scratched on the pad. Some mornings I am convinced it is a dance card with a few names written on the top. Other times I tell myself it's a small sketchpad filled with markings for one of her paintings. In all the times she visits, I look at her white lineless face and I want to reach out and talk to her.

Vêruška, my sister, dancing and laughing down the hallways of our book-lined apartment, the hem of her skirt pulled above her knees.

Many sleepless nights I wondered if I should call out to them. But I always feared the children might hear me — or even Amalia — as sympathetic as she was, and would worry I had finally lost my mind.

But it was no matter. I didn't need to speak. For that is the thing about a haunting, it's almost never communicated through words.

Every time my family came to me, I always knew they'd come back again. The only exception was when they appeared two nights before Jason's wedding. Then I sensed that they were coming for the last time.

I could tell this was their final visit, for when they appeared, they were all smiling. Even my tempestuous little sister's eyes were shining.

I lay on top of my bed, my pajamas damp with an old man's perspiration, and studied them one last time.

Father placed his glasses on his nose, and they were no longer broken. Mother opened her box for me and on top was our group wedding photograph, showing Lenka, the beaming bride.

And Vêruška turned her paper pad to me and revealed a drawing of two clasped hands.

I move to get up and touch them. So real they are to me, shining there in the middle of the night. I am older now than Father is as a ghost — that realization striking me deeply — as I extend my hand to touch him.

How can a son be older than his father's ghost? How can a mother continue to comfort her elderly son from her watery grave? And how can a beloved sister ever forgive her brother when he so clearly let her down?

I am trembling. Convulsing. Wondering if this visit is a signal that I am about to die.

I try to rise, my hands still extended, my legs shaking as I step to where they stand.

I remember the sound of the thud as my body fell to the carpet. I remember vaguely the sound of the door opening, the heavy treading of my son's footsteps coming toward me, and the sensation of his arms pulling me up.

'Dad,' he whispers. 'Are you okay?'

I tell him I am. I ask for a drink of water and he leaves me to fetch it.

I don't remember seeing him return, but when I awake, the glass is there.

I dreamed that it was not my son who brought me back to bed, but the three members of my family. That they had huddled around me and lifted me back onto my mattress, pulled up the covers, and coaxed me back to sleep.

And I knew that from then on, should any of them visit me again, it would no longer be on a sleepless night. It would be the same as when Lenka comes . . . in my dreams.

50

LENKA

In the spring of 1944, we are told that special visitors are coming to visit Terezín and that certain improvements will be made. Commandant Rahm, who is in charge of the ghetto now, orders additional transports east to make room for the 'beautification' of the ghetto. Already eighteen thousand had been transported from Terezín, and now he was demanding that all orphans be sent east. Next were those sick with tuberculosis. A few weeks later, he orders an additional seventy-five hundred prisoners transported. A panic rushes over the ghetto as families are broken apart. One woman begs to be put on a list after her son is selected for a transport. At the station, with the train about to depart, she notices her son is not present and his name not called. Pandemonium breaks out when she is forced onto the cattle car by the SS. She is screaming for the soldiers to remove her, but they cannot make an exception, for the quota ordered by Rahm must be maintained. That evening I see her teenage son crying inconsolably outside the Sudeten barracks. A few people are trying to comfort him, but he is flailing about like a dying animal.

'I'm all alone,' he says over and over. 'I'm all alone.'

That night I can't get the sound of his cries out of my head. I reach over to touch my sister, who now shudders when she feels my fingertips.

She does not awaken from her sleep. But I'm comforted just to have her body close to mine. Anything but to be here all alone.

Terezín is becoming a stage. Over the next few months, fresh paint is applied to the outside of the barracks, a makeshift café suddenly appears, and the fence comes down from the central square.

We see men removing bunks from some of the barracks so that now half as many people will sleep and occupy the space. Many of us, especially the women and children, are given new clothing and shoes that actually fit.

The men who organize the operas and the concerts are told they will be able to perform, and that they should prepare something to impress the visitors.

Hans Krása rallies the children for an encore performance of *Brundibár*. Rafael Schäcter convinces the choir to sing something the observers will never forget.

My father, who, now well into our second year here, is nothing but skin and bones from working so hard, has been told to help create a small sports stadium.

Teams are established for a soccer game. The infirmary is cleaned and provided with fresh linens. The nurses are given crisp new uniforms and the sickest patients are sent on the next transport east. A large circus tent in the ghetto's center, where more than a thousand inmates were forced to do factory work, is dismantled, and in its place grass and flowers are planted. A music pavilion is built next to the square, along with a playground for the children across from one of the barracks.

Three months before the delegation from the Red Cross is to arrive, the guards carry out a search both in the technical department and in František Strass's sleeping quarters. One of the drawings that Haas had sent to the outside has been published in a Swiss newspaper and the Gestapo back in Berlin is up in arms. This will be bad publicity for the Germans, and could undermine their attempt to conceal the true conditions at Terezín from the Red Cross and the world at large.

During the search, the officers in charge find more banned drawings in Strass's barracks, but the compositions are unsigned. The bulk of Fritta's drawings have already been buried in the cylinder Jiří made for him. Otto has bricked his own work within a wall in the Hannover barracks, and Haas has hidden his in his attic room in the Magdeburg barracks. My own painting, thankfully, has been buried, too.

No arrests are made, but the tension in the technical department is thick in the air. Every time I go to work, I smell the fear.

'Keep working,' Fritta tells us as we sit at our drafting tables. 'We must not get behind in our work.'

On June 23, 1944, the Red Cross delegation and members of the Danish ministry arrive. They are accompanied by high-ranking officials from Berlin. Commandant Rahm has scripted a film-worthy scene for their arrival and, in fact, the entire visit is filmed to be broadcast to the world. The movie is entitled *Hitler Gives a City to the Jews*.

As the men disembark from their military jeeps, they are greeted by the most beautiful girls in Terezín, their pretty figures wrapped in clean aprons and rakes in their hands. They sing as the men walk through the gates.

The Terezín orchestra plays Mozart. Fresh vegetables are on display in a shop. White-gloved bakers load fresh bread onto the shelves. There is a clothing store where you can repurchase your own confiscated pants or dress.

Real coffee flows in our 'Jewish café.' Our children suddenly have a real school, more than enough nourishment, and adequate medical care.

We are ordered to cheer when one of the

soccer teams scores a goal. Our plates are laden with food, gravy, and fresh bread, all served on tables with clean cloths and cutlery.

As the Red Cross walks through the camp, a German film crew continues to document their visit.

We curtsy in our new clothes and new shoes, our faces clean and hair neatly braided, as we have been given access to showers and handed brushes and combs. We sleep in barracks with half the normal amount of people, the other half already on their way east. We are allowed to sing and dance. Men line up at the post office to receive fake packages that are filled with nothing. The children perform *Brundibár* and the members of the Red Cross clap with wild approval, not understanding the political implications of the production.

But after their departure a week later, all of the luxuries and added liberties are taken away as abruptly as they had been given. Within twenty-four hours, the extra bunks are put back in the barracks, the stadium is dismantled, and the fence reappears in the central square. The food vanishes, as does the coffee in the makeshift café. The tables with the clean cloth and cutlery end up on a truck headed back to Berlin.

51

LENKA

Shortly after the Red Cross's departure, the technical department is turned upside down. Commandant Rahm storms into our studio with two other SS officers. He screams insults at Fritta and Haas. He demands to see what they have been working on. But Haas does not flinch. He lifts a sign that he has been painting for the ghetto. There is an illustration of a garbage bin and below it the words PICK UP YOUR TRASH. I notice Fritta's hands are shaking as he pulls a booklet of drafting illustrations from his desk.

The two SS officers walk around the room peering over our shoulders.

Rahm stands in the doorway and yells his insults at all of us. He screams that we better not be drawing anything that is offensive to the Reich. On the way out, he takes his crop and smashes a table covered with ink bottles. For the rest of the afternoon, I remain badly shaken. The shattered glass is swept up, but the puddle of black ink seeps into the tile floor. Even after several washings, the stain remains, the shape and color of a storm cloud.

The SS makes more surprise visits to the *Zeichenstube*, as the technical department is called in German. We all continue to work with our heads down and our eyes averted, not even looking at each other. During one inspection, an SS soldier tears a sketchpad from the hands of one of the artists and I feel my heart stop, so afraid for him that a personal sketch might fall out from its pages.

The next week we are each randomly summoned out to the hallway and searched. When my name is called, I feel sick. Faint.

'I said *you*!' the SS officer barks at me. I stumble from my chair and follow him out.

'Arms up and legs apart,' he says.

I place my palms against the wall. My knees are shaking as I spread my legs.

'Am I going to find a pencil here?' he asks, moving his hand between my thighs. His touch is sickening. His breath smells like kerosene. Again he touches me, and I believe I'm seconds away from being raped.

And then I turn my head to face him. He seems taken aback, as though the sight of my eyes has somehow jostled him from his viciousness.

'What the fuck are you looking at?' He shoves me again, but this time I am thrown toward the door. I don't look back. He is now shouting at some other people in the hallway. I run toward the door of the technical department.

Once inside, I rush to my chair and desk. I feel

as though I might vomit up what little is in my stomach.

I try to steady myself. I look at the faces of the people around me who have not yet been called. Everyone is shaking with fear. If I had the courage to depict the scene around me in a painting, all of our faces would be colored a sick, ghastly green.

On July 17, 1944, Fritta, Haas, and the artist Ferdinand Bloch are ordered to report to Commandant Rahm's office. They also call my friend Otto. *No, not Otto*, I pray. My heart rises to my throat. I watch, my body trembling, as Otto rises from his chair. He is visibly shaking when they take him out by the arm, and I desperately want to cling to him, pull him back into his chair. My head is spinning.

His eyes lock with mine, which are wide as saucers. I know I must try to signal to him not to do anything that might anger the officers. I try to whisper to him to remain calm. I want to tell him everything is going to be fine, even though I have a sinking feeling in my stomach that something terrible is about to happen to all three of them.

An hour later another SS officer arrives at the studio and orders the young architect Norbert Troller to report to Rahm's office as well.

Later that evening Petr tells me he spoke to a woman named Martha, a housekeeper in the VIP barracks where Rahm's office is located. She overheard some of the interrogation of my friends. She is a friend of Petr's, having bartered for some of his paintings. Three days before, she had hidden them in a hollowed-out door.

Commandant Rahm does not conduct the artists' interrogation at first. He leaves the first round of questioning to his second-in-command, Lieutenant Haindl. Haindl accuses them of creating horror propaganda that undermines the Reich, and of being part of a Communist plot.

The artists deny everything. They say their only 'crime' is doing a few harmless sketches. They are not Communists, nor are they involved in any plot.

Still, Haindl continues to attack them. He wants the names of their contacts on the outside. He throws down a newspaper from Switzerland and demands to know who painted the image that is reproduced on the front page.

'You ungrateful little shits! How dare you paint images of corpses!' He pounds his fist on the table. 'We fucking feed you, house you. Half the fucking world is starving!'

The artists say they have no idea what he is talking about.

The SS interrogates them separately. They try to get each artist to inform on the others. They hold up one painting after another and demand to know who did it. Every question is answered the same way. The artists insist they 'do not know.'

Haindl and Rahm's tempers rise to a pitch of fury. The artists are beaten. Haas does not scream out as he is kicked over and over again. Fritta swears at his interrogators, but he is silenced with a boot to his mouth. The housekeeper, Martha, says the worst beating was given to Otto. After pummeling him with their fists, they smash his right hand with the butt of a rifle. His cry was so terrible, so gut-wrenching, she says, 'I had to cover my ears . . . Even now, I can still hear the sound of him screaming in pain.'

At sunset, she sees them all being loaded into a jeep that is already filled with Fritta's wife, Hansi, and his son Tommy; Haas's wife, Erna; and Otto's wife, Frída, and their young daughter, Zuzanna. The jeep heads to the *Kleine Festung*. The Small Fortress.

The Small Fortress is on the outskirts of the ghetto, on the right bank of the Ohře River.

We all knew terrible things happened in that place and that no one who was sent there ever returned. There were rumors that the SS made prisoners use their mouths to load wheelbarrows full of dirt, and people were routinely beaten to death or executed.

With our leaders gone, my colleagues and I are losing any confidence we once had.

'We will all be on the next transport,' someone says.

'They won't waste the space on the trains,' says another. 'They'll just hang us all from the gallows.'

'Fucking idiots,' one of the newcomers says, referring to Fritta, Haas, Bloch, and Otto. 'We're all going to pay for what they did.'

'What did they do?' one of the younger girls says. 'What did they do?'

'Shut the fuck up!' Petr slams his fist on his desk. 'All of you just shut up and get to work!'

The technical department now turns into a place of despair.

Over the next couple of days I watched my friend Petr cease to be able to draw. His hands shook uncontrollably. I saw him take one hand and rest it on the other, to try to steady himself and appear as though he was working.

Everyone who works in the *Zeichenstube* finds their barracks have been searched. I watch as soldiers come and ransack our rooms. They turn over our beds, they throw our straw mattresses on the floor. They climb the ladder to the shelves where our suitcases are stored. They unlatch them and empty the contents onto the floor. When mine is opened, I see Mother close her eyes and bow her head to her chest, as if she is praying that I have not done anything foolish.

When my suitcase is opened, all that falls out is a spare pillowcase. She and Marta exhale as it sails silently to the floor.

I am not spared an interrogation, though. Everyone in my department is questioned by the Gestapo.

In a brown-walled room with a single lightbulb dangling from the ceiling, we are each questioned. Drawings depicting the hardships of ghetto life are spread on the table.

Rahm stands over me and lifts one of the drawings. It is a pen-and-ink sketch of the inside of the infirmary. The figures, with sunken faces and hollow rib cages, are drawn in angry, black lines. There are several bodies lying on a single bed. The dead are piled on the floor.

'Does this painting look familiar to you?'

I shake my head. 'No, sir.'

'You mean to tell me you don't know who did this painting?'

Again, I tell him no.

He brings it closer to my face. The piece of paper dangles so close to me I can smell the dampness of the pulpy fiber.

'Look closer,' he demands. 'I don't believe you!'

'I'm sorry, sir. I don't recognize the artist.'

Rahm reaches across the table for another drawing. This one shows the overcrowded interior of a dormitory. I need only a second to see that it is one of Fritta's compositions.

Again and again Rahm pulls paintings from the table. Every one is unsigned, but anyone attuned to nuances of line and composition would be able to identify their creators. I can immediately tell that one is Fritta's by the vigorousness of the line, the way he has of rendering the absurdity and hopelessness of ghetto life. In Haas's drawings, I can sense the anguish in the squiggle of the line, the ghostlike ink washes, and the faces that all but leap off the page like apparitions.

But I say nothing to these German officers

who bark at me, ordering me to identify the artists. They pound their fists on the table and ask me if I know the painters' contacts on the outside. They tell me they have 'intercepted these paintings' and will be able to find others.

'If there is an underground movement within the ghetto, we will root it out and squash it,' Rahm barks at me. Again I tell them I know nothing.

For some reason, perhaps because they are conserving their strength for beating my colleagues, they do not strike me. And finally, after what feels like several hours of incessant questioning, I am told I can leave.

As I go to exit the door, I glimpse on a desk the Swiss paper with the drawing of the camp published on the first page. I want to smile, knowing that Strass's people have been successful in getting one of my colleagues' drawings to the outside world.

Without our colleagues, the technical department seemed devoid of life and full of fear. Those of us who remained did not speak about our interrogations, but I often looked over at the empty chairs where my friends had once worked, and every time I did, I wanted to cry.

Fritta, Haas, and Otto remained imprisoned in the Small Fortress until October. There were rumors that Ferdinand Bloch had been tortured by the Gestapo and then murdered, and that Otto's hand was permanently maimed so he could no longer paint. I began to feel a noticeable difference in the ghetto. The number of transports leaving for the east began increasing, so now thousands of us would disappear overnight. I witnessed the hanging of someone who had tried to escape. The boy was no more than sixteen, and to this day, I can still see his head being forced into the noose as if it just happened. The look of confusion and fear in his eyes as the German officer screamed obscenities just before the floor fell out from under him. Then there was a terrible incident involving a young boy who had climbed the fence to pick some flowers for his girlfriend. 'Flowers?' the SS officer had screamed at him. Seconds later, the officer was seen running the boy over with a tractor, leaving his bloodied body wrapped around a tire as a warning for us all.

In early October, Hans, who is now nearly five, is sent east with his parents. His mother tells me outside the barracks that they will be leaving the following day. She holds Hans's hand, his wrist as limp as a picked dandelion. I extend my hand to run through his brown hair.

'Do you have any pencils, Lenka?' he asks me. His eyes are so sad. I can close my eyes to this day and imagine Hans's, as green as leaves in spring. The shadows of his face seem haunted. I reach into my pockets hoping to find a piece of charcoal to give him, but I find nothing and it agonizes me.

'I will get you some before you go,' I promise. Ilona, his mother, tells me that Friedl, his teacher and my mother's colleague, will be on their transport as well.

I extend my arms and hug them both. I feel the sharpness of their ribs and Hans's heart pounding through his clothes. I whisper into his ear, 'I love you, my sweet boy.'

That night, just before curfew, I find him on the bed in their barracks. I've wrapped two pieces of stolen charcoal in a piece of brown paper. I've drawn a small butterfly on the top in pen and ink. *For Hans, I write, October 5, 1944. With each new journey, may your wings always soar.*

52

LENKA

With the absence of Friedl, my mother and the head tutors of the children's home, Rosa Engländer and Willy Groag, continue to work with the children in Terezín. But with each passing day, we hold our breath, wondering when we will receive our transport papers. On October 16, 1944, Petr's wife is notified of her transport and Petr elects to go with her. He does not tell me about his decision; I find out when I see his empty chair. It is only then, after I ask someone where he might be, that I am told that he has volunteered for that morning's transport.

I feel as though I am beyond emotion. Since my interrogation, I have almost nothing left inside of me. On October 26, we hear that the Gestapo has sent Fritta and Leo Haas on the transport east as well. I find that I am unable to cry. I am like a machine. I exist on almost nothing but air.

In November 1944, my mother is informed of her transport.

That evening, after we hear the news, our family huddles outside the barracks. The air is so cold we see our breath as we speak. Marta holds her hands up to her mouth for warmth. Father's long, weary arm drapes over Mother, who is now so frail, she looks like she might break under its weight.

'Your mother and I have discussed it, children. I am signing up tomorrow to join her on the transport. The two of you will remain here.'

His words ring eerily in my ears. An echo of those years before, when Father had been insisting that I leave with the Kohns and that the rest of my family remain.

'This time you're telling me I cannot go?' I say it in such a way that he has to recognize the irony of the situation.

'Lenka,' he says. 'Please.'

'We came as a family, we leave as a family.'

'No,' he says. 'There is no question about what life is like in Terezín. Your mother and I will rest easier knowing you remain here.'

'But, Papa . . . ' Marta now interjects. 'We can't be separated. Boundaries can be changed during the war, and what if we are forced to remain on one side, you on another . . . '

Father shakes his head and Mother just stands there and cries.

That night, I told Marta not to worry. I would go myself to the Council of Elders and put our names on the transport. And that is exactly what I did.

My father was furious when he discovered my transgression.

'Lenka!' he yelled. His face looked like a skull. A blue bruise was right below his left eye; clearly someone had hit him since I had last see him. 'You and I both know that you are safer here in Terezín than on that transport.'

'The ghetto is changing,' I tell him. 'We no longer feel safe here. What difference will another place make?'

He is shaking now in front of me. I want to reach out and touch his bruise. I want to find twenty kilos of flesh and put them back on his bones. I want to feel that I can hug him again.

'We cannot be separated,' I tell him.

'Lenka . . . '

'Papa, if we separate now, what is the point of my having stayed in the first place?'

I am crying now. My eyes like floodgates.

'We cannot break apart now. Not ever, Papa, not ever.'

He nods his head. His eyelids closing like two paper-thin curtains.

'Come here,' he whispers. He opens his arms and takes me to his chest.

And, for a second, I am able to forget the smell, the dirt, the hollow, concave skeleton that is my father. We are two ghosts sewn to each other. I am his daughter. And my father's heart beats against mine.

There were over five thousand people in our transport that November. We were quarantined the night before. We were roused at the crack of dawn. Then we somberly carried our suitcases and rucksacks, now noticeably lighter than the fifty kilos we had brought to Terezín. We no longer had any food to bring, and much of the clothing we had brought had long since disintegrated. As we walked to the waiting cattle car, newspapers flapped on the empty sidewalk. I strained to read the headlines. One of the men in our transport tried to reach down and grab one, but he was met with a rifle in the back of his head by one of the supervising soldiers.

Do I need to tell you the next part of my story? Do I need to detail what it was like in the cattle car, where we were each pressed so close to one another, how the pot that served as a latrine overflowed over our feet, or how the car was so dark that I only saw the whites of my parents' and sister's eyes? To this day, I can see the fear, the hunger. In one of the last memories I have of my mother, she looks like a starved wolf. Her hair is white and wiry. You could serve soup from the hollow basins of her cheeks or scoop the tears from the valley beneath her eyes.

I remember the sight of my father's emaciated arm slung around Marta. The three-day trip — the starting and stopping of the train — the pitch-blackness of the car, the stench, the near dead pushed to the far corner with the suitcases. We knew that the place where we were going would be even worse than Terezín. Squeezed next to my sister, I hear her whisper words that I have never been able to forget, no matter how many years go by. 'Lenka, where is the Golem now?'

There was a huge jostling when we finally arrived. The door to our cattle car was slid open and SS men with German shepherds straining at their leashes yelled at us to get out. We stumbled into knee-deep snow. Gaunt prisoners in striped shirts and trousers, with caps on shaved heads, carried boxes with blank, tired faces. I saw the sign marked AUSCHWITZ, a name I wasn't familiar with.

I looked at the steel-gray sky and saw chimneys blowing black smoke. *That must be where we'll work*, I thought. Factories for the German war effort.

How wrong I was.

We were told to drop our suitcases into piles. I thought that was strange. In Terezín, we were allowed to carry our own belongings, and as I stared at the large heap of valises and rucksacks, all of which were labeled with the numbers of our first transport but not with our actual names, I wondered how they would ever get the right ones back to us.

The elderly and the youngest children were ordered to the right side. The younger, the more vital of us to the left. My father was shuffled off so quickly I lost sight of him within seconds.

My mother was also sent to the right with the aged, the infirm, and the smallest children. I remember thinking this was a blessing, as she would not have to work as hard as those of us who looked strong. *She will take care of those children,* I told myself. *I will find supplies, just as I did in Terezín, and she will continue to teach them to draw.*

How many times have I returned to that last image of her? My once-beautiful mother standing like an egret. Her long white neck straining above the neckline of her torn, dirty dress. Her bent spine straining to stand straight. She is already an apparition, skin as translucent as eggshells. Watery green eyes. She looks at Marta and me, and through our fear, we communicate. As if through our own private code of secret gestures — the rapid blinking of our eyes, the shiver in our fingers that we are too afraid to raise — I tell my mother that I love her. I bind myself to her, despite my sister and I being in one line and her in another. My mother. I hold her to this day, in an eternal embrace, locked forever in my mind.

We are forced to walk through the snow, in the direction of the black iron gate and the chimneys with their dark plumes of smoke. The drifts feel like icy needles at our skin, soaking through my stockings. My black coat from Prague is worn through and covered with holes.

People are asking for their suitcases. 'You will get your things later,' the SS bark at us. The dogs are foaming at the mouth. I am petrified by the sight of their razor-sharp teeth, the pink of their gums.

There is no Council of Elders to meet us, as there was in Terezín. There are no organized lines proceeding at a slow pace. Instead there is chaos and constant yelling all around. Other inmates hit us with canes and order us in either Polish or German to stay in line. Marta is walking in front of me, her stiff movements suggesting she is in a trance. I want to run up to her, hold her hand, and tell her that we are together — that we will protect each other — but I am too fearful. I see her breath against the cold. I see her legs shaking.

We walk farther, and pass through the gate. I read the sign above in German that says ARBEIT MACHT FREI. Work will make you free.

The watch towers shine tubes of blaring white light. Against barbed wire, I see the bitten-up corpses of those who could not escape the dogs.

We are marched to a bare wooden building and told to take all our clothes off. Inmates sit behind desks and write down where we are from, and our names, and tell us to sign the cards.

We are sent to a hall. We are shivering; our bodies have no fat on them to keep us warm. We see the lines of each other's ribs, and the snakelike outline of each other's spine. I want to put my arms around Marta and cover her, my little sister whom I am powerless to protect.

We all try to cover ourselves with shaking hands, but it is of no use. We are soon ordered to raise our hands as men shave us under our arms and around our genitals. One man works under each arm, another works down below. I would later learn that all the prisoners but those in the Czech transports had the hair on their heads shaved. For some reason, we were allowed to keep ours.

They herd us into another room, where we are hosed down with ice-cold water and given clothes by SS women who are dressed in riding boots and hold crops in their hands. Already I've learned that everything in Auschwitz works efficiently. Everything is as methodical and precise as the assembly lines of a well-run factory.

I am given a brown sack of a dress that is several sizes too big and a pair of wooden clogs that are so ill-fitting I can barely walk in them.

That night we are told to crouch on a cement floor with our heads bowed. If we raise them, we are beaten with a stick.

I am now certain of one thing. Whatever belief I still had in God while in Terezín is now completely gone.

The next morning I find myself lying on the ground. Marta is not beside me, and I am seized with fear. I push myself up and retch, spitting bile onto the snow.

A girl I knew in Terezín is pulling me toward something. 'We're to be gassed,' she whispers. 'You can smell the crematorium, can't you?'

I tell her I don't believe her. 'It's true,' she says as she pulls me farther on. She points ahead to those two tall chimneys I remember from yesterday. 'They burn all day and night,' she says. 'We are all going to die.'

I tell her she is wrong. I tell her this could not be. 'They need us to help with the war. Why would they kill us now after all those years in Terezín?'

She stops talking, but continues to tug my hand as we walk toward the light ahead. She was wrong about what would happen to us. Instead of being gassed, we are sent to a room to have numbers tattooed on our arms.

I received the number 600454, and it was that night that I lost my name, Lenka Maisel Kohn. I was now only to respond to my number, and identify myself by that alone. I was six blue numbers, inked forever to my skin.

We marched toward our barracks and it was there that I found Marta. She was one of ten in the bed. Rolled to her side, looking at her number. She looked at me and I saw that she was too scared — and too tired — even to cry.

We are summoned at the crack of dawn and told to move boulders from one part of the camp to another. It is mindless, stupid work, meant to exhaust and humiliate us. We hear the whistle blow and see the men in the barracks forced to run around in circles. Some, who don't run fast enough, are shot, their blood soaking through the soot-gray snow.

On the barracks walls, the Germans have

painted slogans. CLEANLINESS IS GODLINESS is written on ours. I am enlisted to work painting numbers on plates that are used to mark each barracks.

I find Dina, my old friend from Prague, in our barracks. The last time I had seen her was on the street near our apartment, when she had slipped her yellow star into her pocket so she could see the Disney movie *Snow White*.

Over a year ago, she tells me, she painted a mural on the children's barracks here in tempera paints. She tells me that Freddie Hirsch, whom she knew during her time at Terezín, had asked her to paint it.

'I was in Terezín for only eighteen months. When I first arrived in Auschwitz, a friend took me to the children's barracks, where I saw a huge drab wall in front of me,' she whispers. 'I looked at the wall and pretended it was a Swiss chalet. I began painting flowerpots, then cows and sheep in the distance. As the children came around me, I asked them what they wanted me to paint, and they all clamored that they wanted Snow White.'

I listened to her, mesmerized. 'I had seen *Snow White* several times back in Prague and I had painted it a thousand times in my head,' she said. 'I made all the dwarfs holding hands and dancing around Snow White. You should have seen the look on the children's faces when I was done!'

She told me that the children had even been able to use the mural as a backdrop for a secret play they performed. She made a crown out of paper and painted it gold for the queen. She took black paint and painted strips of paper and attached them to the crown to make it look like black hair.

Even though the play was supposed to be put on in secret, some of the SS watched. 'One of the guards told Dr. Mengele that I was the painter of the mural and now I paint portraits of the Gypsies in his clinic.'

I fell asleep that night, exhausted. Dreaming of my friend's mural. Wishing that all of this were nothing more than a fairy tale, a wretched spell cast by a wicked queen, and that a beautiful Snow White would soon wake up and foil her evil plan.

53

LENKA

There have been so many losses in my life. I can count them like the beads carried by a Bedouin. Each bead warmed and smoothed over by a nervous hand. I hold this rosary in my head, each bead with a color all its own. Josef is the darkest blue, his death the color of the ocean. My parents, who left this world in the most unforgivable chimney of smoke, are the color of ash, and Marta, the purest white. Hers is at the center of my string.

My sister and I worked in Auschwitz together, side by side in a room next to the crematorium. After the SS had ordered the men, women, and children selected for the gas chamber to strip off their clothing, it was our job to go through their things.

There were piles of coats and hats. Piles of dresses and socks. Piles of glass baby bottles. Piles and piles of pacifiers, tiny black shoes. To this day, I cannot look at a pile of heaping laundry in my house. I fold everything and put it away quickly, lest I find myself having to stare at a mountain of clothes and remember Auschwitz.

We were told to dig on our hands and knees and sift through each discarded item. We were told to open up seams and look for hidden pieces o gold, and diamonds sewn secretly into sui linings, and to check for pockets that stil contained money. We also checked inside the heads of dolls, searching for a string of pearls o a bracelet that might have been stuffed inside their ceramic craniums.

Every day we worked from dawn until dusk The gas chambers and the crematorium burned seven days a week, twenty-four hours a day. In the morning we'd arrive and the clothing would be piled almost to the ceiling. Our finger learned to work nimbly, to feel the hem of a skirt, not for the precision of the stitches, bu with the questing touch of a blind person feeling the letters of a book in Braille.

I tried to put myself into a trance as I worked I did not want to think of the poor, desperate woman who sewed her wedding band into the lining of her coat, the diamond earrings tha were stitched inside a collar, or the small piece of gold I found inside the brim of a fur-lined hat

Marta and I were ordered to drop everything we found into boxes. I did as I was told. I did no even look up from my work as I tore open seam and cut through silk linings. I worked like a person who was already dead. How could I no work like that, when I heard the screams of the most recent transport passengers lining up outside, shrieking when they knew they were about to be gassed? And the cries of the children, or the mothers begging for mercy? For every piece of gold I unstitched from the cloth, one of those cries is stitched into me. Until I take my last breath, I will never, ever get them out of my head.

❊

As weak and nearer death as my sister seemed to me with each passing day, there was a defiance to her that I could never quite fathom. As we worked side by side, I would sometimes see her take a piece of jewelry she found and throw it into the latrine.

'What are you doing?' I hissed at her. 'If they see you, they will shoot you!'

'I would rather they shoot me than give them any of this!' She was clutching a woman's velvet skirt and the sight of her hands was ghastly. They no longer looked like the hands of my sister, but like claws. All tendon and bone.

'If the Jew who cleans the latrine finds that diamond, maybe he can barter with it and save his life . . .'

'They will shoot you,' I told her. 'If they knew we were sisters, they'd shoot me first. Make you watch and then shoot you.'

But Marta did not back down. 'Lenka, if I give them everything . . . my life is already lost.'

That night I huddled even closer to my emaciated sister. I felt the thinness of her pelvis next to mine, the near weightlessness of her arm as she flung it over me in her fitful slumber. It was as if I was clasping an empty birdcage, her ribs like wire, her body hollow and without song.

Had I known it would be the last time I would touch her, I would have embraced her so tightly that her bones would have sprung from beneath her thin sheath of skin.

The next morning one of the SS saw my sister throw a brooch into the latrine. He yelled out at her, asking her what she was doing. Marta stood there like a frozen swan. Her white legs poked out from the hem of her brown sack dress, but I did not even detect a shiver. 'Go in and get it, you filthy Jewish whore,' he shouted. She did not move at first. My beautiful redheaded sister. He came closer to her, his rifle sticking right into her face. 'Get into that latrine now, you Jewish piece of shit!' I saw her standing there, looking him straight in the eyes, and not in a whisper, not with a single tremor to her voice, my little sister said her last word, uttered with defiance. 'No.'

And then, right in front of me, with the swiftness that only evil can deliver, Marta was shot in the head.

54

LENKA

My parents vanished into the air of Auschwitz and my sister into its blood-soaked earth. A few weeks after Marta's death, the Germans, sensing that the Soviets would arrive at the camps any day, began moving us by the thousands to other camps farther west. Entire barracks would vanish overnight.

In early January 1945, we were roused just after midnight and forced into the freezing cold. We could see the burning factories in the distance. Even the crematorium seemed to be smoldering.

'They're burning the evidence,' one of the girls whispered. 'The Soviets must be at the borders already.'

After the Germans called out each of our numbers, they began yelling at us to start walking. We were half asleep and were completely emaciated, and many of us stumbled in the snow. Every person who fell was shot. Their bodies did not make a sound as they hit the frozen earth. The only evidence of their deaths was the ribbon of blood snaking from their skulls.

We were driven in the January snow, like cattle they hoped would die before reaching pasture. I watched as nearly each person walking in front of me fell down and did not get up. Others were shot for walking too slow, and some were shot just for glancing at a Nazi with a despairing look. I only survived because there was a woman directly behind me who, in her grief, thought I resembled her dead daughter. When I fell down, she picked me up. When I was near dead from starvation, she made me eat snow. The few times we were allowed to stop for a break, she cupped my frostbitten feet with her hands and tore her head scarf to bandage my bleeding toes. I have no idea what became of her, and to this day, I wish I had had a chance to thank her. Because it was this nameless woman, who wrongly believed I was her daughter, who kept me walking when it was so much easier to die.

We marched for three days before arriving in Ravensbrück, where the SS continued to beat us and shoot whoever was too weak to stand. I remained in Ravensbrück for only three weeks before being transported by train to another, smaller camp called Neustadt Glewe. There, fifteen other girls and I were taken to an airplane factory. For three months, I dug anti-tank ditches, standing in the cold with nothing more than a brown burlap dress and a pair of wood-and-canvas shoes. Every day and every night, the other girls and I would look up at the sky and hear the sound of the American or

Soviet airplanes circling above, and do you know, we did not even think about liberation. We just assumed that they would bomb the factory and we would be unfortunate casualties.

But in early May the unthinkable happened. We woke up one morning to a camp that had been completely abandoned overnight by the SS. They had snuck away like cowards, so when the Americans arrived, all they saw were piles of the dead and those of us who were as near death as the still living could be.

We remained there for a few weeks before the Soviets took over the camp, directing us to displaced persons camps that were being erected throughout Germany. And it was there, in a small camp, outside Berlin, that I first met an American soldier named Carl Gottlieb.

The same way a mother can love an orphaned child or a child a motherless kitten, that is the way Carl fell in love with me.

I could not have been anything much to look at. I was no more then eighty pounds, and though we in the Czech barracks had not had our heads shaved, my black hair was now so dirty and infested with lice that it looked like an old matted rug.

Carl told me that he fell in love with my eyes. He said they were the color of the Arctic. That he saw many a journey in their pale light blue.

I told him, years later, that only with the birth of our daughter had they finally learned to thaw.

I cannot tell you that I loved my husband at the time I married him. But I was a widow, an orphan, and completely alone. I allowed this warm, handsome man to take me under his wing. I let him spoon me soup. I allowed him to escort me to the infirmary for my checkups. I even allowed myself to smile when he danced with his fellow soldiers to the music on their radios.

And when he told me he wanted to take me home to America, I was so tired I did the only thing I could still manage.

I gave him my hand.

55

LENKA

I returned to Prague in the spring of 1945. Carl was unable to go with me because he was not granted leave in Germany, but I insisted that I was strong enough to travel by myself, and he had no choice but to let me go.

How strange it was to travel through war-torn Germany and then to arrive in Prague, which had suffered far less from the bombings and blitzes that blighted much of the rest of Europe. Here was my old city, seemingly untouched. The lilacs were in bloom and the intensity of their scent brought tears to my eyes.

I walked as though in a trance to our old apartment on the Smetanovo nábřeži embankment, and discovered it was occupied by the family of a government official. The wife, who answered the door, had an expression that was close to horror.

'It is our apartment now,' she said, without offering to invite me in. 'You will have to speak to the relocating committee to get new housing.'

I did not know where to go for the night and it was already getting cold. And then I remembered my beloved Lucie.

I walked back to the station and took the next train to her village on the outskirts of Prague.

In a small house, not far from the station, I was greeted not by Lucie but by her daughter, Eliska, my mother's namesake, who was now almost ten. The little girl was the spitting image of Lucie, with the same white skin and black hair. The long, almond-shaped eyes.

'Your mother and I were friends . . . ' My voice began to choke as I tried to explain myself. 'You are named after my mother,' I said through falling tears.

The girl nodded and ushered me into their small living room. On the mantel, I could see the wedding portrait of Lucie and Petr. There were small, hand-painted plates on a dresser and a little wooden crucifix on one of the walls.

Eliška offered me some tea while I waited for her mother, and I accepted. I could not stop myself from staring at her as she lit the stove and pulled some biscuits from a tin box. While we had spent the war dying in concentration camps, she had grown from a toddler to a little girl on the verge of adolescence. I was not bitter, but I was amazed at the transformation all the same.

It wasn't until an hour later, when Lucie walked through the door, that I realized how changed I was myself. Lucie stood in the threshold of her living room and looked at me as though she were seeing someone who had just risen from the dead.

350

'Lenka? Lenka?' she repeated as if she could not believe her eyes. She placed her hands over her face and I could hear her trying to stifle her weeping.

'Yes, Lucie, it's me,' I said as I rose to greet her.

I walked up to her and pulled her palms from her face, grasping her hands. The skin was that of an older woman, though her face was still like my old Lucie, the sharp-cut angles even more pronounced.

'I prayed every night that you and your family would return safely,' she said through her tears. 'You must believe me. I hope you received the packages that I sent to Terezín.'

I did not doubt that she had tried to send us provisions, though truth be told, these packages were often stolen, and we had not received a single one.

'Your mother and father and Marta?' she asked. 'Please tell me they are safe and well . . . '

I shook my head and she gasped. 'No. No. No,' she said over and over again. 'Tell me it isn't so.'

We sat down next to each other and held each other's hands. I asked about Petr, her parents, and her siblings, and she told me that they had struggled during the war, but everyone was alive and well.

'I have never forgotten my promise to your family,' she said. She stood up and went into her bedroom; when she came back she was carrying the basket in which she had so carefully placed mother's jewels years before. 'I still have your mother's things . . . and your things, too, Lenka. They are yours now,' she said, placing them in my hands.

Lucie's little girl came and sat beside her as I unwrapped the pieces one by one. My mother's beautiful wedding band and choker, the cameo from Josef's mother, and my own wedding band, golden and inscribed to me within.

'Thank you, Lucie,' I said, embracing her. I never thought I'd ever have anything of my mother's again.

She could not bear to speak and I kept seeing her glance over to her daughter.

'You are named after Lenka's mother,' she finally told her. 'You will give up your bed for tonight and let Lenka sleep in your room, Eliška.'

The little girl seemed confused by my presence. She clearly had no memory of who I was, much less how, only a few years ago, I watched her take her first steps.

'It is an honor to have you here, Lenka, and I want you to stay as long as you need to.'

I stayed for a week, and in that time learned that the young man, Willy Groag, who had worked alongside my mother, had been liberated from Terezín. He had returned to the city with two suitcases full of children's drawings that mother's colleague Friedl had entrusted to another colleague, Rosa, on the night before she was sent to Auschwitz. There were forty-five hundred drawings.

Leo Haas had also survived Auschwitz and returned to Terezín to unbrick his drawings from their hiding places. He, along with the engineer Jiří, who had also survived the war, went to the farmyard where Fritta's drawings were buried and dug with shovels until they reached the tin canister that contained all of Fritta's work.

Years later, I met up with Haas and learned how he and his wife had adopted Fritta's son, who had been left an orphan after the war. Haas appeared softer than he had been in Terezín. Gone were the dismissive tones that I remembered; he now spoke as if we were equals, as if we had become such just by surviving. Over tea, he told me how he'd carried Fritta, sick and frail from dysentery, out of their cattle car as it arrived in Auschwitz and how he and another colleague tried to nurse him back to health. 'Fritta lasted only eight days, hidden in a barracks,' he said 'A doctor friend of ours tried to administer fluids to him with an eyedropper, but he died in my arms.'

'Petr and Otto?' I said their names tentatively, as if my memories of them were about to shatter in my hands.

'Petr and his wife were gassed a few days after their arrival.'

'And Otto?' My voice was cracking.

'Otto . . . ' He shook his head. 'He was last seen alive in Buchenwald, but he died days before liberation.' Haas, never one to show emotion, struggled to compose himself.

'The last image someone claimed to have seen

of Otto was of him crouching on the side of the road with a lump of charcoal in his left hand, the other hand limp at his side. He was trying to sketch the corpses around him on a piece of scrap paper no bigger than this . . . ' Haas drew a circle around the center of his palm.

I held my hand up to my mouth.

Haas just stood there shaking his head.

As we had never been close, I did not tell him my own story. The story of how I returned to Terezín a few months after liberation.

After bidding good-bye to Lucie, I took a train that followed the same route that I had taken with my family to Bohušovice years before. Although I now carried no rucksack, only a small canvas handbag, the weight of my parents' and sister's ghosts was as heavy as a case of bricks strapped to my back.

I walked silently down the dirt path until I reached the ghetto's gates. I felt as though I were returning to a strange dream, a recurrent dream about a stage play; in this version the set remains the same but the entire cast has vanished. There was no familiar sight of Petr walking down the street with his sketchpad and bottle of ink. Gone was the once-omnipresent sight of a hearse pulling a mountain of suitcases or a gaggle of elderly bodies that could no longer walk. On the contrary, there was hardly a person to be found in a place that was once teeming with people.

I had to blink several times to adjust to the sight of a vacant Terezín. The ghetto had turned into a ghost town.

The barracks, too, were completely empty and

only a few Allied soldiers patrolled the streets.

'What are you doing here?' one of them asked me.

I stopped in my tracks, suddenly terrified, adrenaline coursing through my body. It would take me a lifetime to get over that fear. Even though I was now technically a free person, I did not yet believe it.

'I've left something here.' My voice was shaking. I reached into my purse to show him the identification card I had been given upon liberation. 'I was a prisoner here and want to see if what I am looking for is still here.'

'Is it valuable?' the soldier asked. His smile was crooked and he was missing one of his bottom teeth.

'To me it is. It's a painting I did.'

He shrugged his shoulders, clearly not interested. 'Go ahead, but don't take all day.'

I nodded and walked hurriedly to the Hamburg barracks.

If shadows had a smell, that was the scent of Terezín. I could still smell the wretched odor of packed bodies. The damp walls. The dirt floor. But as I walked down the steps of the basement in the barracks, it occurred to me that this was the first time I had heard the sound of my own footsteps while I was in Terezín. I suddenly felt cold, the very echo of my shoes reinforcing just how alone I really was.

I tried to think of Carl in order to soothe my

nerves. I tried to hear his voice in my head telling me to keep my resolve. I would come here and find my painting. And once I had it in hand, I would leave this place forever.

I had entered an antechamber in the basement, just as Jiří had described. I stood there for a moment like a child in a house of mirrors, not knowing where to look or where to begin my excavation. I kicked the earthen floor with the toe of my shoe. The ground was hard and compact.

I reached into my canvas bag and removed a small spade that I had borrowed from Lucie. I pulled up my skirt and fell to my hands and knees, like an animal digging for something lost.

I told myself I would not stop digging until I found it. I would not stop for a moment. I would unearth the drawing of Rita and Adi, just as I had created it, with torn cuticles, weary hands, and cracked skin, my own blood soaking into the earth.

It took me nearly two hours to find my painting. There it was, just as Jiří had promised, placed within a slender metal pipe.

56

LENKA

I was married to my second husband at the American consulate in Paris. A dozen other couples, all GIs and their European brides, waited outside. On the way there, we bought some flowers on the Rue du Bac and stumbled over cobblestone streets, my feet unused to shoes that fit as they should. I wore a navy suit and did my hair without any artistry, a simple brown barrette tucked above my ear.

After the ceremony, Carl asked me where I wanted to go to celebrate.

All I wanted was palačinka.

'Crêpes,' I told him, and he squeezed my hand as one might a child's. I imagined my younger self at my mother's table. The white eyelet cloth, and the china plate stacked with crêpes filled with apricot jam and dusted with powdered sugar.

'How easy you are to please,' he said, smiling. We found a small café and sat down. I ordered crêpes with melted butter and jam and he a croque monsieur. We toasted each other over warm cups of tea and a shared glass of champagne. I misplaced my flowers on the way home.

That night, in a small hotel on the left bank,

Carl made love to me, whispering that he loved me, and that he was so happy I was his wife. I remember I trembled in his arms. I saw my white sticklike limbs threading through his, my ankles tucked around the barrel of his back. His words sounded to me as if they were actually meant for another person. Who was I to evoke such feelings? I no longer thought of my heart as an organ of passion, but one whose only loyalty was to the blood it pumped through my veins.

Once in America, I strove to be good and dutiful. I bought the Fannie Farmer cookbook and learned to make a good casserole and a raspberry gelatin with tangerine slivers tucked inside. I told my husband how kind he was to give me a vacuum cleaner for my birthday and to bring home white roses on our anniversary.

But in order to survive in this foreign world, I had to teach myself that love was very much like a painting. The negative space between people was just as important as the positive space we occupy. The air between our resting bodies, and the breath in between our conversations, were all like the white of the canvas, and the rest our relationship — the laughter and the memories — were the brushstrokes applied over time.

When I held my husband of fifty-two years, I could never quite hear his heartbeat the way I did Josef's in those handful of days and nights we lived together. Was it because I had grown more plump over the years, and the extra padding against my chest prevented me from feeling the rush of blood in his body in the way I remembered it flooding through Josef's? Or was it that with a second love, we are not as attuned? My heart was thicker with my second love. It had a casing around it and I wonder what else it shut out over the years.

There were also cracks in my heart where feelings so deep and raw managed to flood through. The birth of my daughter was one of those times. When I held her in my arms and saw my reflection in her blue eyes, I felt a more overwhelming sense of emotion than I'd ever felt before. I traced each one of her features in their newborn perfection, and saw my father's high forehead, my small narrow chin, and my mother's smile. And I saw for the first time how, despite the isolation of our own lives, we are always connected to our ancestors; our bodies hold the memories of those who came before us, whether it is in the features we inherit or a disposition that is etched into our soul. As I grew older, I realized how little control we really have over what we are given in this world. And I no longer battled with my demons. I just grew to accept that they were a part of me. Like an ache in my bones that I try to shake every day that I awaken, an internal fight within myself not to look back, but to focus on each new day.

I named my daughter Elisa, to honor the memory of my mother. I dressed her in beautiful clothes and gave her a sketchbook when she was barely five. When I watched her clutch the colored pencils for the first time, I knew she had inherited her talent from my family. She knew not just how to replicate what she saw before her but to see beyond it, beyond the surface. To see beneath the line. My own hands were damaged from the years of deprivations, the cold, and the conditions in Auschwitz. But sometimes, for the sake of instruction, I would clutch the stem of a pencil or the handle of a paintbrush and push through the pain in order to illustrate a concept to my ever-eager daughter.

I never told my daughter when she was young the details of my life before she came into this world. She simply knew that she was named after my mother.

But the smoke of Auschwitz I did not speak of. That blackness, the mental scars — the reason for the pain in my hands — I kept a secret. Like a slip of mourning hidden beneath my clothes, sewn to my skin. I wore it every day. But I revealed it to no one.

Not even my painting did I share. Some nights when Carl and Elisa were fast asleep, I would walk into my bedroom closet, turn on the light, and close the door. There, in the corner, behind my sewing box, my plastic containers of shoes and slippers, I kept my treasured painting. It pained me that I kept it among such pedestrian things, that I had not the courage to display it or tell my family about its existence. But it was like a raw wound that I kept hidden, but nursed secretly at night. On the evenings when I could not sleep, when my nightmares got the best of me, I would pull it out from its cardboard tubing and stare at the faces of Rita and her newborn son. I would hear Carl's breathing, imagine my sweet daughter sleeping next door, and I would finally allow myself to cry.

57

LENKA

I gave birth to only one child. A daughter. Carl and I tried for years for another baby, but it was as if my body couldn't produce more than one offspring. Every stretch of vein, every bit of bone, was pulled from me to make that perfect one.

Elisa grew up strong and tall. She had her father's American limbs. She ran fast like a colt, her amber legs stretching in mighty leaps. When I saw her on the playground as a little girl racing against the boys, I remember gasping for breath. Who was this child who could leap faster then a gazelle, who tore out her tight braids because she loved the sensation of the wind in her hair? She was mine, but she was so wild and free.

I loved that about my daughter. I loved that she was fearless, that she had passion in her heart, that she thrilled to the sun on her face and rushed to the shoreline, just so she could feel the lapping of water at her toes.

I would be the one who secretly worried. I never told her how each night I had to fight the anxiety that raced through my head, the worry that something awful might befall my child.

I would wrestle the thoughts in my head like they were lions inside me. I would fight with myself not to let the blackness of my past seep into any part of Elisa's life. She would have a pure, golden life without shadow, I swore. I swore it up and down.

My daughter was five when she first asked about my tattoo. I will never forget the near weightlessness of her finger tracing the numbers on my arm.

'What are those numbers for?' she asked, almost mesmerized.

I had dreaded this day since her birth. What would I tell her? How could I spare her the details of my past? There was no way on earth I'd allow a single image of my nightmare to sneak into her beautiful, angelic head.

And so, that afternoon, as Elisa sat in my lap, her finger against my skin, her head against my breast, I lied to my daughter for the first time.

'When I was little, I always got lost,' I told her. 'This was my ID number in case the police needed to know where to return me.'

She seemed to accept this for a while. It was when she became a teenager that she learned about the Holocaust and figured out what those numbers really meant.

'Mom, were you in Auschwitz?' I remember her asking the summer she turned thirteen.

'Yes,' I answered her, my voice cracking. *Please. Please*, I prayed, my heart thundering in my chest. *Please don't ask me anymore. I don't want to tell you. Leave that part of me alone.*

I could see her eyebrows rise as my own body

stiffened, and knew she had recognized the fear crossing my face.

She looked at me with those ice-blue eyes of hers. My eyes. And in them I saw not only sadness, but also my daughter's capacity for compassion.

'I'm so sorry, Mom,' she said, and came over and wrapped her long arms around me, then rocked my head against the thinness of her chest.

And she knew enough not to ask me anything more.

Although I never uttered another word about Auschwitz to my family, I still dreamed of it. If you have lived through such a hell, it never leaves you. Like the smell of the crematorium that is forever in the back of my nose, my dreams of Auschwitz are always at the back of my mind, despite all the efforts I've made to push them away.

How many times did I dream of the last time I saw my mother, my father, my sister? Every one of their faces appeared to me like apparitions over the years. But it was the dream where I am in Auschwitz with my daughter, Elisa, that was always the worst. That one, when it came, tortured me for days at a time.

The dreams changed as Elisa changed. When she became a teenager, my daughter grew lazy like her American friends. How many times did I ask her to clean her room, pick up her clothes, or help me peel a bowl full of vegetables before her father came home from work? But Elisa never tolerated such tedium. It was all about meeting her friends or boys.

And in those years, my dreams always began with the selection process at Terezín. She is standing next to me, my beautiful daughter. And in my dream I am begging the SS officer to send her to the right with me. I tell him: 'Please! She is a good worker!' I beg him to send her to the line that I am in. But always in the dream he is prying our hands apart. He sends my daughter to the left. And I awaken, my nightgown wet with perspiration and Carl comforting me, whispering that it was only a terrible dream.

It was always in those moments, when my husband held me, that I knew that I was lucky to have found him. Those hands on my shoulders never lost their warmth during all the years of our marriage. They were always the hands of the young soldier who found me in the DP camp. Who brought me a blanket and a warm meal. Who told me in broken German that he was Jewish, too.

Every night as I went to bed, I looked at the black-and-white photograph of him in his army uniform. His thick head of hair, his dark brown eyes full of the compassion he had since that first day. This is how I filled the canvas of our marriage. I filled it with gratitude. For no matter what else happened, I would always think of Carl as the one who saved me.

He Americanized my name to 'Lanie,' and gave me a good life with a healthy daughter. She learned the highly prized craft of art restoration and became a mother herself to my beautiful Eleanor. Eleanor, who inherited her swanlike grace from my mother and made heads turn whenever she walked into a room. She took to languages the way a duck takes to water. At her graduation from Amherst, she took home nearly every prize.

When Carl fell ill, I finally became the caretaker in our marriage. I held his head when he needed to vomit, and I made him only soft food when his stomach couldn't digest anything else. When the chemo claimed his thick white hair, I told him he was still my handsome soldier. I held his brown-spotted hand to my lips and kissed it every morning and every night. Sometimes I'd even place it in the center of my half-buttoned nightgown so he could feel the beating of my heart. I could see the end of the painting of my marriage, and I was racing to fill it with just a few strokes more.

I will tell you, though I am a deeply private person, that our last moment together was perhaps our most beautiful. That final night after he had been tucked into bed. I had given him his pain medicine and was getting ready to take a bath.

'Come here,' he managed to whisper. 'Come next to me, before the medicine clouds my head.'

I believe those who have the luxury to die in their own bed can often sense when the end is near. And this was the case with Carl. His breathing suddenly became labored, his skin took an unearthly pallor. But in his eyes, there was a fierceness — a determination to use every ounce of his powers to see me clearly for the last time.

I took his hand in mine. 'Put the music on, Lanie,' he whispered. I stood up and went to the old phonograph and put on his favorite record by Glenn Miller. Then I returned to sit next to him, slipping my old wrinkled hand in his.

With all his strength, my Carl gently raised his arm as if he were about to lead me in a dance. He swayed his elbow and my arm followed his lead. He smiled through the cloud of medication.

'Lanie,' he said. 'You know, I have always loved you.'

'I know,' I told him, and squeezed his hand so hard, I feared I might have hurt him.

'Fifty-two years . . . ' His voice was now barely a whisper, but he was smiling at me with those dark brown eyes.

And then it was as if my old heart finally tore open. I could feel the shell that I had so carefully maintained for all those years come undone. And the words, the feelings inside, seeped out like sap from an old, forgotten tree.

It was there, in our bedroom with the old faded curtains and the furniture we had bought so many years before, that I told him how much I loved him, too. I told him how for fifty-two years I had been blessed to spend my life with a man who held me, protected me, and gave me a daughter who was strong and wise. I told him

366

how his love had turned a woman who only wanted to die after the war into someone who had a full and beautiful life.

'Tell me again, Lanie,' he whispered. 'Tell me again.'

And so I told him again.

And again.

My words like a kaddish for the man who was not my first love. But a love all the same.

I told him until he was finally gone.

Dear Eleanor,

It is hard for me to believe that tomorrow you will be getting married. I feel I have lived so many lives in my eighty-one years. But one thing I am sure of is that the days on which you and your mother were born were the two happiest days of my life. On the day I first saw you, the sight of your red hair, your white skin, I was struck speechless — I could not help but think of my mother, your great-grandmother, and my beloved sister. How wonderful for this color hair to reappear in the family after all these years. You remind me so much of my mother. You have her lithe frame, and that long neck that turns like a sunflower up toward the light. You have no idea how this makes me feel, to see her in you. To see her live through the blood in your veins, the sparkle in your eyes.

I pray you will understand the wedding gift I am giving you and Jason. I have carried it with me for over fifty-five years. I made it for a dear friend, who is no longer here. I made it in honor of her child, who she was only able to hold in her arms for a few short hours. This painting was done with my heart, my blood, every part of me wanting to make something to keep this moment alive for my friend.

It was buried through the war under a dirt floor, hidden there by a man who risked his life to hide hundreds of paintings that were done by men and women like me who needed to record their experiences in Terezín.

I returned to Terezín after the war and dug it up myself. My hands worked quickly, as my spade dug through the earth to find the tin canister in which it was rolled. I eventually found my buried painting and wept with joy that it was still there. My friend, you see, was now with her child and her husband in whatever heaven there is. But the drawing remains as a testament to their lives, cut short but filled with love nonetheless.

I have waited until now to share it. I have not wanted to burden your mother's life or yours with stories of what I endured during the war. But this painting should no longer be hidden in my closet. It has spent its life in darkness. It deserves to be seen by eyes other than my own.

Eleanor, I am giving you this painting not as a sign of morbidity, but because I want

*you to be its guardian. I want you to know
the story behind it. To see it as a symbol not
just of defiance, but of eternal love.*

I placed the note on the canvas and rolled the
painting up.

58

JOSEF

I dress myself the day of my grandson's rehearsal dinner with a careful reverence. I had laid out my clothes the night before. The navy-blue suit, and the white shirt that I sent to the laundry the week before. I think of Amalia on this day, how happy she would be to see our grandson with his beautiful bride. It will be a grand wedding. The bride's family is sparing no expense for their only child, a girl who looks so familiar to me, I can hardly say why.

I shave my face slowly, below my neck and the line of my slackening jaw. The mirror is merciless. My once-black hair, and my eyebrows, are as white as cotton. Somewhere deep beneath the lines, and beneath my paunch, there is a young man remembering the day he got married. His bride waiting for him under a white lace veil, a trembling body that would receive his gentle hand. I have so much love for my grandson. To see him getting married is a gift I never thought I'd live long enough to receive.

I pull on my undershirt, slip my arms through my shirtsleeves, and button myself carefully so as not to miss a single hole. I dab a little pomade on my hands and smooth out my few remaining curls.

Isaac arrives at four o'clock. The salt-and-pepper hair he had at Amalia's funeral has now turned completely white. He comes into my room and stands behind me, both of our reflections cast in the mirror above Amalia's old vanity. I can see his eyes fall to the porcelain tray that still holds her silver-plated brush, her pot of cold cream, and a tall green bottle of Jean Naté that she never felt she had the occasion to open.

He is not carrying his violin case, and somehow the sight of him without the leather case, the bow tucked inside, is soothing to me. I marvel at the sight of his two unencumbered arms, dangling like a schoolboy's from the dark sleeves of his suit, his gray eyes sparkling like two silver moons.

Jakob has come out of his room and greets us in the hallway. My fifty-year-old son surprises me with a smile.

'Isaac,' he says, nodding a friendly hello. 'Dad,' he says. I see him clasping his hands to steady his nerves. 'You look great.'

I smile at him. He looks handsome in his suit, the first sprouts of gray hair around his ears remind me of my own. His eyes remind me of Amalia's.

'What a night,' Jakob says as the three of us walk out under the canopy of my building. The doorman whistles for a cab. The moon is shining over the skyline. The air smells of autumn. Crisp as apples. Sweet as maple sugar.

The three of us slide onto the cab's blue vinyl

seats and fold our hands in our laps on the way to my grandson's wedding rehearsal.

I look out the window as we drive across town, through the channels of a jewel-lit Central Park, and think I have lived to be eighty-five years old, to see my grandson on his wedding day. I am a very lucky man.

Epilogue

At a table in the back of the restaurant, long fingers of moonlight strike an aging couple. The bride-to-be and the future groom are dancing.

Her sleeve is now pulled upward. It is not the six blue numbers that have made the old man weep, it is the small brown birthmark on the flesh just above them. He trembles as his old finger reaches to touch it, that small raisin shape he had kissed a lifetime ago.

'Lenka . . . ' He says her name again. He can barely get the word out of his mouth. It has been stuck there for sixty years.

She looks at him with eyes that have seen too many ghosts to believe he is who she thinks he might be.

'I am Lanie Gottlieb,' she protests weakly.

She touches her throat, encircled in a seed-pearl necklace that once belonged to an elegant redheaded woman in Prague. She glances over to her American granddaughter, her eyes filling with tears.

He is about to apologize, to say that he must be mistaken. That for years he thought he has seen her face in the subway, the bus, in a woman on line in the grocery. Now he fears he has finally lost his sanity.

She pulls down her sleeve and looks directly into his eyes. She studies him as a painter might study a canvas that she had long abandoned. In

373

her mind, she colors his white hair black, and traces the arch of his brow.

'I am sorry,' she finally says with a shaking voice and tears in her eyes. 'I have not been called Lenka in nearly sixty years.' She is covering her mouth, and underneath a fan of white fingers, she whispers his name: 'Josef.'

He is trembling. She is once again before him, a ghost who has miraculously come to life. A love that has been returned to him in his old age. Unable to speak, he lifts his hand and covers hers with his.

Author's Note

This book was inspired by several people whose stories are woven throughout its plot. I had planned on writing a novel about an artist who survives the Holocaust, but ended up writing a love story. With any novel, unexpected plot and other developments typically arise, and you find yourself going in a direction that you hadn't originally planned. In this case, while getting my hair cut one afternoon, I overheard a story told by a guest at a recent wedding where the bride's grandmother and the groom's grandfather, who had not met prior to the ceremony, realized they had been husband and wife before the Second World War. The story stuck with me, and I decided to use it in the first chapter of my novel. I then created two characters and set out to fill in the space of the sixty years they spent apart.

Lenka's experience is partly inspired by one of the actual characters mentioned in the book, Dina Gottliebová, who studied art in Prague and later worked for a short time in the Lautscher department in Terezín painting postcard scenes before she was deported to Auschwitz. She immigrated to the United States after the camps were liberated, and died in California in 2009. The United States Holocaust Memorial Museum in Washington, D.C., proved to be invaluable in providing an oral testimony of Dina Gottliebová's experiences, working both in Terezín and in

Auschwitz, where she created the mural of *Snow White and the Seven Dwarfs* for the Czech children's barracks. The mural came to serve as a comfort to the children, and also helped to save Dina's life. After she completed it, an SS guard informed Mengele of her artistic talent. Mengele then promised to spare her and her mother's lives if she painted life portraits of the men and women he used in his horrific medical experiments.

Several other characters who appear in the book were also actual people. Friedl Dicker Brandeis arrived in Terezín in December 1942, and almost immediately began teaching art classes for the children there. In September 1944, upon hearing that her husband, Pavel Brandeis, was being transported east, she volunteered to follow him on the next transport. She perished shortly after her arrival in Auschwitz. Prior to her transport, however, she gave two suitcases, containing 4,500 drawings, to Rosa Englander, the chief tutor of the young girls' home in Terezín. At the end of the war, Willy Groag, the director of the girls' home, was entrusted with those suitcases, and hand-carried them to the Jewish community in Prague. Of the 660 children who created art with Friedl Dicker Brandeis in Terezín, 550 were killed in the Holocaust. All of the remaining drawings are now in the collection of the Jewish Museum of Prague, and many are on display for all the world to see.

Bedřich Fritta perished in Auschwitz on November 5, 1944. His wife, Johanna, died while in Terezín, but miraculously, their son Tommy survived. Leo Haas made it through the war and returned to Terezín to find the artwork he had hidden in the attic of the Magdeburg barracks. With the assistance of an engineer, Jiří Vogel, he was able to recover the hidden paintings made by Fritta and their other colleagues from the technical department: Otto Ungar, Petr Kien, and Ferdinand Bloch, who had all since perished. Upon hearing that Tommy Fritta was left orphaned, Haas and his wife, Erna, adopted the boy and moved back with him to Prague.

While visiting the Czech Republic, I was able to meet with Lisa Miková, an artist who worked in the technical department of Terezín. Even so many years later, she was able to vividly describe the unusual circumstances in which artists were assigned to create blueprints and various drawings for the Germans while smuggling art supplies from the office in order to do their own work at night. She shared with me how the paintings had been bricked inside the walls of Terezín and how Jiří Vogel buried Bedřich Fritta's work after placing it in a metal canister.

I am indebted to many people who shared their stories with me, and am so grateful for the opportunity to help preserve their legacies. Without them, this book would not have been possible. They are Sylvia Ebner, Lisbeth Gellmann, Margit Meissner, Lisa Miková, Nicole Gross Mintz, Iris Vardy, and Irving Wolbrom. I would also like to thank Dagmar Lieblova, who so generously gave me her time, her contacts, and a personal tour of Terezín during my stay in Prague. Also, Martin Jelínek at the Jewish Museum in Prague and Michlean Amir of the United States Holocaust Memorial Museum, for the invaluable research assistance they provided me, both during and after my trips to these wonderful institutions; Jason Marder, for his early work as my research assistant; Alfred Rosenblatt and Judith and P. J. Tanz, for providing me with additional background material; Andy Jalakas for his unwavering support; Linda Caffrey, Antony Currie, Marvin Gordon, Meredith Hassett, Kathy Johnson, Robbin Klein, Nikki Koklanaris, Jardine Libaire, Shana Lory, Rita McLeod, Rosyln and Sara Shaoul, Andrew Syrotick, Ryan Volmer, my husband, my mother and my father, for their careful readings of early drafts of the novel; Sally Wofford-Girand, my wonderful agent who pushed me further than I thought I could ever go and made the book all the better for it; my fantastic editor Kate Seaver; Monika Russell, for her stories and her assistance with everything from Czech translation to diminishing my daily chaos and always showing me and my children such love. And to my children, parents, and husband — a special thanks for your infinite patience and love.

Other titles published by
The House of Ulverscroft:

TELL THE WOLVES I'M HOME

Carol Rifka Brunt

Fourteen-year-old June Elbus, shy at school and distant from her older sister, has only ever had one person who truly understood her: Finn Weiss — her uncle, godfather, confidant and best friend. So when he dies, far too young, of a mysterious illness, June's world is turned upside down. At the funeral a strange man lingers beyond the crowd. A few days later, June receives a package in the mail. Inside is a beautiful teapot she recognizes from Finn's apartment and a note from Toby, the stranger, asking for an opportunity to meet. Then, as they spend time together, June realizes she's not alone in missing Finn, and if only she could trust this unexpected friend he might just be the one she needs the most.

THE COVE

Ron Rash

In the shadow of a deep cove, Laurel Shelton and her brother Hank have built a home. The locals whisper about the cove being cursed — good fortune rarely seems to reach their little cabin in the woods. But when a stranger turns up, hiding among the trees, the course of their lives seems altered. The mysterious Walter begins helping Hank on the farm and brings Laurel the only real comfort she's ever known. Finally the dark cloud hanging over the cove lifts, but then a secret is uncovered which threatens to shatter their newly found happiness. As their neighbours begin to stoke a fire of rage against the cove and its inhabitants, Laurel, Hank and Walter come to understand the profound danger they are in . . .

THE PARISIAN'S RETURN

Julia Stagg

In the commune of Fogas in the French Pyrenees, Stephanie brains an intruder with a stale baguette, little realising that he's the new owner of the épicerie. Fabian's welcome gets worse when his attempts to modernise the shop are met with a resounding *non!* by the locals. Ready to admit defeat, he's suddenly hit by a *coup de foudre* and falls in love. Stephanie herself is too busy for *l'amour*. Working at *l'Auberge* and getting her garden centre off the ground are all-consuming. She doesn't even notice that her daughter Chloé has something on her mind. Troubled by a sinister stranger in the village, Chloé has no one to turn to. Her only hope is that someone hears her cries for help before it's too late.